SEBASTIAN DARKE

DARKE

Prince of Explorers

PHILIP CAVENEY

Illustrated by Julek Heller

RED FOX

SEBASTIAN DARKE: PRINCE OF EXPLORERS
A RED FOX BOOK 978 1 862 30258 7

Published in Great Britain by The Bodley Head,
an imprint of Random House Children's Books
A Random House Group Company

The Bodley Head edition published 2009
Red Fox edition published 2010

1 3 5 7 9 10 8 6 4 2

Copyright © Philip Caveney, 2009
Cover illustration by Jonny Duddle
Inside illustrations by Julek Heller
Illustrations © Random House Children's Books, 2009

The Random House Group Limited supports the Forest Stewardship Council
(FSC), the leading international forest certification organization. All our titles that
are printed on Greenpeace-approved FSC-certified paper carry the FSC logo. Our
paper procurement policy can be found at www.rbooks.co.uk/environment.

Set in 11/16pt Palatino by Falcon Oast Graphic Art Ltd.

Red Fox Books are published by Random House Children's Books,
61–63 Uxbridge Road, London W5 5SA

www.kidsatrandomhouse.co.uk
www.rbooks.co.uk

Addresses for companies within The Random House Group Limited can be found
at: www.randomhouse.co.uk/offices.htm

THE RANDOM HOUSE GROUP Limited Reg. No. 954009

A CIP catalogue record for this book is available from the British Library.

Printed and bound in Great Britain by
Printed in the UK by CPI Bookmarque, Croydon, CR0 4TD

To my daughter, Grace.
Sebastian Darke was created
with you in mind . . .
and like me,
a part of him will always belong to you.

PART ONE

THE VILLAGE

CHAPTER 1

LOST

The small expedition plodded wearily along the jungle trail in the terrible afternoon heat.

It comprised four people and three beasts, and they had been moving in this frustratingly slow fashion for several weeks now. When they first found the trail, they had been excited, feeling that they were finally on the brink of making a discovery; but now it seemed as though it was leading them nowhere.

At the front of the column walked a young elfling, thin and wiry and dressed in the sweat-stained remains of what had once been a sailor's outfit, now little more than a collection of rags. The tricorn hat perched on his head was battered and misshapen. He was using a broad-bladed machete to hack his way through the thick tangle of ferns and vines that overhung the trail, and the effort of swinging it back and forth had brought a thick sheen of perspiration to his pale but – some would say – handsome features. His hands and fore-arms were badly scarred by thorns and his palms were blistered where they had been rubbed raw by the handle of the machete.

He was called Sebastian Darke and he had once advertised himself as a jester, the celebrated Prince of Fools. Every step he took on this desperate journey served to assure him that he might have been a little hasty in abandoning that title.

Just behind him trudged a powerful warrior, sweating copiously in the chain-mail singlet and metal breastplate that, despite the awful heat, he stubbornly refused to take off. He was called Cornelius Drummel; he was a Golmiran and very small – unlike most men of his profession – less than half the height of Sebastian. His smooth baby face was set in a scowl and he was still limping noticeably from a recent wound incurred on the open sea, where he had suffered a minor disagreement with a young kelfer. The disgruntled expression on his face might have had something to do with the fact that his short stature prevented him from taking a turn at the head of the column. He simply couldn't reach high enough to cut aside the overhanging greenery that drooped down into the other men's faces. It was an un-fortunate situation but it was one that none of the others dared comment on.

Next in the column was a great shaggy brute of a buffalope,

his massive shoulders and flanks laden with heavy equipment – ropes, tools, food, lamps, cooking pots – all strapped
higgledy-piggledy around him. His name was Max and,
unusually for him, he wasn't complaining. Having moaned
incessantly for several days, he had lately taken to sulking in
silence and his huge head was bowed until his snout barely
skimmed the ground. He had been plodding along like this
for the best part of a day and it was a situation that was
unlikely to last much longer, so Sebastian and Cornelius were
making the most of it.

After their recent hair-raising adventures in Ramalat, the
three friends had been hired by a rich merchant named
Thaddeus Peel to seek out the legendary lost city of Mendip;
and if they found it, to bring back proof of its existence. The
city had been talked about for centuries. Many claimed that
it contained fabulous treasure. Others said that the place was
cursed and that ill-fortune awaited anyone who chanced
upon it.

Behind Max walked the hired hands – two big, muscular
men from Ramalat who rejoiced under the names of Karl and
Samuel. Neither of them had been employed for their witty
conversation, but for their ability to travel mile after mile
without complaint. Each of them led a small mule laden with
equipment. Like their owners, these beasts, known as Betty
and Jasper, were not the brightest of their species. On the first
few days out from Ramalat Max had made valiant attempts

to engage them in polite conversation, using the common language of the plains, but he now preferred to leave them to their own devices; when he had something to say, he directed his remarks to the two-legged members of the expedition.

And it was to Cornelius that he finally addressed his first question in several hours of travelling.

'I don't suppose there's any chance of stopping for a rest?'

Cornelius sighed. 'I thought it was too good to last,' he muttered. He glanced back over his shoulder. 'We can't stop here, can we?'

'Why not?'

'It's too narrow. We need to find a clearing.'

Max considered this for a moment. 'Couldn't we make a clearing?' he asked. 'With the machete.'

Sebastian laughed at this idea, though there wasn't much energy in the laugh. 'I love the *we*,' he said. 'What you actually mean is, *I* could make a clearing. But that would involve cutting down entire trees and I'm exhausted enough as it is. We'll just have to keep going a while longer.'

Max gave a low, mournful sigh. 'Oh yes, well, that's just the standard reply on this trip, isn't it?' He modulated his voice to mimic Sebastian's. *'We'll just have to keep going!* Well, we've been going for what must be weeks now and what have we found? Absolutely nothing! When Thaddeus Peel told us this was an errand for the foolhardy, he wasn't kidding!'

'Give it a rest, can't you?' growled Samuel, from behind

Max; and everyone turned to look at him in surprise. It was virtually the first time he had uttered more than a grunt since they had set off.

'Oh, excuse me!' said Max haughtily. 'I was only expressing an opinion.'

''Pinion or not, here we be, like it or lump it,' said Samuel emphatically. 'Ain't no use in complainin'.'

'Arrr,' added Karl. For a moment it seemed as if he might be about to add something else, but he must have thought better of it.

Max swung his head back round and continued for some distance in silence, mulling over what had just been said. But Sebastian knew that it was only a matter of time before he returned to his theme.

'What I mean to say,' continued Max, 'is: how long are we going to go on with this fiasco? At exactly what point do we say, *Well, we've given it our best shot, we're now completely and utterly lost and it's time to head back to Ramalat?*'

Sebastian paused mid-swing and considered that one. He had to admit, it was a good question. He glanced back down the line and gestured to Karl. 'You want to take over for a while?' he asked.

Without a word, the big man strode forward, took the machete in one great fist and forged ahead, the arcing blade felling great swathes of forest. Cornelius dropped back to take Betty's rope, a look of resignation on his face. Sebastian realized how humiliating it must be for him to be unable to do his fair share, but knew there was nothing he could do about the situation, short of carrying him on his back while he swung the machete, and he simply didn't have the energy for that.

He resumed walking just a short distance ahead of Max.

'I know it's frustrating,' he said, 'but Mr Peel is paying us a great deal of money to be here. And, should we find anything of value, he'll pay us a great deal more.'

'I'm aware of that,' said Max. 'But for goodness' sake, all we've seen in this hell-hole is jungle, jungle and more jungle. What do you suppose are the chances of happening upon an ancient city in the midst of all this?'

Sebastian was about to reply when he broke off at a sudden chattering in the treetops to his left. Everyone stopped and turned to look. Cornelius's hand dropped instinctively to the handle of his sword but he grinned when he saw the creature that had made the sound – an agile, furry little beast that was swinging about in the trees, its face contorted into a comical expression.

'What on earth is that?' he wondered aloud.

'It's a boobah,' Sebastian told him. 'Don't you remember? Princess Kerin had one just like it.'

The mention of the name made him thoughtful. There was a time when it would have hurt him to speak of her; but that seemed an age ago, before his trip to Ramalat and before he'd met Captain Jenna Swift, the commander of the *Sea Witch* and his current true love.

Max, of course, couldn't resist commenting on the name. 'Ah yes, the fair Princess Kerin . . . or perhaps I should say *Queen* Kerin. Lovely girl. You know, I always rather hoped that we'd head back in the direction of Keladon one day. The royal stables did a marvellous lunch – one of the finest I've ever eaten.'

'And you've eaten a lot of lunches,' observed Cornelius slyly.

'Indeed, I do think of myself as something of a connoisseur,' said Max, missing the dig entirely. 'Speaking of which, I wonder what delights we'll have for our supper this evening. If I have to eat any more of that rotten— Ah! At last we're coming to a clearing!'

Sebastian saw that he was right. The trail was finally widening out into a small opening in the midst of the dense ranks of greenery. There were more boobahs here, he noticed, swarming merrily amidst the lower limbs of the trees, chattering and gesticulating at each other, a great animated troop of them.

'Perhaps we should try and catch one,' he mused aloud. 'They make good pets.'

'Be my guest,' muttered Cornelius, sinking down under the shade of a tree. 'If you have the energy.'

Sebastian considered for a moment and then decided that,

quite frankly, he didn't. He followed his friend's example and dropped down beside him. He unstrapped his canteen and took a large swig of warm, foul-tasting water.

'At least there's no shortage of this stuff here,' he said brightly, offering the canteen to Cornelius.

The little warrior nodded and took a gulp himself, then pulled a face. 'Not like the sweet cold waters of Golmira,' he observed.

Max snorted. 'Oh well, naturally! According to you, nothing's as good as it is in Golmira! It's a wonder you've never taken us there if it's so blooming marvellous.'

'I will, one day,' Cornelius told him. 'I'll take you both there and introduce you to my parents.'

'Oh goody, I can hardly wait.' Max glowered resentfully at the two mules, who had lowered their heads and were chomping energetically at the lush green grass all around them. The two handlers had sat down under another tree and taken out pipes, which they were charging with tobacco.

'Of course, it's hardly likely to live up to this charming spot,' continued Max. 'I mean, look around! We've got dense, stinking vegetation everywhere. We've got two mules demonstrating the fact that they're the most ill-mannered creatures in existence. And we've got their owners, who seem intent on polluting the already foetid atmosphere with their pipe smoke.'

'Why don't you belt up and browse a bit of grass?'

suggested Sebastian irritably. 'It might help keep your energy up.'

'Energy!' Max gave him a disbelieving look. 'I ate two mouthfuls of that stuff the other day and I was awake with raging wind all night!'

'Yes, we *did* notice,' said Cornelius pointedly. 'But don't worry, I've made myself a set of ear plugs for tonight.'

'Oh, ha ha! Please desist, I'm in danger of splitting my sides laughing.'

Sebastian and Cornelius grinned at each other. Taunting Max was one of the few pleasures they'd had on this trip.

'We've got company,' observed Samuel; and everybody looked up to see that a couple of the boobahs had clambered down from the trees and were advancing cautiously across the clearing, ready to run if they needed to. Sebastian laughed at the anxious expressions on their faces. They were holding out their hands as if begging.

'What do you suppose they want?' he asked.

'Food, I shouldn't wonder,' replied Cornelius. 'But I'm afraid we have none to spare. In fact . . .' He reached down to his belt and took out the various pieces that comprised his miniature crossbow. He began to slot the pieces together with well-practised ease.

'What are you doing?' hissed Sebastian.

'I'm wondering if these creatures are good to eat,' muttered

Cornelius. 'It would be nice to have a change from javralat and wild rusa.'

Sebastian reached out a hand to stay his arm. 'You can't,' he whispered. 'They have faces like little people . . .'

'It's not their faces that interest me,' said Cornelius. 'It's their chunky little arms and legs. They'd roast up nicely over the fire.'

Sebastian made an expression of distaste. 'But they're pets, Cornelius! It wouldn't be right.'

'You said yourself last night that you were desperate for a taste of something different.' Cornelius had now finished assembling the crossbow and was pulling back the string. 'We'll just take one for now – see what it tastes like. And if—'

He broke off in surprise as the boobahs suddenly looked over their shoulders in alarm. One of them issued a loud warning screech and they bounded away across the clearing before anybody had a chance to react. In an instant the whole troop had vanished into the surrounding vegetation.

'Shadlog's teeth!' said Cornelius. 'What could have tipped them off?'

'Shush!' said Max. 'Listen.'

'I don't hear anything,' said Sebastian after a few moments.

'Exactly,' said Max.

CHAPTER 2

RUMBLE IN THE JUNGLE

Sebastian realized that Max was quite right. A terrible silence had descended, where an instant earlier there had been a rich cacophony of birdsong and insect chirrups.

'I don't like this,' said Max quietly. 'This is definitely not good. Reminds me of when we met that blooming tree serpent.'

Cornelius and Sebastian got warily to their feet. The Golmiran slotted a bolt into his crossbow and Sebastian pulled out his sword. The two Ramalatians, alerted by the reaction of their employers, put away their pipes and drew their weapons. Everybody stood there, gazing around, straining to see into the depths of the jungle.

There was a rustle in the bushes, and Sebastian's keen eyes caught a glimpse of something moving from left to right across his vision. He thought at first he was looking at another boobah. There was a glimpse of ginger hair and a grizzled face staring at him through a thick screen of bushes . . . but then he registered that this creature was the size of a full-grown man and that its wild eyes were glaring at him from beneath the brim of a metal helmet.

'Cornelius,' he whispered, 'I just saw—'

He broke off at a sudden hissing noise, which sounded unnaturally loud in the silence. A short distance in front of him, Karl's body jolted and he gave a dull grunt of surprise. His sword slipped from his hand and fell to the ground. Everyone stared at him in horrified fascination. He turned to face Sebastian; he was looking down at his own chest in wide-eyed horror. The feathered shaft of an arrow protruded from its centre. He opened his mouth to say something, but all that emerged was a slow exhalation of air. Then his body crumpled and he fell to the earth, his eyes open but sightless.

Sebastian stared down in astonishment at the fallen man, unwilling to believe the evidence of his own eyes. He stood mesmerized, and it was only when Cornelius bellowed at him and struck him hard across the hip that he came out of his trance, into a world of chaos.

He could see them now – scores of great armour-clad shapes, shambling through the gloom of the jungle, shrieking and jabbering and waving their swords. Something whizzed past his head and thudded into the trunk of a tree beside him. Another arrow. Cornelius discharged his crossbow bolt, and across the clearing one of the hairy beasts gave a yelp of pain and fell backwards into the undergrowth.

Sebastian glanced at his little friend and saw that he was grinning gleefully, never more happy than when he was in a situation like this.

'Cornelius,' he said, 'maybe we should—'

He was interrupted by a deep bellowing as one of the mules raced past him, terrified, stampeding back down the trail. Sebastian made an instinctive grab for the mule's bridle as it raced past, but the creature was going so fast, the impact nearly jerked his arm out of its socket. He clung on for a short distance, then lost his footing and went tumbling in the dirt.

He staggered back to his feet and saw that Cornelius was running across the clearing towards the enemy, his sword raised. He was roaring in anger at his attackers. Max had lowered his head and was advancing too, his great horns poised to strike at whoever came within reach; the great piles of equipment on his back jigged and clattered as he went.

'I knew it was too ruddy quiet!' Sebastian heard him say as he raced after Cornelius.

'Hey, wait for me!' shouted Sebastian. He started after his friends – they clearly hadn't realized he wasn't still with them – but then blundered into Samuel, who was staggering back towards him, his eyes wide and staring, his arms held out in front of him as though begging for mercy. He grabbed hold of Sebastian and hung onto him tightly, his weight bearing the slim elfling down onto his knees, making him drop his sword.

'What are you doing?' gasped Sebastian – but in the next instant his question was answered. He saw a long wooden shaft sticking out of Samuel's side.

'Pull it out,' gasped the big man. 'It hurts. Pull it out!'

Sebastian stared at Samuel for a moment. There was such fear written on the man's normally placid features – he couldn't leave him. He took hold of the arrow in one hand, but before he could exert pressure on it, a second arrow thudded into Samuel's broad back, finishing him off. His pleading eyes glazed over and the strength flowed out of his arms. He tipped sideways and hit the ground, staring up at Sebastian as if in silent accusation.

Sebastian shook his head. This couldn't be happening! He told himself that perhaps he was asleep and dreaming . . . but then he saw a smear of bright crimson on his hand and knew that this was no nightmare: it was really happening and, for the moment at least, he had no idea where his friends were.

He was getting back to his feet when one of the attackers ran at him, a great hairy brute encased in crude armour and waving a huge two-handed sword. There was no time to think. Sebastian snatched at his own sword where it lay on the ground. His scrabbling fingers closed on the hilt and he brought the blade up as the creature closed the distance between them. The sword shuddered as it punched its way through metal and into the flesh beneath. The beast went flailing over him in a sprawl of arms and legs, then struck the ground heavily and tumbled over and over, until at last he came to a halt and was still.

Sebastian remembered to draw breath. He got to his feet and turned to look in the direction that Cornelius and Max had taken. They were up there somewhere – he could hear them crashing through the undergrowth, Max bellowing for all he was worth. It might not be too late to catch up. He took a step forward and then the arrow hit him in the chest.

It was like being struck with a wooden club. The impact made him reel back several steps and the air was driven abruptly from his lungs. Liquid fire seemed to trickle from his breastbone to his groin, and when he tried to take another step, it was as if the muscles in his legs had gone. He sank to his knees, gasping for breath. A short distance away he could see Samuel's dead face staring sightlessly up to the canopy of leaves high above them.

And then he saw them coming. Two more of the creatures, their pale faces arranged into masks of grinning triumph, shambling along on their short bow legs, their long arms holding crudely fashioned, heavy swords. Sebastian looked around helplessly. There was no sign of Cornelius or Max. He was on his own. He tried to lift his own sword but it took a terrible effort to even raise it to chest height and he was

horribly aware that his strength was failing as the blood trickled out of him.

The nearest of the beasts slowed to a walk, baring his yellow, misshapen teeth. He lifted his sword in both hands, ready for the death blow. Sebastian steeled himself for the impact of the blade against his neck. But then there was a loud hiss: another arrow seemed to bloom like a strange flower out of the creature's chest and his face contorted in agony. He fell backwards onto the ground and lay there, writhing and gasping for breath.

The second creature was still shambling forward, but now he was no longer staring at Sebastian but at something or someone behind him. The beast raised his sword and then a lithe figure leaped past Sebastian to meet the attack – a tall, dark-haired warrior dressed in animal skins. The two swords clashed together, striking sparks, and the creature grunted, disengaged his blade and tried to swing again. But the newcomer was too fast for him, ducking under the blow and driving a smaller, lighter blade straight up into the beast's throat, dropping him in his tracks.

Now more of the newcomers came into view from behind Sebastian and raced past the first warrior, into the jungle where Cornelius and Max had gone. As they ran past the fallen beast, one of them finished him off with an almost casual flick of his blade.

The first warrior made no attempt to follow the others but

turned to look at Sebastian. He heard his own voice give what seemed like a distant gasp of astonishment. The warrior was a young woman. She was gazing down at Sebastian, her dark brown eyes like those of some wild creature. She crouched down in front of him, opened her mouth and said something that might have been a question, but Sebastian could hear nothing above the slow rhythmic thudding of his own heart.

He tried to speak but could not shape an intelligent sound. He was dying now – he was sure of it. His head seemed to fill with bright light that bleached out everything around him except the woman's face and her brown eyes, which were still staring at him in open curiosity. She reached out a hand and touched his face. Her fingers were warm and he dimly registered that they gave him a feeling of comfort. Perhaps the last he would ever know. He thought of Jenna, away on her ship somewhere, gazing out across the endless ocean and never knowing that he had fallen in this lonely spot. He would have cried if he could have stayed awake.

But the white light obliterated everything and then a darkness fell, deep, black, sweeping him into its cold embrace.

CHAPTER 3

TIME HEALS

For what seemed like the longest time, he only had glimpses of life . . .

His eyes would open for an instant and he would register what was happening. But his eyelids were heavy – they came crashing down again, shutting off his vision. He could not tell how long passed between each glimpse. Every time he woke, it was with a sense of surprise.

The first time his eyes opened, he registered that he was lying on his back and could see Cornelius just a short distance away, his face lit by the glow of a lantern. The little man's baby-like features were creased into an expression of anguish and there were tears on his cheeks. Sebastian would have liked to ask him what was wrong but he could not stay awake long enough to do so.

The next time he woke, he was staring at a ceiling made

from what looked like woven leaves and branches. He was aware of a deep, rhythmic drumming from somewhere nearby, and the air around him was smoky and scented with a strange musty perfume. Then he drifted back into oblivion.

More visions followed, each as brief and insubstantial as the last:

His eyes opened. A couple of dark-haired children, dressed in animal skins, were staring at him intently. He tried to say something to them but sleep was tugging at him and he could not resist. He went down into darkness . . .

His eyes opened. An old, white-bearded man was pushing his fingers into a large bloody hole in Sebastian's chest and the pain was unbelievable. As he gasped and stared, there was a sudden wrench and the fingers emerged, gripping a large stone arrowhead. The cessation of the pain was such a relief that he slipped back into unconsciousness once again.

His eyes opened. Daylight. The white-bearded man was kneeling beside him, shaking some kind of decorative rattle over his head while he chanted in a long, low monotone. 'Go away,' said Sebastian, quite clearly; and the man stopped chanting for a moment and stared down at him in surprise. Then he resumed his chanting and Sebastian slept once more.

* * *

His eyes opened. The woman – the one he had seen at the fight – was sitting beside him, and once again her hand was on his face, stroking it, following the contours of his profile with her fingertips, as though she had never seen anyone like him before. He managed to lift a hand to hold her wrist, but she pulled it away from him and he did not have the strength to hold on. He slept.

Between each vision he was aware that time had passed – but he could not say if it was hours, days or moons.

And then came the day when he awoke and was able to stay conscious for long enough to take stock of his surroundings. He saw that he was lying on a bed of straw in a large hut made of slender branches and woven vegetation. A short distance away from him, a metal pan bubbled over a fire, which accounted for the smoke in the air. Through an open doorway he could hear the sounds of people – children laughing and calling to each other, mutts barking; the general unidentified sounds of habitation. There was a thick woven blanket over him and he eased it back gingerly to look at his bare chest. The wound was livid red and seemed to be packed with a poultice of mud and leaves, but it looked as if it might be healing. Merely breathing caused him considerable discomfort, and when he coughed un-expectedly, the pain was so intense that he slipped back into unconsciousness again, fighting it all the way . . .

He woke again and knew that this time he would be able to stay awake for a while. It was dark and the hut was lit by the glow of a lantern. A small figure was slumped beside him on a seat made out of bales of straw. His head was bowed; he was obviously asleep. Sebastian made an effort and cleared his throat, though the action caused a stab of pain to lance into his chest.

Cornelius jerked awake and raised his head. He looked a lot happier than the last time Sebastian had seen him. He leaned forward and placed a hand on Sebastian's shoulder. 'How are you?' he asked.

Sebastian tried to speak but his throat was so dry, all that emerged was a croak. Cornelius picked up an animal skin and lifted it to Sebastian's mouth, allowing a stream of water to trickle down his throat. It was warm and brackish, but at that moment it was the best thing that Sebastian had ever tasted.

'Careful now,' Cornelius advised him. 'Just a little bit at first.' He eased the water away and beamed at his friend. 'It's good to have you back,' he said. 'For a while there, I was sure we were going to lose you. You were very close to death, my friend – as close as you'll ever get without slipping into the deep.'

Sebastian nodded. 'I . . . I believe you,' he murmured. 'It felt as though I was close.' He lifted his head to gaze around. 'Where exactly are we?' he asked.

'We're in the village guesthouse,' said Cornelius.

'The . . . village?'

'Yes. It belongs to a tribe who call themselves the Jilith. I don't know how much you remember about the fight . . .'

'I remember . . . those awful creatures . . . and then some people arrived . . . they saved us . . .'

'That's right. A hunting party chanced upon us when we were under attack. They came to our rescue.'

Sebastian began to remember more details. 'Karl and Samuel . . .' he said. 'Those great hairy brutes came out of the jungle . . . and killed them!'

Cornelius sighed. 'It was a terrible end for them both,' he said. 'I can't help but feel responsible for what happened.'

'But . . . those *things*. . . what . . . what were they?'

'They were the Gograth – sworn enemies of the people of this village. As far as the Jilith are concerned, anybody who the Gograth attack are friends of theirs. That's one of the reasons why they helped us.'

Sebastian gestured for more water and Cornelius helped him to take a couple of mouthfuls before setting it aside again.

'There was a woman . . .' said Sebastian. 'I believe she saved my life.'

'That's Keera,' said Cornelius, smiling. 'Trust you to

notice *her*! Maybe you're not in such bad shape after all.'

Sebastian attempted a smile, but it must have looked more like a grimace, because Cornelius stood up as if to leave.

'Perhaps I should let you rest,' he said. 'You're still very weak.'

I've done enough sleeping,' protested Sebastian. 'How long have I been lying here, anyway?'

'Four days and four nights,' Cornelius told him. 'We really thought you wouldn't make it through the first night. The arrowhead was buried deep in your chest and it was hard to dig it out. Keera insisted on bringing Danthus, the tribe's medicine man, to tend to the wound . . .'

'The man with the white beard?' Sebastian touched the wound on his chest gingerly. 'I remember. I woke for a moment when he was . . . pulling the arrowhead out.'

Cornelius shook his head. 'I must say I had my doubts about his approach to medicine. He made up a poultice from wildflowers and mud and packed that into the wound. But' – he peered at Sebastian's chest – 'I have to say, it does look like it's improving.'

'Tell me about Keera,' said Sebastian.

Cornelius chuckled. 'Why do you want to know about her?' he asked.

'I told you. She saved my life.'

'Well, she's a pretty important person in the village,' Cornelius said. 'Her father, Maccan, is the big chief here. He wasn't so keen on having us in the village at first, but Keera talked him round.'

'She was touching my face,' murmured Sebastian. He could feel sleep tugging at him again, his eyelids growing heavy, and though he struggled to fight it off, he was rapidly losing the battle. 'She was . . . staring at me . . .'

'That's not so surprising,' Cornelius told him. 'You see, she claims to know who you are.'

'Hmm?' Even so close to sleep, Sebastian registered how strange this remark was. 'But . . . how could she? I've never been here before . . . and she . . . presumably, has never . . .'

Cornelius patted him on the shoulder. 'Stop fighting it,' he advised. 'We'll talk again later, when you've rested a bit more.'

'Rest . . . yes . . .' Even as he was sinking into sleep, a thought occurred to Sebastian. 'Max!' he whispered. 'I haven't asked about Max. Is he all right?'

'Max is . . . worried.'

'A-about me?'

'Well, yes, of course . . . but it's not just that. You see, amongst the Jilith, buffalope meat is considered a real delicacy. He is convinced that everywhere he goes, the people of the tribe are sharpening their knives and salivating.'

If he had possessed more strength, Sebastian would have laughed at this. But he could hold out no longer. His fingers lost their precarious grip on consciousness and he fell, slowly, tumbling over and over into a deep dark void that seemed to have no end . . .

He woke again and felt much stronger this time. He was aware of a raging hunger within him; and as if in answer to that, a figure stepped in through the open doorway of the hut carrying what could only be a bowl of food. The woman came to kneel beside the bed and he saw that it was the one called Keera. She looked at him for a moment with those dark brown eyes and smiled.

'You are hungry?' she asked him.

He nodded.

'This will make you stronger,' she assured him. She dipped a rough wooden spoon into the bowl and lifted it to his lips. It was some kind of thick, meaty soup. He took a gulp of it and was aware of it trickling down into his insides, warming him. 'You must take it slowly,' Keera told him. 'You have only had milk and water for the last few days.' But she raised the spoon again and he swallowed the contents gratefully. Then a terrible thought occurred to him.

'What's in this?' he asked. 'It's not . . . buffalope, is it?'

She shook her head. 'Don't worry, it's rusa. The little warrior has warned everyone in the village that the buffalope is special and anybody who harms him will answer to his sword. We saw the Golmiran fight – nobody here is in a hurry to cross swords with him.'

Sebastian smiled. 'He's only little but he fights like ten men,' he said. 'Mind you, you're no mean fighter yourself. I saw you take on those two creatures . . . what is it you call them? Golgath?'

'Gograth. Our mortal enemies.' She stared thoughtfully into the bowl of soup. 'They grow in numbers all the time,' she said. 'And day by day they venture closer and closer to the village.' She seemed to make an effort to put her thoughts aside and gave him another spoonful of soup.

In his haste to swallow the contents, Sebastian made a loud slurping noise. 'Sorry,' he said, licking his lips.

'That's all right. Amongst the Jilith, it's considered good manners to slurp your food.'

'Really?' He managed a smile. 'Then my buffalope, Max, must be considered the best-mannered creature of all.'

Keera laughed, displaying even, white teeth. 'I have never heard a beast that can talk like him! The children of the village are afraid to go near him because he is so magical.'

'There are many words I'd use to describe Max,' said Sebastian. 'Magical isn't one of them.' He opened his mouth and accepted another spoonful of soup. 'How do your people come to be living in the middle of the jungle?' he asked.

She shrugged. 'It is where we have always lived. Not in this same village – we move around from time to time.'

'What makes you move?'

'There can be many reasons. Perhaps the hunting becomes

bad and we have to move in search of fresh game . . . perhaps the water supply dries up . . . or perhaps the Gograth grow too strong and threaten to wipe us out. The elders of the tribe are saying that we should move soon, before they mass together and finish us for good.'

'Why would they do that? I mean . . . what harm are you to them?'

Keera gave him a last spoonful of soup and then set the bowl aside. 'It's not about harm. It's about a grudge that goes back to the beginning of time. There's a story about how in the ancient days there were two tribes in the jungle and the gods decided to grant one tribe the gift of intelligence and beauty and to curse the other to be beasts for all eternity.'

Sebastian smiled. 'It's easy to see which tribe was blessed with good looks,' he said; and Keera lowered her eyes, made suddenly self-conscious by the remark.

'I do not know if this is a true story,' she told him, 'but that is supposed to account for the Gograth's hatred of us. They are jealous of the gift we were given. And ever since, it has been their intention to destroy us.'

'And could they do that?'

Keera sighed. 'A few moons ago, I would have said no. The Gograth were spread out in little groups all over the jungle. They were bad enough but they had no real strength. Then General Darvon came along.'

Sebastian frowned. 'Who's he?'

'A Gograth with high ambitions and just a little more brains than the rest of them. He's been going around uniting all the little bands into one big army. He's made it clear that he believes there's room for only one tribe in the jungle. He claims that he can talk to the ancient gods and they have commanded him to destroy the Jilith.'

'And people believe that?'

'You've seen the Gograth,' Keera said. 'Did they strike you as creatures with a lot of intelligence? They believe what they're told. I suppose we could move on, but they'd no doubt follow us. You know, I was pondering the matter when we chanced upon you and your companions – and then I knew I had an answer. You have come to our aid, as promised.'

Sebastian gazed at her, puzzled. 'What do you mean?' he asked her. Then he remembered something that Cornelius had told him. 'I was told that you claim to know me . . .'

Keera smiled and nodded. She reached into a little animal-hide pouch that hung from her belt and drew out what looked like a piece of parchment. She unrolled it carefully, handling it as though it were some precious artefact. 'This scroll has been passed down through the generations,' she said. 'It is given to each chief of the Jilith when he takes up his position. It is said to be part of an ancient prophecy and speaks of a mysterious half-man who will come to the aid of the Jilith in their darkest hour. Look . . .'

She turned the scroll round and held it out so that he could see it. The scroll showed a painting of a lean, wiry young man, dressed in long boots and what looked like a tricorn hat. Sebastian could see that the character had pointed elvish ears – he couldn't deny that there was a strong resemblance to him. In the picture, the figure was wielding a sword and was about to plunge it into the breast of a hairy beast-like creature that was evidently a Gograth.

Sebastian opened his mouth to say something but couldn't seem to find any words. In the end he just said, 'Oh.'

'Don't you see?' said Keera excitedly. 'Your arrival was foretold. You are the saviour who was sent to free my people from the terror of the Gograth!'

CHAPTER 4

ELF LORD

In the silence that followed Keera's remark, Sebastian considered his options. He could hardly ridicule what she'd just said. After all, she'd saved his life. But at the same time, the thought of taking on the might of the Gograth army was not a particularly appealing one. He'd met up with just a small band of them and had very nearly paid the ultimate price. Still, he had to say *something*. She was looking at him expectantly, waiting for his words of wisdom.

'Umm . . . well, Keera, that's . . . that's . . . remarkable. I admit, it does look a bit like me, but—'

'*A bit?* Look at the clothes. Look at the ears!'

'But, Keera,' he said, 'do you not think that all this – strange as it may seem – could simply be some kind of coincidence?'

Keera smiled and brushed back her long hair with her fingers. 'Forgive me, but I know better than that,' she said. 'I mean, think about it. A strange half-man comes into the jungle from the outside world. He brings with him a tiny but mighty warrior and a magical talking buffalope. And what's the first thing he does when he arrives? He takes on the arch-enemy of the Jilith. You are the Chosen One, the Elf Lord that we have been promised for so long.'

'They attacked me! And I nearly got killed! That doesn't seem very heroic, does it?' The act of raising his voice sent a jolt of pain through Sebastian's chest and he grimaced.

'But it is spoken of in the ancient stories,' said Keera. 'The half-man will suffer terrible tribulations, but he will weather the violence and will rise up stronger than before. Then he will smite our enemies with such force that they will be vanquished for ever!'

'I . . . I'm not awfully big on smiting,' protested Sebastian.

'Of course you are!' said a voice from the doorway; and looking up, Sebastian saw Cornelius leaning against the doorframe, his arms crossed, a big grin on his baby face. 'Ignore him, Keera, he's just being modest. Why, if I were to tell you of all his victories, I'd be here till tomorrow evening.'

Sebastian stared at the little warrior in exasperation. 'Tell her!' he protested. 'Tell her I'm not a hero!'

'I will do no such thing,' retorted Cornelius. 'This is just like you, Sebastian, trying to downplay your abilities. But your modesty is misplaced. You should celebrate your magnificent victories, just as *ordinary* men do.' He smiled at Keera. 'The

Chosen One is still weak and a little confused. If the two of us could talk alone for a few moments . . .'

'Of course.' Keera rolled up the parchment and replaced it carefully in her pouch. Then, retrieving the bowl, she got up, bowing respectfully first to Sebastian and then to Cornelius as she went past.

The little warrior waited until she was out of hearing, then strolled into the hut, beaming. 'I'm rather enjoying being the friend of the Chosen One,' he said. 'I've never been so indulged. I simply snap my fingers and I get whatever I want!'

'Cornelius!' Sebastian glared at his friend. 'What's all this "Chosen One" nonsense? And why are you allowing Keera to believe such a ridiculous notion?'

'For very good reasons,' Cornelius assured him. 'While you've been sleeping the days away, I've been using my time to good purpose . . . But more of that later. For now, I have a surprise for you.' He glanced back towards the open doorway. 'Come on, shaggy. He's clearly well enough to entertain visitors.'

A great mournful head ducked in through the doorway and there stood Max, regarding Sebastian with evident relief. 'My prayers are answered!' he exclaimed. 'The young master is healed!'

'I wouldn't go quite that far,' Sebastian told him. 'But I'm certainly on the mend – and though I never thought I'd say it, it's good to see your face, Max.' He thought for a moment. 'Who exactly did you pray to?'

'Why, the great buffalope-god Colin, of course.' Max looked quite indignant at the question. 'Who else?'

'But I didn't think you believed in him,' persisted Sebastian.

'I don't really. But in a situation this grave, I wasn't taking any chances.'

Sebastian laughed at this and instantly regretted it as another stab of pain went through him. Cornelius came and sat down cross-legged beside the straw bed. Max ambled closer too.

'Oh, young master,' he said. 'I can't tell you how happy I am. Even in this terrible place, where everybody seems to want a portion of me!'

Cornelius laughed heartily. 'It's lucky for you you're the magical assistant of the Chosen One,' he said. 'Otherwise you'd be nothing but a handful of spare ribs. I swear there's one fellow in the tribe who can't look at you without drooling!'

'There you go again!' hissed Sebastian. 'You must put Keera straight about this. It's not fair to let her go on thinking . . . well, that there's something special about me.'

'But who's to say there isn't?' argued Cornelius. 'You've seen the scroll. And I've spent some time listening to the old stories. There are some startling similarities: for instance, the

Chosen One – that's what the Jilith call this Elf Lord – he's supposed to come from a desert region, just like your home-land Jerabim. He's supposed to have brought down kings and witches, just as you have. And—'

'Yes, but these are just coincidences! There's nothing special about me.'

'I can vouch for that,' said Max. 'I've seen his jester's routine.'

'You *are* special. We all are, and you'd better get that into your thick skull,' said Cornelius.

'But can't you see? It's wrong to allow Keera to deceive her-self after she saved our lives and everything. If you won't say something to her, then I will.'

Cornelius shook his head. He reached into his singlet and took out his tobacco pipe and pouch. 'You'll do nothing of the kind,' he said calmly. 'For one thing, tell her that and poor old Max here will be on a roasting spit before he has time to blink.'

'Do you really think so?' asked Max warily. 'I'm nervous enough as it is without that kind of talk!'

'And secondly,' continued Cornelius, 'if we can convince the Jilith that you are who they think you are, they'll give us the location of the lost city of Mendip.'

'What are you talking about?' asked Sebastian. 'Nobody knows if there is a lost city . . . do they?'

'Well, hear me out a moment and see what you think.'

Sebastian was beginning to tire but he listened to Cornelius's story and marvelled at his friend's cleverness. It was clear that despite his concerns for Sebastian's welfare, the little warrior's mind had remained active enough to spot golden opportunities. He had noticed that Keera seemed to be in awe of Sebastian from the very start, treating him with great care and reverence, as though attending to the needs of a king. He had taken his first opportunity to ask her about it.

Soon enough she had told him the story and shown him the ancient parchment. At that point, Cornelius could easily have dispelled the notion, but he had decided that it would be in their interests to allow it to develop. It was Keera who had convinced her father that the strangers in the camp were not ordinary men; and that their appearance here at the village had great significance for the future.

'I've spoken with Keera's father, the chief,' said Cornelius; 'a powerful warrior called Maccan. I asked him if he had ever heard of an ancient lost city in the jungle. He replied that of course he had – it had been a familiar story since his child-hood. Not only that, but an old man of the tribe called Joseph claimed to have visited it when he was a little boy.'

'Could he lead us there?' asked Sebastian, trying to hide his mounting excitement.

'Joseph is very old and infirm, not capable of making a long journey – but Maccan thought that he might be able to give us directions to it. I told him,' said Cornelius, puffing away on his pipe, 'that the reason we were sent here was to find the lost city. And for that we would require a guide.'

'I see,' murmured Sebastian. His eyes were growing heavy but he was determined to stay awake a while longer. 'So . . . did you talk to this . . . Joseph character?'

Cornelius frowned. 'Not yet,' he admitted. 'But it's on my list. I thought I'd wait till you were a bit stronger. I'm sure you'd like to meet him. The thing is . . .' He puffed on his pipe for a moment, emitting great clouds of fragrant smoke. 'Keera told me that nobody from the tribe would be willing to undertake a long journey at the moment – not with the Gograth threatening the village as they are. So I was obliged to promise her . . .' He hesitated and threw a cautious look at Sebastian.

'What?' prompted Sebastian. 'What did you promise her?'

'That, er . . . we'd rid her of that little problem before we left the village.'

Sebastian stared at him. 'What . . . little . . . problem?'

'The Gograth. I told her we'd ensure that they were never a threat to the Jilith again.' Cornelius blew out another cloud of smoke. 'So we just have to work out exactly how we're going to do that,' he said.

'Cornelius,' sighed Sebastian, 'how can you hope to achieve it?'

The little warrior smiled. 'I'm already working on it. My plan is to train the Jilith up as an army so they can give the

Gograth the trouncing they so obviously deserve. Maccan has already approved my plan.'

Max snorted and shook his great horned head. 'Why does it always come down to fighting with you people?' he asked. 'Surely there's some other way. Couldn't you go to the Gograth and offer them your hand in friendship?'

Cornelius looked doubtful. 'Did they strike you as the kind of people who are open to reason?'

'They didn't even strike me as *people*,' said Max. 'More like overgrown boobahs with shorter tempers.'

'Well, there you are then,' said Cornelius. 'Offer them the hand of friendship and they'd most likely chop it off and cook it for dinner.'

'But . . . from what Keera was saying,' murmured Sebastian, 'they greatly outnumber the Jilith.'

Cornelius made a dismissive gesture. 'Numbers mean nothing! The Gograth look like they need help to do up their buttons. All the Jilith needed was a mighty general to teach them the finer points of warfare.'

Max looked glum. 'Yes, but where are they going to . . . ?' He glared at Cornelius. 'Not you, surely? You're only a captain!'

'Shadlog's beard! Keep your voice down, you great oaf! I've told Keera I'm a general, just like this General Darvon that everybody's so stirred up about. That way she'll feel more confident about me training the villagers.'

'It doesn't matter how trained they are,' protested

Sebastian. 'If they're outnumbered twenty to one they'll be slaughtered.'

'In a stand-up fight, yes,' admitted Cornelius. 'That's where we need a really great bit of strategy.'

Sebastian and Max looked at him expectantly.

'I'm . . . working on it,' he said. 'Now' – he got to his feet and nodded to Sebastian – 'you get some more sleep. You'll find that each day now, you'll manage to stay awake a little longer. You've been very lucky, my friend. I saw them take out that arrowhead – it was right next to your heart.' He held his forefinger and thumb slightly apart. 'That close.' He looked at Max. 'Come on,' he said. 'We'll let him sleep.'

'Very well.' Max gave Sebastian a mournful nod. 'Goodbye, young master, I'm pleased you're not dead. I'll see you later.'

Max and Cornelius left the hut, and within moments Sebastian was asleep and dreaming. He dreamed that he was sitting on a great golden throne, in the centre of a huge marble palace. Below him he saw Keera coming slowly up a long flight of steps, holding a jewelled casket out in front of her, her brown eyes gazing up at him in utter devotion. She knelt before him and held out the box like an offering. He took it from her, placed it on his lap and opened it. Inside was an ancient scroll. He took it out, unrolled it and studied its contents, realizing with a dull sense of surprise that it was a list of his father's jokes, written in elegant calligraphy.

He looked back down the steps to see that behind Keera

were lots of people in animal skins, who he presumed were the rest of the Jilith tribe. They were all kneeling and looking up at him expectantly. He recognized others too. There was King Septimus glowering up at him in silent hatred; there was Leonora watching him knowingly with her pale yellow eyes. There was Jenna Swift and Queen Kerin and lots of other faces he never expected to see in this strange place.

They all seemed to be waiting in silence.

So he read out the first joke – the one about the man who had a little mutt that chewed somebody's hat. He came to the punch line, paused for dramatic effect and then delivered it clearly. He waited for the laughter and applause. He waited and waited but the crowd were just looking at him blankly. And that was when he felt the big beads of sweat break out on his forehead.

He tried the next joke. And the next. Nobody laughed. Not a titter. Not a chuckle. Just silence and those terrible bemused faces.

And though he knew he was asleep and dreaming, he couldn't seem to make himself wake up, no matter how hard he tried . . .

CHAPTER 5

COME TO THE FEAST

The days passed and Sebastian was finally strong enough to get up and take his first brief forays outside, seeing the village for the first time. He discovered that it was composed of around twenty small round huts and several oblong communal guesthouses, one of which had been allocated to him and Cornelius. The jungle had been systematically cleared for a good distance all around the encampment so that there was no cover where enemies could hide. In and around the huts, the Jilith worked, played or just sat and passed the time.

They were a handsome people, with olive skin and dark hair. The men sported beards, which they kept neatly trimmed, and wore rough animal hides. Though they had no armour and their weapons were crude things, they were clearly capable of defending themselves. Sebastian noticed that whatever they were doing, they kept their swords,

43

shields and spears within reach. Keera had told him that parties of Gograth might launch armed raids on the camp at any time. It had been a while since the last raid and everyone was on edge, waiting for the next one.

The women of the tribe seemed to be at work of some kind every hour of the day. They were scraping hides to make clothes, washing them in the stream that meandered a short distance from the village, fetching firewood or searching for edible roots in the jungle. They seemed to accept the work with quiet good humour and Sebastian never saw any looking disgruntled with their role in life.

The children were everywhere, running around in laughing, yelling gangs, playing with their home-made toys or chasing one of the many mutts that seemed to hang around the village. The older boys trailed after the hunting parties to learn the skills that would take them through to adulthood.

Sebastian would sit on a log by the entrance to his hut, sipping a cup of chai, the spicy green tea the villagers loved to make, and he would marvel at the wonderful community spirit that seemed to radiate from these people. They had never seen the wonders of cities like Ramalat and Keladon, but they had riches that money could not buy – an affinity with the land in which they lived. As far as Sebastian could see, they had no kind of currency, but seemed to share whatever they had, as though they had no notion of greed or any wish to acquire material possessions.

Most afternoons, Sebastian sat beside Max and the two of them watched as 'General' Cornelius put his troops through their paces. The Jilith tended to fight as individuals, but he had told them that if they wished to vanquish the Gograth, they would have to learn to work as a team. To help them with this, he had introduced them to a game that was popular in Golmira. A piece of animal hide was stuffed with straw and stitched into a ball. Two teams of warriors kicked the ball backwards and forwards, trying to get it through two upright sticks at each end of a clearing. One warrior was assigned to defend the opening and was allowed to touch the ball with his hands – the others could only use their feet.

'Does this game have a name?' Sebastian asked Cornelius one afternoon.

The little warrior thought for a moment. 'It's called *kick-the-ball*,' he said.

'Wouldn't *football* be a better name?' asked Max. 'It has a certain ring to it, does it not?'

Cornelius bristled. 'It's called kick-the-ball,' he repeated firmly. 'It has been played in Golmira for centuries. There are ancient cave paintings showing warriors kicking a ball, all dressed in brightly coloured clothing, with numbers written on their chests.'

'It looks like fun,' said Sebastian. 'Maybe I'll take a turn at it myself when I'm a bit stronger.'

'It seems completely mindless to me,' observed Max

disparagingly. 'Kicking a lump of hide around a field – where's the skill in that?' He nodded his head towards the straggle of running, shouting warriors on the pitch. 'They're half killing each other out there.'

Cornelius smiled. 'Yes, but they're starting to think as teams,' he said. 'Let's hope they do as well when they face up to the Gograth.'

As one day blended into another, Sebastian rapidly grew stronger. Soon he was able to go on short walks around the village without struggling for breath and every day saw a marked improvement. All that was left of his close brush with death was a livid scar, and a dull pain in his chest whenever he brandished a sword. He began to train with the weapon for a short time each day, aware that before very much longer he might be called upon to face up to the Gograth once again.

Then, one morning, Keera arrived with an invitation. She told them that her father, Maccan, the village chief, had decided that it was finally time to meet the Chosen One face to face.

'He bids you come to his hut tomorrow,' she told them. 'There will be a great feast in your honour.'

At this news, Max brightened considerably. 'A feast,' he said. 'Lovely. What's on the menu?'

Cornelius gave him a sly look. 'Let's just hope it's not buffalope steaks,' he said; and walked away laughing.

* * *

The drums started at twilight the following day. At first Sebastian was startled, thinking that it was the sound of an advancing army, but it was too close at hand, and a quick glance outside confirmed that it was emanating from the centre of the village. A big fire was burning outside Maccan's hut and the enticing smell of roasting rusa filled the air.

'They're getting ready for our shindig,' announced Cornelius, who in spite of the heat was dressing himself in full armour. 'Looks like it's going to be quite a party.' He glanced disparagingly at Sebastian. 'Don't you think you should make an effort to smarten yourself up a bit?' he said. 'I mean, you're supposed to be the Chosen One, not a down-and-out.'

'What would you suggest?' Sebastian spread his arms in a gesture of helplessness. 'All my spare clothes were packed into the saddlebags of that mule, and I must have lost my tricorn hat back in the jungle. All I've got left is what I'm wearing.'

'Well, you could at least wash your face. It looks like it hasn't seen a bowl of water in an age!'

Sebastian took the hint. He stripped off his tunic, poured fresh water into a bowl and washed himself down. Then he spent some time twisting the ends of his long black hair into braids and tying them with leather thongs, a task made doubly difficult by the absence of any kind of mirror.

'You had a word with Max?' asked Cornelius.

'Yes, he's given me my orders,' said a mournful voice from the doorway; and they turned to see Max's head gazing resentfully in at them. 'I'm to mind my manners and not speak out of turn. And I'm most definitely not to have any alcohol.'

'I don't think they know what alcohol is,' said Sebastian. 'The only drink I've seen around here is chai.'

'Oh, they'll have alcohol,' Cornelius assured him. 'All people do, of one kind or another. They just might not know it by that name. And as for chai, we all know what effect that has on Max!' He scowled. 'You know, perhaps it would be best if he didn't come with us. We don't want him interrupting the chief with great gusts of wind, do we?'

Max looked hurt. 'Don't fret,' he said. 'I'll take special care not to disgrace myself. Besides, they'll want to see me – I'm the magical talking buffalope, am I not? Let's face it, I'm one of the strongest cards you have. When it comes to magical properties, you two aren't much to write home about, are you?'

Cornelius looked doubtful. 'Whatever we are, we can't afford to mess this up. Sebastian, you'll have to convince Maccan that you are the Chosen One. So far, he's accepted you purely on the word of Keera and me. If he's confronted with a bumbling, babbling twit, he might think again.'

'What are you trying to say?' muttered Sebastian.

'Oh, come on, you know you've an uncanny ability to put your foot in it. Just think before you open your mouth, that's all I ask. And remember, both of you, that I am now a *general*. When I outline my plans to defeat the Gograth, I don't want one of you piping up with some stupid remark.'

Sebastian looked at him. 'We'll do our best,' he said quietly. 'I'm sure we don't want to mess things up for you, do we, Max?'

'Oh, don't be like that!' protested Cornelius. 'I was only—'

'Somebody coming!' announced Max; and he drew back from the doorway.

A few moments later, a tall sinewy warrior stepped into the hut and greeted them with a bow. Sebastian knew that he was called Cal and that he was highly regarded in the village. He wore his long black hair tied back. There was an old scar running down his left cheek and he had cunning grey eyes that seemed to look deep inside a man and read any secrets that lay hidden there. Sebastian had only spent a short time in his presence but he always felt somewhat nervous of him. Cal bowed politely enough but there was a sardonic smile on his face as he spoke.

'Maccan has bid me come and summon our . . . *distinguished* guests to the feast,' he announced.

Sebastian was still tying off the last of his braids. 'Please tell Maccan that we are greatly honoured by his kindness and that we will be along presently,' he said.

'As you wish,' purred Cal. 'I shall tell him that the Chosen One is still . . . combing his hair?'

'Braiding it,' Sebastian corrected him. 'I'm braiding it, if you must know. Now, you go back. We won't be a moment.'

'We are preparing a fine fat rusa for you,' said Cal. 'I think you'll find it to your taste. I killed it with my own hands. I put them around its throat and throttled the life out of it.'

'That's, er . . . nice,' said Sebastian awkwardly, and was aware of Cornelius shooting a despairing look at him. 'We are indebted to you,' he added, thinking that this might sound a little more regal.

'Cal is the finest hunter in the village,' explained Cornelius. 'His skill with a throwing spear is exceptional.'

'Is that right?' Sebastian wondered what else he could add to the subject. 'That's terrific. Well done! It's, er . . . good to . . . kill rusas,' he offered. 'Where I come from, we have a saying. *The only good rusa is a dead rusa.*'

Cal looked at him blankly. 'Which means?'

'Well, blessed if I know, really. It's just a saying.'

'In a day or so the hunting party will be setting out to look for fresh game,' said Cal. 'Perhaps you would both like to accompany us?'

'We'd love that,' said Cornelius, without hesitation. 'Wouldn't we, Sebastian?'

'Er . . . yes. Great. Just . . . try and hold me back.'

Cal bowed again and left the hut without another word.

Sebastian waited a few moments until he was out of earshot. 'Is it my imagination, or does that man dislike me?' he muttered.

'Oh, he feels a bit of friendly rivalry, I suppose. After all, until we came along he was the big fish in this pond. And . . .'

'And what?' asked Sebastian suspiciously.

'By all accounts, he's rather sweet on Keera. In fact, as I understand it, he was hoping to marry her.'

'So?' Sebastian looked at Cornelius indignantly. 'I haven't done anything to change that . . . have I?'

Cornelius smirked and lifted his bronze helmet onto his head. 'Oh, not much! Let's face it, Cal's got eyes – he can see that Keera is interested in you, so—'

'Don't be ridiculous! She's not interested in me. Is she?'

'Oh, what have I said?' groaned Cornelius. 'I assumed you *knew*!'

'Well, she *has* been coming around here a lot, but I didn't think . . .'

Cornelius stood up. 'Just forget about it,' he said sternly. 'Right now that's a complication we don't need. Don't do anything to encourage her. Got that?'

'I suppose . . .'

'Good! Now, how do I look?'

'Hmm . . . ?' Sebastian studied the little warrior for a moment. 'Very noble,' he said. 'What about me?'

'Like you've been dragged through a swamp backwards,

but there's not much we can do about that. Come on, it doesn't do to keep Maccan waiting.' He handed Sebastian a dagger. 'Here, take this,' he said.

'What's this for?' asked Sebastian.

'It's customary to offer the chief a gift when you meet him. I bought that in Ramalat – I'm sure he'll like it. Unless, of course, you'd like to give him that fancy amulet you wear around your neck?'

'Princess Kerin gave me that back in Keladon,' protested Sebastian.

'Hmm. Yes, I didn't think you'd be ready to hand that over.' Cornelius looked shrewdly at his friend. 'If I didn't know better, I'd say there's still a part of you that carries a torch for your first love.'

'What nonsense,' said Sebastian, a little too quickly. 'I'm with Jenna now.'

The two of them went out into the open, where Max was waiting for them. They gazed towards the chief's hut, where the thunder of drums was steadily rising to a crescendo. 'We'd better get this over with,' said Sebastian apprehensively. 'What are we supposed to do exactly?'

'Perhaps you could try them with a few highlights from your old jester's routine,' suggested Max. 'It went down a storm in Keladon.'

'Oh, very amusing,' snarled Sebastian.

'Actually, no, that was the problem.'

'Stop bickering, you two,' snapped Cornelius. 'And wherever possible, leave the talking to me. Just try and look regal, Sebastian . . . and as for you' – he glanced at Max – 'keep your lip buttoned! Come on.'

CHAPTER 6

MACCAN'S WORD

They walked the short distance across the village, the thudding of the drums getting louder at every step.

As they drew closer, they could see the huge carcass of a rusa boar sizzling over the fire. Around it, several male and female dancers, wearing carved and painted wooden masks, were leaping and jerking to the primitive beat. A short distance beyond them, in front of the chief's hut, they saw a figure that could only have been Maccan. He was seated on an ornate wooden throne and dressed in elaborate regalia made from what looked like leaves and quills and woven reeds. He had a beautifully carved wooden crown on his head; beneath it, his face was dark and weather-beaten, and his long hair was decorated with animal teeth and shells. His deep-set brown eyes regarded the three latecomers expressionlessly as they approached.

On his left side sat Keera, wearing a long gown of roughly woven blue cloth, her hair tied up in an intricate arrangement of decorative plaits. The colour of her cheeks and lips had been artificially accentuated with some kind of pigment and she looked beautiful. She regarded Sebastian demurely from beneath lowered lashes, and though a smile plucked momentarily at her lips, she managed to keep it in check.

On Maccan's right side sat the stick-thin, white-bearded figure of the shaman, Danthus, whom Sebastian had not seen since the old man had pulled the arrowhead out of his chest. Sebastian smiled and nodded but Danthus gave no indication that he had even noticed the gesture. His thin, almost cadaverous face remained expressionless, his pale grey eyes staring straight ahead, his blue-veined hands resting on the handle of a rough-hewn stick.

Sebastian supposed that there would once have been a wife sitting on Maccan's right side, but Keera had told him that her mother had died years ago from a fever and that her father had never sought another partner.

The three friends walked round the fire and came to a halt a respectful distance from the chief. He sat there regarding them for a few moments, then raised his arms and clapped his hands together once. As if by magic, the music came to an abrupt halt, the dancers stopped in their tracks and Sebastian had an immediate impression of this man's incredible power over the village. Clearly he demanded – and received –

complete obedience. When he spoke, his voice was deep and full of authority.

'The Chosen One and his companions are most welcome in our village,' he said. 'Please' – he indicated a couple of vacant seats beside his daughter – and a pile of fresh straw that had been thoughtfully left for a buffalope to recline on – 'take your places beside us. You honour us with your presence.'

Sebastian smiled and was about to do as he was told when he felt a surreptitious jab in the side from Cornelius's elbow and realized he was supposed to respond. He bowed his head.

'On the . . . contrary, Great Chief, it is we who . . . are honoured,' he insisted. 'And we humbly . . . thank you and the people of the village for the . . . the help you have given us.'

He looked back up at Maccan but the chief was still gesturing to the empty places, so he went and sat next to Keera. He glanced at her nervously and was rewarded with a fleeting smile. Cornelius took his seat and then Max, trying his very best not to knock anything over, lowered his prodigious bulk into the available space. Glancing around, Sebastian saw that the men, women and children of the tribe were arranging themselves cross-legged on the ground. Every pair of eyes was staring directly at him and he began to feel extremely nervous, particularly when he noticed Cal a short distance away, a superior sneer on his face.

There was a long silence, broken only by the snapping of twigs in the fire. Then Maccan spoke.

'My daughter has told me of your quest to find the lost city.'

Sebastian nodded. 'It was our main reason for coming here,' he admitted.

'My daughter also spoke of the mighty pool of water upon which you have travelled?'

'Oh yes, Great Chief, the ocean! We have travelled upon the waters in a vast ship and had many adventures. We have fought pirates and kelfers – terrifying sea beasts with great snapping jaws – and escaped to tell the tale.'

'I should like to see this mighty water for myself,' said Maccan.

'Well, unfortunately it's a great distance from here – many moons of travel away.'

Maccan nodded gravely. 'Still,' he said, 'perhaps one day something could be arranged?'

There was a long silence.

'Er . . . why not?' said Sebastian. 'I'm . . . I'm sure something could be sorted out. A kind of . . .'

'Sightseeing tour,' suggested Max. 'Yes, we could have a jolly trudge all the way back to Ramalat and the chief could take in all the hot spots. The harbour . . . the taverns . . . maybe even a little trip out in a boat.'

'Er . . . yes, why not?' said Cornelius feebly. 'We'll, um . . . have to see how we're fixed.'

Maccan frowned. He glanced at Danthus, who shrugged his narrow shoulders. 'It sounds good,' said the chief.

'You'll love it,' Max assured him. 'It's a fun town.'

Another silence; then Maccan clapped his hands together. 'And now,' he went on, 'a gift for the Chosen One!'

A woman came forward carrying a headdress made from bones and multicoloured feathers. She stopped in front of Sebastian and lowered the thing carefully and respectfully onto his head. She stepped back, bowed and moved away.

Sebastian sat there, feeling vaguely foolish. He glanced at Cornelius. 'How does it look?' he asked.

'Very regal,' said Cornelius; but it was obvious that he was stifling a laugh.

Sebastian glanced at Max. 'Oh yes, young master,' said the buffalope, a little too quickly. 'You look a right . . . Jilith!'

'Thanks very much,' muttered Sebastian.

'And now it's your turn,' whispered Cornelius.

'Huh?'

'The knife, you nitwit!'

'Oh yes.' Sebastian got to his feet, walked across to Maccan and put the dagger carefully into his hands. 'A small token of our respect,' he said.

Maccan grinned and lifted the dagger so that his people could see it. A great cheer went up. Sebastian bowed his head and returned to his place.

'He seems to like it,' muttered Max, sounding genuinely surprised. 'He's easily pleased.'

Now Maccan slipped the dagger into his own belt and clapped his hands a second time. 'Bring my guests some icara!' he commanded.

Immediately tribeswomen appeared carrying jugs and clay cups, one of which was pushed into Sebastian's hand and filled with a dark red liquid that looked suspiciously like blood; but when he sniffed at it surreptitiously, he got the unmistakable aroma of wine. He saw with a sense of misgiving that a big bowl had been placed in front of Max and that it was being filled to the brim.

'This is . . . alcoholic?' asked Sebastian nervously.

Maccan was lifting his own cup to his mouth. 'I do not understand this word, Elf Lord,' he said.

'It makes you . . . happy?'

'And then some,' said Maccan, grinning for the first time. 'So . . . drink!'

'What do I do?' hissed Max, under his breath.

'Drink it,' whispered Cornelius.

'But you said—'

'We can't insult the chief. Drink!'

'All right, but I'm taking no responsibility . . .' Max plunged his snout into the bowl and started lapping enthusiastically.

'Sip it!' said Cornelius through gritted teeth.

Sebastian lifted the cup to his lips and took a generous gulp. At first it tasted deliciously sweet, but this was followed by a sensation of being punched in the stomach; his vision seemed to waver and shimmer as though he'd imbibed several flagons of the strongest ale. He gasped, then disguised it as a cough.

'Wow!' he said. He glanced around at the crowd behind him, who were just sitting there, watching in silence. 'Is nobody else having any?' he asked.

Maccan wiped his mouth with the back of his hand. 'Icara is too precious to give to just anyone,' he said. 'It's harvested once a year from a secret grove and then allowed to ferment for many moons before it is ready. You like?'

'Very nice,' said Sebastian. 'Very . . . refreshing.'

'Refreshing? It's sensational!' said Max. 'You must let me have the recipe!' He was licking the last dregs from the bowl as he spoke.

Cornelius rolled his eyes in despair. 'I believe the great chief just told us that it's a very *special* drink,' he said. 'So I don't think he'll want to give you the recipe, will he?'

'Pity.' Max looked up and caught the eye of one of the serving women. 'Hey, love! A drop more over here, if you don't mind!'

'Max!' hissed Sebastian. He smiled at Maccan. 'You must forgive him, he's . . . very excitable!'

'He's a comical creature,' enthused Maccan. 'He speaks as

well as any man. Are there many such creatures where you come from?'

'Not like him,' murmured Cornelius, watching in disbelief as the bowl was filled for a second time. 'For goodness' sake, Max, take it easy,' he whispered.

'Make your mind up,' said Max. 'A moment ago you said—'

'I know what I said!' Cornelius tried to mask his anger with an unconvincing laugh. 'Great Chief, we were talking with Keera the other day about the threat of the Gograth.'

'Ah yes.' Maccan was getting his own refill from one of the women. 'Yes, it's a worry.' He reached out a hand and patted his daughter on the shoulder. 'Keera and the others are valiant in the way they take on those beasts, but we cannot hope to prevail for much longer. They are so savage. I cannot begin to tell you the horrors they have visited upon my people. Warriors slaughtered by the score – even women and children. They are merciless and it seems they are intent on persecuting us to extinction. You promised to help us fight them, but my warriors tell me that you are training them to kick balls around.'

'Umm . . . well . . . that's just part of what we're doing. You see, although your warriors are excellent hunters and they fight very well as individuals . . . even in small teams . . . the Jilith must learn to fight as an army.'

'This has never been our way,' said Maccan.

'I understand that, but you must fight fire with fire. General Darvon has a powerful army and the Jilith cannot hope to defeat it unless they have one too. So I am teaching your people to fight as one. We have already made great improvements and I have formulated an ingenious plan to defeat the Gograth. I would like your permission, Great Chief, to begin preparations for a final conflict. One that will rid you of their threat for ever.'

Maccan looked thoughtful. 'I admit it sounds like a wonderful thing – and it *is* foretold in the old stories that the Chosen One will come to rid us of our enemies.' He glanced at Danthus. 'What say you, shaman? Can the Chosen One and the little general do what they promise?'

Danthus frowned. He reached into the animal-skin pouch that hung around his neck and pulled out what looked like a series of strangely shaped bones. He crouched down and threw the bones onto the ground. Then he stared at them intently, as if puzzling them out.

'What's he looking for?' muttered Max ungraciously. 'A weather forecast?'

'Shush!' hissed Sebastian.

Now Danthus was waving a gnarled hand over the bones, his eyelids fluttering. 'Okrin, the goddess of the forest, speaks to me,' he announced.

Max glanced around. 'I didn't hear anything,' he muttered.

He looked at Cornelius. 'Did you hear anything?' Cornelius glared at him.

'She tells me that we should trust the strangers,' said Danthus. 'She says that they are capable of making good on their promise.'

'She's clearly no mug,' observed Max, and then winced as Cornelius's hand came out and slapped him across the rump. 'Ow!' he complained. 'Do you mind?'

'But Okrin says that if they do not succeed, they must be banished from this place and never allowed to return.'

'Oh, well, that's charming, isn't it? Of all the ungratefu—' Max broke off abruptly because Cornelius had now moved across to him and clamped his jaws shut.

The Golmiran bowed to Maccan. 'Ignore the buffalope, Great Chief,' he said. 'The icara has made him talk nonsense. And fear not, I shall deliver you from the Gograth. All I ask is that you help us with our quest to find the lost city of Mendip.'

Maccan bowed in return. 'Rid me of my enemies and I shall do whatever you ask,' he said. 'You have my word on it.' He looked around. 'And now,' he roared, 'music! Dancing! And more icara!'

CHAPTER 7

A CUNNING PLAN

Sebastian woke the next morning to the sounds of industry: the thudding of axes against wood, the crunching of spades delving into stony soil and the unmistakable noise of Cornelius barking orders.

Sebastian groaned and shook himself awake. The party had gone on until dawn and he felt quite exhausted. He remembered dancing wildly with Keera at one point, and Cornelius had been dragged from his seat by a huge woman with red hair and thrown around like a rag doll. Sebastian and Cornelius had stopped drinking icara pretty quickly, but unfortunately Max had not. He had even joined in the dance, flailing around madly, kicking up his hooves and bellowing some old buffalope songs. At one point a back leg had flung up the embers from a fire and scattered them in all directions, sending people running for cover.

Sebastian glanced around the interior of the hut and saw the strange bone-and-feather headdress that Maccan had presented to him; it rested on the handle of a sword, its blade stabbed deep into the earth. Outside, people continued to work, and though he really felt like pulling the animal-hide covers over his head and going back to sleep, he realized that he would have to show willing. He dragged himself up, pulled on his clothes, then stumbled outside, blinking in the harsh light of the early morning.

A short distance from the guesthouse, a couple of burly warriors were assembling a rough wooden structure that looked like a large cart. They were using primitive tools and Sebastian noticed a pair of rough-hewn wheels waiting to be fitted – though he had previously seen no evidence that these people even knew about wheels.

A little way further on, a second group of warriors were digging a shallow trench, big enough to enclose the central cluster of huts. A group of women followed behind them, packing the trench tightly with large bales of what looked like straw. Sebastian spotted Cornelius and Max supervising one group of diggers and wandered over to them.

'What's going on?' he asked feebly. 'And whatever it is, do you have to do it quite so early?'

'Ah, Sebastian, I was wondering when you were going to surface!' said Cornelius. 'What's the matter? You look a little weary.'

'Can you wonder?' he cried. 'We only got to sleep a few moments ago. Aren't you tired?'

Cornelius shrugged. 'I felt a little bleary-eyed when I got up at first light,' he admitted, 'but that soon passed. And besides, there was work to be done.'

'What about you, Max?' ventured Sebastian. 'You must be feeling rough after all the icara you put away.'

Max affected a look of unconcern, but his eyes were strangely unfocused and Sebastian could tell he was suffering. 'We buffalope are renowned for our hardy constitutions,' he said. 'And luckily, I was pacing myself. I know when to say "enough".'

'Really? I didn't hear you mention that word last night,' said Sebastian disparagingly. 'I believe I heard you yell "more"quite often, though.'

Max rolled his eyes. 'Such an exaggerator,' he said. 'I only drank that stuff to be polite.'

'And you're feeling terrible?' Sebastian asked him.

'Not one bit.'

Cornelius gestured around at the partially completed circle. 'Well, what do you think?' he asked.

Sebastian frowned. 'Umm . . . well, at first glance I thought you were digging a trench, but it's clearly not deep enough to hide men in; and besides, you're packing it with that yellow stuff.'

'Well spotted.' Cornelius and Max exchanged knowing

looks. Then the little warrior leaned down and scooped up a handful of the straw-like substance. 'This "yellow stuff", as you call it, is called conflagrus: it grows wild in the jungle. The Jilith have been using it since time began. Watch this.' Cornelius stepped away from the circle and dropped the lump of weed onto the ground. Then he knelt down beside it and took his tinderbox from his belt. He struck one spark and let it fall onto the weed. Immediately the clump erupted into flame, a high bright flame that seemed to give off intense heat. 'The Jilith use this stuff as kindling and to make torches,' he said. 'It burns hot and bright and for a surprisingly long time.'

'So?' Sebastian was feeling too tired to do much thinking.

'So it's going to be one of the secret weapons that will give us total domination over the Gograth,' said Cornelius.

'I don't understand,' said Sebastian.

'One spark in this lot and it'll go up like a whole pile of thunder-sticks,' said Cornelius. 'They won't know what hit them.'

'What if it rains?' asked Max.

Cornelius glared at him. 'It won't rain,' he said. 'It hasn't rained since we arrived here.'

'It must rain *sometimes*,' said Max. 'Look at all the greenery around us. I bet it rains for days on end. How will you set light to it then?'

'It *won't* rain,' said Cornelius, through gritted teeth. 'Suffice it to say that when the Gograth attack the village, the conflagrus is going to be one of the elements we shall use to destroy them.'

'Don't you mean *if* they attack the village?' said Sebastian.

'No, I mean *when*. And fire will be only one of our weapons.'

'The other one is me,' said Max, looking rather pleased with himself. '*I'm* secret weapon number two, but don't tell anybody – it's a secret.'

'Not *just* you,' Cornelius reminded him. 'Max will be pulling the war wagon.' He pointed to where the warriors were piecing together their wooden contraption. 'My own design, adapted from a Golmiran battle sleigh. Those poor Gograth don't know what they're in for.'

Sebastian stared at the trenches. He wasn't yet sure exactly how they were going to work; indeed, there was part of him that didn't really *want* to know. 'What about Max?' he asked. 'Won't he be very vulnerable?'

'Yes,' said Max, suddenly looking a little worried. 'Won't it be dangerous?'

'Not at all,' snorted Cornelius. 'You remember – we discussed this. You're to have your own armour.'

'Armour?' said Sebastian.

'Yes. We're going to make him a special suit made from layers of rusa hide, tough enough to withstand attack from arrows and spears.'

Max smiled proudly. 'Oh yes, I forgot about that bit. Cornelius says I'll be like some invincible beast rampaging through the midst of the enemy. He says I'll probably be part of the Jilith's stories in years to come.'

Sebastian frowned. 'Hmm. The one about the fabulous talking buffalope that turned into a great hairy pincushion?'

Max's mouth fell open. He looked at Cornelius. 'I thought you said my armour would be tough enough to stop arrows!'

'It will be!' Cornelius glared at Sebastian. 'Stop trying to put the wind up Max,' he growled. 'He already has more than his fair share!'

'You don't think you're rushing things, do you?' said Sebastian. 'I mean, you've only been training the Jilith for a short time – I'm not at all convinced that they're ready.'

'Of course they're ready!' snapped Cornelius. 'You'll see when the Gograth attack—'

'You keep saying that, but how can you know that they will?'

'Because we'll provoke them into it. I'm tired of waiting around for something to happen. You see, up until now the Jilith have always adopted a defensive role. Oh, they fight like demons when they are attacked, but they have always allowed the Gograth to make the first move. This time *we'll* strike the opening blow, we'll draw the first blood. Then we'll retreat in apparent disorder, back to the village. If this General Darvon is the kind of creature I think he is, he'll see this as a terrible insult – he'll *have* to come after us. We'll lure his army into the trap . . . and then we'll deal with them.'

Sebastian nodded. 'It seems thorough enough,' he admitted. 'If a bit brutal.'

Cornelius raised his eyebrows. 'Brutal?' he echoed. 'The Gograth were hardly gentle with us, were they?'

'Well, no . . .'

'They tried to kill us on sight and you were lucky to survive the attack. And you heard the stories Maccan told us about them – the terrible things they've done to this tribe. Women and children murdered in cold blood. I wouldn't waste any time worrying about them.'

'Yes, but . . . it sounds like you're planning to destroy their entire tribe.'

'That's about the size of it,' agreed Cornelius.

'Good enough for 'em!' sniffed Max. 'Great hairy bullies, the lot of 'em. The jungle will be a better place without 'em.'

'You may be right,' agreed Sebastian reluctantly; but somehow he couldn't convince himself that this plan was acceptable. 'I mean, yes, the Gograth are brutal – but is that any excuse to sink to their level?'

'Sebastian!'

He turned and saw Keera coming towards him from the direction of the huts. She was carrying a large wooden bowl filled with green liquid.

'Good morning,' she said. 'I'm surprised to see you up so

early. I thought you might be feeling tired after last night's celebration.'

'Me? Oh no . . . I'm right as rain,' said Sebastian. 'We've all been up for ages working on the battle plan, haven't we, lads?'

Cornelius and Max exchanged sardonic looks.

'And you,' said Keera, looking at Max. 'You drank a lot of icara last night. It's powerful stuff if you're not used to it.'

Max affected a devil-may-care laugh that wasn't entirely convincing. 'Oh, don't worry about me. We buffalope can handle our drink.'

Keera looked relieved. 'Oh, that's all right then.' She nodded at the bowl of green liquid. 'I was just bringing you this special medicine. But as you don't need it—'

'Medicine?' said Max.

'Yes. It can cure a headache instantly. The Jilith have used it for generations. But as you're feeling all right—'

'Well, let's not be too hasty!'

Before Keera could react, Max had lunged forward and thrust his snout into the bowl. He began gulping down its contents eagerly. 'Yes!' he said, between slurps. 'I can feel it working . . . or rather . . . I probably *would* . . . if I had a bad head in the first place. Which I haven't. Actually . . . it's quite tasty!'

Keera was staring at him in dismay. 'You're not supposed to drink it,' she said. 'I was going to rub it onto your forehead.'

'Really?' Max stepped back, looking worried. 'I don't suppose it'll do any harm,' he muttered. 'What's in it?'

Keera thought for a moment. 'Let me see now . . . You crush tree beetles, green worms and white lizards in a gourd and then you add some rusa spit . . .'

Max blanched. 'Excuse me,' he said; and hurried away behind the nearest hut. After a few moments they heard the sounds of him being spectacularly unwell.

'Oh dear,' said Keera.

'Don't worry about him,' Cornelius reassured her. 'It's not the first time he's been like that. Now, umm . . . was there some other reason you came to see us?'

'Oh yes. I've come to take you to meet Joseph,' she said. 'Remember, the old man who visited the lost city?'

'Ah, excellent,' said Cornelius. 'I've been looking forward to this.'

Max came stumbling back from behind the hut.

'Did you hear that, shaggy?' said Sebastian. 'We're going to meet Joseph.'

'Oh, goody,' said Max.

'Just give me a moment.' Cornelius moved away and had a quick word with the trench-diggers, then returned to the others, smiling. 'Let's go,' he said to Keera.

She led them amongst the huts. The villagers were up and about, preparing fires and brewing their first shot of chai. Many bowed their heads respectfully to Sebastian as he passed. More worryingly, he noticed that some of the younger women were whispering to each other and giggling.

Keera saw his nervous look and tried to reassure him. 'Many of our girls think you are good-looking,' she told him. 'You set some hearts aflutter last night with your wonderful display of dancing.'

'Is that what he was doing?' muttered Max. 'I thought a spark from the fire had gone down his breeches.'

'Do you mind?' growled Sebastian.

'Not at all,' said Max.

'So you are already making ready to face the Gograth?' observed Keera, changing the subject.

'Oh yes,' said Cornelius. 'We believe in striking while the metal is hot. But everything must be ready, I want to leave nothing to chance. In a couple of moons, all the preparations will be ready.'

'The young master seems to think we shouldn't be so hard on them,' observed Max gleefully. 'If it was up to him, he'd give them nothing worse than a good telling off!'

Keera looked at Sebastian in surprise. 'This is true?' she asked him.

'Not really. As usual, he's twisting my words.' He thought for a moment. 'I think they deserve a harsh lesson, of course, but killing every last one of them . . . ? Wouldn't it be enough to destroy *some* of them and let the others understand that it will happen to all of them if they don't mend their ways?'

Keera shook her head. 'I'm afraid you do not know the Gograth,' she told him. 'They are animals, not men. Allow just one warrior to escape and he will keep his hunger for revenge alive in his heart. He would not have a moment's rest until he had taken it. They are hateful creatures, totally without conscience or remorse.'

'But how can that be?' reasoned Sebastian. 'There must be families amongst them – husbands, wives, children. There has to be *some* love there, surely? Some . . . compassion.'

'For their own kind perhaps . . . but not for anybody else, of that you can be certain. We have had to live with their barbaric ways for a long time now; and I have seen many of our best people die at their hands.'

Sebastian was about to say something else, but he saw that Keera was heading towards the doorway of a small hut. It was dark and smoky inside. She bowed her head and spoke softly into the gloom.

'Joseph?' she murmured. 'I have brought the visitors to meet you.'

There was a short silence; then a croaky voice said, 'Bring them inside.'

CHAPTER 8

JOSEPH'S STORY

Keera went in first; Sebastian followed, bowing his head to avoid banging it on the lintel. Cornelius strolled through easily, but Max's huge shoulders would not fit through the narrow opening, so he had to stand with his head poking through the doorway.

There were just two people inside. At first glance Sebastian took the first, tending a metal pot over a fire, to be a long-haired boy of perhaps fourteen summers; but as the figure turned to look at him, he realized that it was in fact a skinny girl, who regarded him with bright green eyes. It occurred to him that under the layers of grime that covered her face, she might actually have been quite pretty.

A few steps away from her, sitting up in a low bed, was an old man. He was skeletal beneath the animal-skin clothes he wore and his face was etched deep with the lines of a long, hard life. His grey hair hung to his shoulders and around his skinny neck was an assortment of beads and charms, worn one on top of the other as though he had acquired more and more of them over the years.

'Please be seated,' he said, indicating a rug laid out beside the fire. He watched in silence as the visitors settled themselves down. Then he gave them a gap-toothed grin.

'You are welcome to my home,' he croaked. 'Keera has told me much about you, but this is the first time I have seen you for myself. My legs are not good these days – I seldom leave the hut.' He looked at Sebastian – 'You are the Chosen One who seeks the lost city' – then pointed a bony finger at Cornelius – 'Obviously you are the little warrior who fights like twenty men.' His gaze shifted to the doorway. 'And this must be the magical talking buffalope.' He smiled at Keera. 'You described them well,' he said.

'Well, he's certainly got the measure of us,' said Max; and Joseph gave a wheezy gasp of delight. He looked at the girl beside the fire. 'You were right, Salah, he *does* sound like he has the intelligence of a man!'

Max looked affronted. 'Judging by some of the people I've met,' he said, 'that's not saying very much!'

Joseph cackled again, as though this was the funniest thing he'd ever heard. 'Do you hear him? The brute clearly has quite an opinion of himself.'

'*Brute?*' echoed Max. 'Well, really!'

Sebastian spoke in a hasty attempt to defuse any argument. 'Thank you for taking the time to speak to us,' he said. 'You clearly know quite a bit about us.'

'Oh, Salah here brings me all the news of the village,' said Joseph. The girl grinned self-consciously and stirred the brew with a length of stick. 'She's my niece. Her parents both died in a Gograth raid some time ago and she hasn't uttered a single word since that day. I'm afraid I'm all she has left in the world.'

Sebastian was about to ask how Salah could tell Joseph any news if she couldn't speak, but at that moment she turned to the old man and made some swift gestures with her hands.

Joseph nodded. 'She asks if you would like to partake of a cup of chai,' he said.

'We'd be delighted,' said Sebastian.

Salah nodded and began to ladle dark-green liquid from the cooking pot into clay cups, which she handed round to everybody.

'I drink ten cups every day,' said Joseph. 'That's why I've lived to be as old as I am.'

Max looked hopefully at the others. 'Couldn't I have a little drop?' he asked pitifully. 'I'm parched.'

'You know the effect it has on you,' warned Cornelius.

'Yes, but my back end's not even in the hut. And I need something to take away the taste of that medicine. Surely it can't do any harm?'

Salah looked enquiringly at her uncle and the old man smiled and nodded.

'Pour the beast a hot sup,' he told her. 'Since he seems to think he's the equal of any man, we'll see what he thinks of our chai.'

Salah took a bowl to the doorway, set it down reverently in front of Max as though he were some kind of sacred cow, then backed away. He fell to, making loud slurping noises as he drank.

'That's very good,' he observed, between slurps. 'Quite the nicest I've tasted.'

Joseph laughed. 'I never dreamed I would live to see the day when a buffalope congratulated me on my chai,' he observed. 'What a world we live in!' He settled himself back against his cushions and studied Sebastian and Cornelius with interest. 'So . . . you wish to know about the lost city of Mendip?'

'Yes, please,' said Cornelius. 'We have been sent here to find it – and Keera tells us that you have actually been there.'

'That's true enough,' Joseph said, 'though it was many, many summers ago. I was but a boy then, not much older than Salah. My father used to tell me stories about the place, but I never dreamed that there was any truth in them. Then, one day . . . I went out on a hunt with some of the warriors of the village.'

'Yes, but which village?' asked Sebastian. 'I know that you

move around from time to time, so . . . would you be able to find the place again?'

Joseph smiled. 'I believe so. You see, I think it was *this* village.'

Sebastian looked puzzled.

'We often return to former sites,' explained Keera. 'It means that we have very little work to do when we get there: we just patch up the huts we made before. We have lived in this place many times.' She turned to Joseph. 'But how can you be sure?' she asked him. 'This happened when you were a boy and you must have lived in so many different places. How do you know it's this one?'

'I'm pretty sure it was here,' he told her. 'I may be long in the tooth but there's nothing wrong with my memory.' He returned to his story. 'We set off along a rusa trail heading west and walked for the best part of two days. Then we reached a place where a fast-flowing river crossed our path. It was wide and rapid and we stood there, wondering how we would ever get across it.'

He paused for a moment and lifted his cup to his lips. Sebastian saw that Salah was listening intently, her eyes on the old man's face. She was smiling knowingly – this was no doubt a familiar story.

'Then one man noticed something a short distance down river,' continued Joseph. 'He lifted a finger to his lips and pointed. We looked and, to our delight, we saw a huge tree.

It had thick black roots coming up out of the ground, forming deep hollows, and amongst the roots lay a family of rusa – a big male, several sows and their babies. It was like a gift from Okrin. The men turned and began to creep forward, spears raised. I did likewise.'

He pointed in front of him as though he could actually see the animals waiting there for him. 'The boar rose up, squealing with anger, tusks glittering in the sunlight. It saw the ring of men advancing upon it and searched for the weakest point.' Joseph smiled. 'I was head and shoulders shorter than the others, so of course it went for me. It moved fast for such a heavy beast. Before I knew it, it had slammed into me and was swinging its head to try to get its tusks into my flesh. I didn't have time to think. I grabbed two fistfuls of hair and hung on for dear life.'

Sebastian stared at the old man, trying to imagine him as a young, inexperienced boy plunged into such a desperate situation.

'I heard the yells of the other men as they turned in pursuit, but I didn't dare let go, lest I be trampled underfoot. Of course, I had forgotten that behind me was the river. In its rage the rusa had forgotten also. Suddenly the ground was gone from beneath my feet and we were falling, the rusa and I.' He shrugged his skinny shoulders. 'I had expected to hit the ground,' he said; 'to have the life crushed out of me. When we splashed down into freezing water, the shock made

me cry out in terror; and the next instant the rusa was gone and I was being swept along at incredible speed, held in the chilly embrace of the water.'

Joseph shook his head and his ancient eyes mirrored the terror he must have felt at the time. 'I was not a good swimmer – far from it – and I panicked every time my head went below the surface. The warriors pursued me along the bank for some distance, but they could not keep up and were soon left behind: I was quite alone . . .'

There was a long silence, during which the tiniest sound would have seemed like an intrusion. That was Max's cue to break wind with incredible ferocity. Everybody turned to look at him indignantly.

'Sorry,' he said. 'Must have been the chai.'

'Please ignore his behaviour,' hissed Sebastian, his face reddening. 'Go on with your story.'

The old man nodded. 'I do not know how long I was swept down that river,' he said. 'I was bounced off rocks, tumbled through rapids, dragged deep under the surface. At one point, just as I was grabbing a tree branch, the rusa came hurtling down the river and crashed into me. Its tusks snagged in my clothes, and for a moment I feared it would drag me down, but then it was carried away and I never saw it again. I came close to drowning many times, but at last a fallen tree trunk came down the river. Darkness fell and I was exhausted but I clung onto that tree all through the night as the waters dashed me here and there. When the dawn came, I was still hanging on. I kept trying to kick my way towards the bank but the current was strong and I was exhausted. I dared not release my hold. Finally . . . finally I blacked out and I knew nothing. I had fully expected to die.'

'You didn't though, did you?' asked Max; everybody glared at him. 'I was only asking,' he said.

'When I next opened my eyes,' said Joseph, 'I found myself lying on a low bank of shingle that extended down into a big pool. I was battered and exhausted, but grateful to be alive.'

He smiled, reliving the joy he'd felt at escaping death. 'I lay there for a very long time – I must have slept for several hours. When I awoke, my strength had returned and I felt able to rouse myself. I realized, of course, that I could follow the river back until I either found my comrades or located the trail that would take me to the village, but as I stood there and looked around, I saw something through the trees that made me stare in astonishment.'

There was a long, pregnant silence.

'What was it?' asked Cornelius at last, trying not to show his impatience.

'It was a building,' said Joseph, sounding as though he still could hardly believe it. 'Right there in the middle of the jungle; a building overgrown with vegetation. Not a simple hut like the Jilith would make, but a great grey stone edifice, the like of which I have never seen before or since. Of course

I had to go and investigate. I was young and fascinated by the unknown. So I walked through the trees until I came to the building, and then I saw that it was only one of many, stretching away into the jungle before me. I stood there, looking around me in astonishment for I had never seen such things. They were like . . . the temples of the gods.'

'And was anybody living there?' Sebastian asked.

Joseph shook his head. 'I walked amidst them for what seemed half the day, but I saw no human life, only the occasional javralat and rusa wandering through the desolation. It was as though whoever had lived there had fled suddenly in the middle of the night and never returned.'

'Did you go into any of the buildings?' asked Cornelius.

The old man shook his head, his expression sheepish. 'I . . . I was young and inexperienced. I *wanted* to go inside but I was afraid to. I thought that there might be ghosts or demons waiting for me, just as my father's old stories had said. I looked in through doorways and windows, but there were dark shadows and I was fearful. And I had the uncanny sensation that someone or something was watching me the whole time – something powerful and evil. So after a while I turned round and retraced my steps. Eventually I found my way back to the river and began the long walk home, following its course. I did not reach the village until many days and nights had passed; then there was dancing and feasting in my honour, because of course my parents were sure that I had perished.'

'And you never returned to the city?' asked Sebastian.

'Never.' Joseph smiled. 'Oh, I thought about it many times and I even told others about what I had seen, but they all advised me never to go back. Most of them thought that the place was cursed – returning there might direct the curse at us. But I wasn't sure. I think if I'd managed to persuade a group of warriors to come with me, then I might have returned. Now, of course, it's too late.'

'You . . . perhaps might have brought something back with you?' ventured Cornelius. 'A memento of such a great adventure?'

The old man gazed at him thoughtfully for a few moments before replying. 'There is *something*,' he said, and gestured to Salah, who went across the hut to a large clay bowl. She lifted its lid and revealed something wrapped in a piece of cloth. She withdrew the bundle and brought it back to Joseph, who began to unwrap it, handling it gingerly as though afraid it might burst into flames. Everybody leaned forward, eager to see what it contained; and even Max tried to press in closer, making the flimsy doorway creak in protest.

Joseph finally revealed what looked like a glass dome with a flat base. Within the dome was a tiny city, carved in intricate detail from what looked like smooth wood or bone. Sebastian caught his breath: he had never seen such craftsmanship before. Then he noticed that the city was covered by water.

'It reminds me of the Angels' Lair,' he whispered. Joseph gave him a quizzical look and he elaborated. 'A sunken city we saw beneath the waves on the way to Lemora.'

'Yes, but watch this,' said Joseph. He gave the globe a quick shake, and suddenly the water was full of tiny white flakes. When he stilled his hand, the flakes came drifting down onto the city.

'Shadlog's teeth!' cried Cornelius. 'It's snow!'

Joseph stared at him. 'What's that?' he asked.

'Oh, I've *heard* of it,' said Sebastian, 'but I've never seen any. It's supposed to be cold, isn't it?'

'Oh yes. Snow is little flakes of frozen water that fall from the sky,' Cornelius told him. 'Like rain, but . . . firmer. Where I come from in Golmira, it snows all the time. It gathers in great drifts on the ground and you have to wrap yourself in fur in order to go out in it. You can pat it into shapes and even make houses from it. It's marvellous stuff.' He gestured at the globe. 'Mind you, I've never seen anything like this.'

'What's it for?' asked Sebastian, puzzled.

'I have no idea,' said Joseph, handing the object to him. 'I found it lying on the ground – just waiting to be picked up. You see, it fits in the hand very well – almost as though it was meant to. But it doesn't really do anything. It just . . . looks . . . *interesting*.'

Sebastian took the globe and examined it carefully. He tried to imagine the kind of skill it would require to craft such a thing, but he wouldn't have had the first idea how to go about it. He couldn't even see an opening where the water had been poured in.

'Does it feel cold to the touch?' asked Cornelius.

'Not really.' Sebastian passed the globe to him and the little warrior gazed at it intently.

'Why doesn't the snow melt in the water?' he muttered.

'I've no idea,' Sebastian told him. 'What do you think it's for?'

Cornelius frowned. 'It can't be a weapon,' he surmised. 'It's heavy enough, but it looks like it would shatter if you smashed someone on the head with it.'

'Be careful,' Joseph advised him. 'You might break it. I've kept that for many years.'

Cornelius nodded and handed it to Keera. 'I have seen this many times,' she said, gazing into it thoughtfully. 'When I was a child, I used to think that it was some kind of magical world, and that if I wished hard, one day I might shrink until I was small enough to go into one of those tiny houses. I wished and wished every day, but alas, Okrin never granted me my wish.'

'I don't suppose you'd be interested in selling the globe . . . ?' asked Max, and everyone turned to look at him. 'Well, if Joseph would sell it to us, we could take it back to

Thaddeus Peel as proof and save ourselves the trouble of a blooming long trip into the jungle.'

'What does he mean, *sell* it?' asked Joseph, mystified. Clearly this was not a word he understood.

'Oh, ignore him,' said Cornelius. 'As usual, he's just trying to get out of work. The globe is a wonderful thing, but it could have come from anywhere. It's not the proof we seek.'

'But none of us can say what it is,' reasoned Sebastian. 'And if Joseph says it comes from the lost city, I believe him.'

'So do I! I'm merely saying that it will not be proof enough for Thaddeus Peel. No, we have to try and find the city for ourselves and obtain something more conclusive.' Cornelius looked at Joseph. 'If you are right about your journey starting from this village, then it would simply be a case of finding the river and following its course.'

Joseph nodded. 'It would seem so,' he agreed. 'But listen – when you undertake this trip, I would be obliged if you would take Salah with you.' He waved a bony hand at his niece. 'She has always been fascinated by my story and would like to see the city for herself. I have warned her that it may be a cursed place, but the young care nothing for such thoughts. She will be able to guide you as far as the river and she's a fine hunter – as good as any boy in the tribe.'

'But who will look after you while she is away?' asked Keera.

Joseph waved a hand. 'I have any number of friends in the

village who will be happy to fill in for her. What do you say? She has pestered me about this ever since she learned of your plans.'

'Pestered you?' Max snorted. 'She hasn't uttered a sound since we arrived.'

'Yes, but she does the most energetic sign language you've ever witnessed. Will you take her?'

'Why not?' agreed Cornelius. He studied the girl for a moment. 'You would work hard and do as you are told?' he asked.

Salah smiled and nodded eagerly. She pointed to the cooking pot and gestured wildly with her hands.

'She is telling you that she will do the cooking,' explained Joseph.

'Well, thank goodness for that,' said Max from the doorway. 'Neither of these two have the first idea about how to make decent food!'

Joseph laughed again and slapped a bony hand against a skinny leg. 'I'll bet that one is hard to please!' he observed.

'You have no idea,' said Sebastian.

'So . . .' Joseph studied them thoughtfully. 'It's settled then. You will take Salah with you.'

Sebastian smiled at the girl. 'Happily,' he said. 'She is a bit of a chatterbox, but I suppose we'll manage.'

She grinned back delightedly.

'When will you be ready to leave on your quest?' asked Joseph.

'Soon,' said Cornelius. 'There's a small matter to deal with first. Speaking of which . . .' He got to his feet and bowed politely to the old man. 'If you will excuse me, I have some more preparations to attend to.'

'Of course,' said Joseph, waving a hand in dismissal. 'It has been a pleasure to meet you.'

'Shall I come too?' asked Sebastian.

'No, you stay and rest,' said Cornelius. 'You'll need to be fully recovered if we are to lead the battle against the Gograth army.' He turned. 'Come on, Max, you can help. Or would you rather stand around drinking chai all day?'

'Do I get a choice?' asked Max, but he backed his huge frame out of the doorway. Cornelius followed him, leaving Sebastian and Keera sitting side by side. Sebastian glanced at her and saw that she was still staring into the globe, as though imagining herself in that tiny city.

'She is pretty, is she not?' said Joseph unexpectedly; and Sebastian glanced up in surprise. Keera lifted her head too, her face reddening.

'Umm . . . yes. Yes, she is,' agreed Sebastian, 'now that you mention it.'

Joseph grinned and glanced knowingly at Salah. 'Makes you wonder about the prophecy, doesn't it?' he said.

The girl nodded gleefully.

'The . . . prophecy?' echoed Sebastian.

'You are not familiar with the story?' Joseph asked incredulously.

'Umm . . . well, some of it. The bits that Keera has mentioned to me. All that stuff about smiting the Gograth. I mean, I'm not a professional smiter or anything, but I'll give it my best shot.'

'She didn't tell you about the last part?'

'Umm . . . which part is that?' asked Sebastian nervously.

'Where the Chosen One takes a woman of the Jilith tribe as his wife?'

Sebastian stared open-mouthed at the old man. Then he looked at Keera, but she lowered her gaze demurely and said nothing. He was beginning to get a very bad feeling about all this.

'A . . . wife?' he said feebly. 'Oh, crikey!'

CHAPTER 9

DAY OF RECKONING

Sebastian woke suddenly from a deep sleep. A hand was shaking him roughly by the shoulder. He opened his eyes and blinked up into the grinning baby face of Cornelius.

'It's time,' said the little warrior.

'Time?' Sebastian sat up and yawned. He was quite healed from his injuries, but he had got used to sleeping late. 'Time for what?'

Two moons had passed since he had visited Joseph's hut, and during this time Cornelius had finalized his preparations for the battle with the Gograth. Only the previous night, he had told Sebastian that everything was ready: they would go into action just as soon as an opportunity presented itself. Judging by the jubilant expression on his face, that opportunity had arrived.

'Time to do some smiting,' he said.

Sebastian glanced apprehensively through the open doorway of the guesthouse. He saw that it was still dark outside. 'The . . . the sun's not even up,' he protested.

'It's just before dawn. Cal is here. He and his hunting party have chanced upon a group of Gograth sneaking around close to the village. Obviously they mean to launch an attack, but we shall turn the tables on them.'

'Uh . . . yes, but . . . does it have to be right this instant? Couldn't we attack them at a more reasonable hour? After breakfast or something?'

'Time waits for no man,' Cornelius informed him. 'And this is a perfect opportunity.' He slapped Sebastian on the shoulder. 'Come on, dress yourself and prepare for battle. If you get a move on, you'll have time for a cup of chai.'

Sebastian groaned, but nodded. Cornelius went outside and Sebastian dragged himself out from under the fur covers and pulled on his clothes and boots. He strapped on his sword and stumbled out into the chill air of early morning. Cornelius was crouched beside the campfire with Cal and his hunting party. The rest of the villagers were waiting expectantly in a large circle around them.

Cal studied Sebastian with insolence in his eyes. His fellow warrior, Galt, was with him – a big shambling fellow with muscular arms and a shock of red hair. Unlike most of the Jilith, he wore his beard long and scruffy, and though of a cheerful disposition, he didn't seem all that bright. The two men looked like they ate, drank and slept for the pursuit of wild beasts.

'This one's getting too used to lying around.' Cal grinned and handed Sebastian a cup of chai with perhaps rather less reverence than the elfling had become accustomed to. Cal made no secret of the fact that he took the Chosen One legend with a large pinch of salt. He had even said, in Sebastian's presence, that as far as he was concerned a man made his own luck and that legend had very little to do with it.

'I need my rest,' Sebastian told him. 'Because I, er . . . have to preserve my powers. Particularly when there's a battle coming up.'

'Hardly a battle,' Cal assured him. 'A small hunting party – nothing special. We could take them all like *that*.' He snapped a dirty thumb and forefinger together.

'Yes, but we don't *want* to,' Cornelius reminded him. 'We only want to kill *some* of them. The rest must be allowed to escape so that they can summon help. And remember, when they arrive in greater numbers, we have to retreat. They must believe that we are scared.'

Cal scowled. 'It is against my nature to run from any enemy,' he said.

'I understand that. But the shame will be worth it once we have them within range of our spears and arrows.' Cornelius turned to address the other villagers. He climbed up onto a log so everyone would have a clear view of him. 'The moment is at hand,' he roared. 'You all have your appointed tasks. See to it that you carry them out to the best of your ability. And remember, when we come back, there won't be much time. Every one of you must be ready to fight to the death.'

'Excuse me . . .' interrupted a mournful voice.

Sebastian looked up in surprise. A strange apparition was lumbering towards them. It resembled one of the huge lizards he had fought on the treasure island of Callinestra, but there was no mistaking the voice. Max was encased in a curious assortment of armour. A huge padded saddle of rusa hide covered his flanks, a metal-studded breastplate hung around his neck, and some enterprising villager had even fashioned him a kind of helmet, which fitted ingeniously around his curving horns and protected his nose and cheeks. His brown eyes stared dolefully through two tiny slits. 'I feel ruddy stupid,' he complained. 'When you mentioned armour, I imagined something majestic-looking. But I just caught sight of my reflection in a pool of water and I look like a yarkle.'

'Not at all,' Cornelius told him. 'You look . . . noble. Doesn't he, Sebastian?'

'Er . . . yes,' said Sebastian, trying very hard not to laugh. 'You look . . . like a . . . force to be reckoned with. I certainly wouldn't want to face you in battle.'

'You're just saying that,' grumbled Max. 'I can see you're trying not to laugh.'

'No I'm not! Anyway, I'd rather look a bit of a twit than wind up with twenty arrows sticking out of my backside. Remember the fuss you made on the plains of Neruvia, when those Brigands shot just *one* arrow into you. You claimed you were dying.'

'I thought I was,' said Max gloomily. 'How was I to know it was just a flesh wound? Oh well then, if that's all the sympathy I'm going to get, I'll return to my chariot.' He turned and trudged away, revealing that the armour was ingeniously styled to allow his tail to poke through. Again Sebastian felt an irrational urge to laugh out loud, but managed to restrain himself. This was no time for humour.

'Come on,' said Cornelius. 'Cal, you lead the way.'

Cal and Galt set off into the jungle, carrying their throwing spears. Sebastian and Cornelius fell in behind them.

'Are these the only warriors we're taking?' asked Sebastian nervously.

'Of course. We want the Gograth to come after us, don't we? They won't do that if we have half the village in tow.' Cornelius grinned delightedly. 'We must be heavily out-numbered. That will embolden them, make them want to crush us. Hopefully they'll throw caution to the wind.'

Sebastian shook his head. 'You're loving this, aren't you?' he observed.

'Of course!' Cornelius chuckled. 'These are the days I live for, when the blood runs hot and the foe is at hand.' He gazed up at Sebastian. 'It's not for you, though, is it? Oh, you'll give of your best when push comes to shove, but I expect there are many things you'd rather be doing.'

'I have to admit, fighting's not my favourite pastime,' said Sebastian.

'Hmm.' Cornelius lowered his voice so that Cal and Galt would not overhear. 'You know, somebody was telling me a bit more about that prophecy last night. It seems that the Chosen One is expected to take a wife from amongst the women of the village.'

Sebastian shrugged. 'It's just an old folk tale,' he said. 'I wouldn't put any faith in it. Besides, what would Jenna say if I returned to Ramalat with a wife on my arm?'

'Something fairly salty, I should imagine. So . . . Jenna's still uppermost in your mind, is she?'

'Of course. Just because we're apart doesn't mean I've forgotten her.'

Cornelius smiled. 'Good for you,' he said. 'She's a special lady, that one.'

They followed the narrow trail as it led deeper and deeper into the jungle. Sebastian wondered how Cal and the others managed to find their way through the thick undergrowth. To him, every trail looked the same. He started to ask Cornelius something but Cal turned and lifted a finger to his lips.

'Quiet now,' he whispered. 'We are close.'

Sebastian did as he was told. He watched Cal and Galt creeping along the trail without making a sound and tried hard to emulate them, horribly aware of twigs cracking beneath his boots and foliage rustling as he brushed by. He couldn't help feeling like a great clumsy oaf beside them.

Now Cal paused for a moment, listening intently. He pointed into the jungle to his left and stepped off the trail, gliding in amongst the trees with the grace of a panther. The others turned to follow and now Sebastian found it really hard going. Ferns and thorns snagged against his clothing, insects buzzed around him and he was aware of a thick sweat beading his forehead. By comparison, Cal and Galt looked as if they had set out on nothing more than a pleasant stroll.

Suddenly Sebastian flinched as he heard a noise coming from up ahead: the unmistakable clink of armour. He watched as Cal knelt behind a screen of bushes and peered through them. Sebastian crouched down and took a quick peek. Ahead of him, a party of Gograth were moving slowly and silently towards the village, their swords held ready for action. It was clear that they were about to attack the Jilith.

Taking a deep breath, Sebastian slid his own sword from its scabbard as quietly as he could. He watched and waited, his heart beating rapidly. Beside him, Cornelius was expertly assembling his miniature crossbow. Once he had slid a bolt into place, he lifted the weapon and took careful aim on one of the creatures in the midst of the group. There was an abrupt hiss and then the Gograth warrior halted in his tracks; the bolt had struck him in his thick neck, just above the breastplate. He fell to the ground and his companions stopped and stared stupidly down at him.

'Now!' roared Cornelius. And they all burst out from cover and ran straight at the enemy.

It went exactly as planned. Taken by surprise, the Gograth put up only a token resistance, and in a matter of moments half their number had fallen beneath the flashing blades of their enemies. The rest turned and retreated in complete disarray. Cornelius managed to rein in Cal and Galt, allowing the surviving Gograth to make their escape.

'Tell General Darvon that this is how the Jilith vanquish all their enemies!' Cornelius bellowed at their retreating backs. 'Tell him that the Gograth are cowards who hide behind the backs of their women.' He seemed to be searching for more insults, so Sebastian weighed in with one of his own.

'Tell him that the Gograth smell of rusa poo!' he yelled.

Cornelius gave him a pitying look. 'Embarrassing,' he said. 'Don't you know how to give a decent insult?'

'We don't need to insult them,' said Cal. 'Killing them will be enough.'

'What do we do now?' asked Sebastian.

'We wait,' said Cornelius calmly. And he settled himself down on the ground and took out his pipe.

* * *

They didn't have to wait very long. Soon enough, they heard the booming of drums, the blasts of great horns; and something else – a distant rumbling that seemed to shake the earth beneath them.

'What was that?' muttered Sebastian. 'Sounded almost like thunder.'

'That *was* thunder,' muttered Galt. He lifted his head and sniffed the air. 'Rain's coming,' he said matter-of-factly.

'What?' Sebastian looked at Cornelius. 'Did you hear that? Rain!'

'Yes, yes,' said Cornelius, waving a hand dismissively.

'But . . . what if it starts falling before the Gograth reach the village?'

'Don't worry, it's nowhere near us,' insisted Cornelius, but his smile had lost some of its confidence.

'If we can't set light to that conflagrus—' began Sebastian.

'You're sounding more like Max every day,' snapped Cornelius. 'Now stop griping for a moment and let me listen.' He did exactly that for a moment, then nodded approvingly. 'Sounds like they've summoned plenty of reinforcements,' he said. 'Good. The more the merrier.' He glanced sternly at the two Jilith men. 'Don't forget what we agreed now. We have to run. If you try to stand and fight, you'll mess up the whole plan.'

'Yes, yes.' Cal nodded but he looked far from happy. 'I just don't like to think of them boasting about how we ran before them.'

Cornelius gave a grim smile. 'Don't worry – if everything goes according to plan, by sundown there won't be many of them left to boast about anything.' He lifted his head. Now the approaching sounds were unmistakable: the dull clunk of armour, the crunching of vegetation being crushed underfoot and the rising clamour of drums. And then, booming above them, another peal of thunder, closer this time.

'Cornelius, that doesn't sound very far away,' whispered Sebastian.

'Will you pipe down? Here, Cal, be a good lad and climb a tree. Let's see how many of them are coming.'

Cal sprang to the nearest trunk and vanished up into the canopy in a couple of lithe bounds. Everyone waited below. Sebastian felt beads of sweat welling on his neck and running down his spine. For what seemed like an age there was silence from above. Then he heard Cal say, 'Okrin's blood!' A moment later he came scrambling down again, and though he tried to act casual, his face had gone several shades paler.

'How many?' asked Cornelius.

'More than I've seen in my entire life,' admitted Cal. 'At first I thought a great wind was flattening the jungle. Then I looked again and saw it was the Gograth. Looks like the whole tribe's turned out.'

Cornelius grinned. 'Excellent,' he said. He slapped Sebastian on the back. 'Come on,' he said. 'Let's make for a clearing and give them a good look at us. We want to be sure they follow us all the way back to the village . . .'

CHAPTER 10

BATTLE ROYAL

When they finally made it, breathless and sweating from their frantic flight through the jungle, Sebastian was relieved to see that all the villagers were at their battle stations. But at the same time he was worried to note how dark it had become; and when he looked up at the sky, he could see that a mass of bruise-black clouds were rolling overhead.

The young men of the tribe, and many of the women, were standing in a defensive line around the huts, each clad in a suit of rusa hide and holding a sword and a large wooden shield. A short distance behind them stood a ring of archers, each equipped with a bow and a quiver of arrows; burning torches of conflagrus were stuck in the ground beside them. Sebastian knew that the older people and the children were sheltering in the communal huts in the very centre of the village; but they too were armed and would fight to the last if necessary.

'Come on,' said Cornelius. 'Let's take our places. Our guests will be arriving at any moment.'

As Sebastian slotted himself into the circle of warriors, he noticed Keera standing a short distance away, armoured and armed just as the others were. Beside her stood Maccan, dressed in full ceremonial regalia, clutching a huge curved sword in each hand, his face painted into a terrifying mask.

Thunder rumbled again, and off beyond the trees there was a brief flare as lightning split the sky.

Sebastian glanced around but could see no sign of Max. After a few moments he noticed a large pile of straw standing a little way inside the circle and surmised that Max and the battle wagon must be hidden beneath that. Evidently Cornelius was using every opportunity to take the Gograth by surprise. Somebody handed Sebastian a heavy shield; he took it and unsheathed his sword. The shield was rather cumbersome but Sebastian knew that it would play a big part in the coming battle. Then Salah appeared carrying Sebastian's headdress. She motioned to him to bend down and placed it respectfully on his head. Then she bowed and pushed her way back through the ranks to the village.

'Do I have to wear this?' whispered Sebastian.

'Of course you do,' said Cornelius. 'You've got to look like a chief.'

'Yes, but I *feel* like a great ninny.'

'Stop complaining and start acting regal. Remember, you're in charge of all this.' Cornelius waved a hand at the waiting warriors. 'It's you they look up to. You're the Chosen One.'

'Yes, thanks for reminding me,' said Sebastian. 'And I have you to thank for that.'

Cornelius grinned. He reached up and lowered the visor of his helmet. 'They're close,' he said.

Now Sebastian was aware of a new sound coming out of the surrounding jungle, drawing closer and closer. It was a thudding noise, the clamour of scores of swords crashing against the sides of many shields. He glanced down at Cornelius, who grinned back up at him.

'Relax, lad,' said the Golmiran. 'That's just the enemy making a pathetic attempt to strike fear into our hearts!'

Sebastian swallowed hard. *It's working*, he thought, but said nothing to Cornelius. His friend did not seem to know fear and was never very sympathetic when he observed it in others. But there was something else he wanted to say.

'Cornelius, if I should fall today—'

'Don't be ridiculous!' cried the little warrior. 'What can happen to you? You're the Chosen One!'

'Yes, but . . . seriously, if I don't make it through this battle . . . there's a note in my pocket . . . for Jenna . . . I would appreciate it if you would make sure she receives it.'

Cornelius made a dismissive gesture. 'Don't worry,' he said. 'Today is not your day to die.'

'How do you *know* that?' protested Sebastian.

'Because you've already had one close call with the Gograth. I didn't nurse you back from the brink just to have you lose your life to those brutes. You'll be fine, provided you follow my instructions to the letter. Now stop worrying and get ready. I think I see our first customers . . .'

Sure enough, figures were emerging from the green depths all around them; great shambling shapes dressed in primitive armour, armed with shields and swords and throwing spears. Their faces were contorted into expressions of rage and they were making horrendous gibbering sounds as they marched forward. Sebastian's blood seemed to run cold in his veins.

'Nobody make a move,' roared Cornelius. 'Stand your ground until I give the word!'

Arrows began to fly out from the advancing ranks and somewhere to Sebastian's left there was a scream of pain and a Jilith warrior fell to the ground.

'Shields!' bellowed Cornelius and, as one, each man lifted a heavy shield to cover the top half of his body. No sooner had Sebastian lifted his than he felt the impact of arrows thudding into it. He peered out and saw a seemingly endless wave of armoured warriors coming towards him.

'Cornelius,' he said, 'we need to—'

'Wait!' yelled Cornelius. 'They have to be inside the ring.'

A spear glanced off the top of Sebastian's shield and went

spinning end over end behind him. He glanced back and saw that the archers were waiting, their first arrows nocked and ready. Their faces were impassive, betraying no sense of fear.

Perhaps it's just me, thought Sebastian. *Perhaps I should drop the tough-guy routine and take up embroidery or something.*

Another arrow thudded into his shield. This time, the stone head actually broke through the wooden barrier and stopped a few finger-widths away from his face. Sebastian gulped and risked a glance round the side of his shield. The nearest of the Gograth were already well inside the ring but many of the others were not.

'Cornelius,' he hissed, 'we can't wait much longer—'

'Hold your nerve,' snapped Cornelius. 'They'll stop firing arrows now for fear of hitting their own men. I want them all inside the circle, or it won't work.'

Something struck Sebastian's shield with a force that nearly smashed it out of his grasp and then fell at his feet. He saw that it was a crudely made stone axe.

'Oh, nice,' he said. 'Really nice.' Then he felt something even more worrying. A droplet of water landed on his head. Then another, and another . . .

Rain. It was starting to rain! He remembered Max's doleful expression when he'd asked the question: *What happens if it rains?*

Cornelius seemed not to have noticed. 'Wait for it . . .' Sebastian heard him say. 'Wait for it . . .' And then, at a volume that seemed to shatter Sebastian's eardrums, he screamed, 'ARCHERS!'

The archers needed no second bidding. As one they plunged the heads of their first arrows into the flaming brands, took aim and fired. Sebastian was only dimly aware of plumes of smoke whizzing up into the rain-streaked air behind him and curving down to land behind the ranks of advancing warriors. In fact, so puny did the first volley appear that many of the Gograth stopped in their tracks to point at the passing arrows, laughing derisively at what they assumed was a miserable attempt to hit them.

The arrows trailed down out of sight, and for the longest time nothing happened. Sebastian felt an awful sinking feeling in his stomach. 'Cornelius,' he said, 'I don't think—'

And then the world seemed to explode in a great burst of orange flame, the ring of fire leaping up like something alive and clawing at the sky. Sebastian lowered his shield a fraction and felt the intense heat on his face. He saw that the Gograth were turning round in panic, unable to deal with this sudden explosion of the thing they feared most in the world.

'DOWN!' shouted Cornelius. Sebastian and the others in the front rank dropped onto one knee.

'ARCHERS!' screamed Cornelius again, and the ring of bowmen unleashed a second volley; this time they used ordinary arrows and their aim was deadly. The Gograth fell like wheat before a deadly scythe as the arrows thudded into their unprotected backs. Bewildered, they turned to face the enemy and were hit by a third volley, which dropped scores more. Now there was confusion among their ranks. Some shambled forward, others turned back towards the flames. In the chaos, a fourth volley hit them and now they were sprawling one on the other, screaming in panic, wanting to flee but unable to brave the wall of fire that hemmed them in.

'ARCHERS . . . STAND DOWN!' yelled Cornelius. 'WARRIORS . . . FORWARD!'

The front rank of warriors jumped back to their feet and surged forward to strike the Gograth in their moment of disarray. Sebastian ran at the closest man and cleaved him across the shoulders with his sword. The man fell aside, arms flailing, revealing another warrior who was turning back to the fight; Sebastian ran him through, the razor-sharp blade crunching through his breastplate and dropping him where he stood.

Sebastian caught a glimpse of Keera, her sword felling Gograth warriors at every stroke, and then he moved forward again, stepping on the bodies of the fallen, blind to anything but the need to swing his sword at anyone who opposed him.

'FALL BACK!' Cornelius's voice cut through the noise of battle and he reacted automatically, dropping back with the others, raising the heavy shield as he did so: Cornelius had warned him that once the Gograth had recovered from their surprise, they would regroup, taking heart from their superior numbers. Through the smoke and haze of the still blazing fire, Sebastian saw Cornelius's grime-streaked face winking at him.

'MAX!' he roared.

Sebastian lifted his head and saw the huge mound of straw where Max was concealed suddenly burst apart as the buffalope sprang forward, dragging the heavy war chariot behind him. He moved slowly at first but rapidly increased his speed; now Sebastian could see the Jilith's best archers standing in the back of the wagon, their bows ready to fire. Max lowered his head and thundered towards the nearest ranks of Gograth. His horns made contact with armour and the warriors were flung aside like broken dolls. For a moment it was like a great tidal wave passing through the press of bodies; the Gograth could do nothing but try and scramble out of the way. Many were flung into the air, to come crashing down onto the heads of their comrades. Those who avoided the horns were felled by the archers as the wagon moved on.

'Go on, flee, you scum!' Max was bellowing. 'You tried to kill my master, you hairy brutes! Now see how you like it.'

Arrows thudded into the buffalope's padded flanks but he paid them no heed. He just kept galloping onwards, an unstoppable force.

Cornelius was laughing delightedly. 'What did I tell you?' he yelled. 'It worked in Keladon and it's working here.' He waited until the war chariot had gone past and then lifted his sword and signalled to those behind him. 'Come on!' he cried. 'Let's finish them.'

As if to punctuate his cry, there was a sudden brilliant flash of lightning; and in that instant the heavens opened and the rain came down. Sebastian hesitated for a second, shocked by the ferocity of the downpour. It was a deluge – he could feel the rods of rain bouncing off his head and shoulders, and thought how disastrous it would have been if it had come down like this a few moments earlier; but he could not allow himself to be distracted. He put his head down and ran after Cornelius.

Everybody surged forward and went to work on the Gograth who were left, but by now they were demoralized: many were simply looking for a way out through the flames.

Max came round the circle a second time, smashing down any Gograth who dared to oppose him.

'Behold the power of Max the Mighty!' Sebastian heard him bellow; followed by a rather less majestic, 'Ouch! Who left that there?' But then the war chariot thundered by, its wheels flinging up two fountains of water in its wake.

Sebastian ran forward to deal with those few warriors who were still left standing. He squared up to one mighty creature, ducked beneath a savage sword blow and was offered an open shot at the Gograth's head.

But something stopped him from making the killing blow – he could see blind terror in the Gograth's eyes. As he stood back, the once-proud warrior dropped his weapons and turned to run towards the flames, which were now dying down beneath the falling rain. Grey smoke billowed across the clearing and in a moment the fleeing creature was lost to sight.

Sebastian stayed where he was and lowered his shield. He suddenly felt very weary. He lifted the headdress off and tilted back his head to let the chill rain wash the blood and sweat from his face. Max came thundering round for a third time, but already there were fewer targets for him to chase and he was having to weave from side to side in order to make contact with them.

Then Sebastian saw a figure cut off from the rest, a huge, imposing warrior dressed in more sophisticated armour than his companions. He was standing on a heap of fallen bodies and fighting with all his might. His shoulder pads carried the insignia of a leader and his helmet sported a purple plume. This, Sebastian knew, had to be General Darvon.

He was surrounded by Jilith warriors, each of them eager to be the one to claim his life, but none of them reckless enough to attack him face to face. The huge two-handed sword he brandished lashed left and right, keeping them at a

distance. The general was staring through the pouring rain, wide-eyed with shock, unable to believe that his mighty army had been so thoroughly vanquished in what seemed like a matter of moments. As he stood there, the last of his warriors threw down their weapons and ran; he was alone. He glanced towards the ring of fire, now little more than a circle of smoke.

Then Sebastian saw Cornelius running towards the general, slipping and sliding on earth that was rapidly turning into a quagmire, clambering across the ranks of the fallen in his haste to reach his enemy. Sebastian dropped his shield and sword and ran after him, his long legs covering the distance faster than Cornelius ever could. He caught up with the little warrior a short distance from his quarry, grabbed him around the shoulders and wrestled him to the ground.

'What are you doing?' bellowed the Golmiran. 'Let me go, you fool, he'll escape!'

'Cornelius, it's over,' Sebastian shouted back. 'He's finished, let him go!'

The general took one last despairing look across a battle-field littered with dead and dying Gograth. He gave a final roar of defiance, then turned and fled towards the smoke.

Cornelius struggled to free himself from Sebastian's grasp, but the elfling hung on tight and they both watched as General Darvon flung himself through the wall of smoke and disappeared from sight.

'You bloody fool!' roared Cornelius. 'You've let him escape. We could have finished him!'

But Sebastian shook his head. He released his friend and gestured around him. 'He *is* finished,' he said. 'Look.'

Cornelius gazed around at the devastation: the piles of sprawled bodies, the pools of blood thinning in the rain, the lifeless eyes staring towards the dark-grey sky. He opened his mouth to say something, but words seemed to fail him. His eyes widened and a look of profound shock came over his features, as if he were seeing the scene for the first time.

'Shadlog's teeth,' he whispered at last. He got to his feet and continued to stare at the battlefield.

The dead must have numbered into the hundreds. Here and there, Jilith warriors were moving through the fallen men, finishing off those who were still breathing. As far as Sebastian could tell, the Jilith had lost fewer than a dozen men. He saw Keera walking across the battlefield. Her face was bloody but she seemed unharmed. She lifted a hand and waved to him.

'You did it, Cornelius,' he said quietly. 'You destroyed them, just as you said you would. Perhaps you truly are a general.'

But Cornelius was still staring around at the carnage. Sebastian saw, with a stab of shock, that the little warrior's eyes were filling with tears.

'Cornelius?' he said. 'Is something wrong?'

Cornelius shook his head. 'It's the smoke from the fire,' he said; and he turned and walked away through the falling rain, picking his way carefully through the lifeless bodies.

Sebastian stared after him, then turned at the sound of a familiar voice. Max was approaching, pulling the heavy war wagon behind him. His rusa-hide armour was literally bristling with arrows, making him look like an oversized hedgehog.

'So it doesn't blooming rain here . . .' said Max. He shook his head, flinging droplets of water in all directions. 'That's a good one. What does he call this then – light refreshment?' He glanced around. 'What's up with little britches, anyway? I saw him walking off as though he'd found five croats and lost ten. He should be celebrating his great victory.'

Sebastian shrugged his shoulders. 'I think he got a bit of a shock when he saw how many we'd killed.'

'What did he think we were doing with them, reading 'em bedtime stories?' Max was clearly overexcited by his recent experiences. 'How did you do, young master? I did pretty well myself. I *had* meant to keep count, but it got a bit confusing out there and I stopped after thirty or so.'

Sebastian turned to Max and rubbed him fondly on the head. 'Thirty, eh? I didn't get anything like as many as that. You're not injured then?'

'In about twenty places, but I don't like to make a fuss. This armour isn't as tough as Cornelius said it would be. Typical.

But then, they never tell you the truth, these generals. That's how they get people like me to follow them.' He licked his lips. 'I could do with a drink though.'

'I'll find you some water,' suggested Sebastian.

'Water?' Max looked offended. 'After a battle like that, I would have thought a bowl of icara would be more in order.'

Sebastian smiled. 'I'll see what I can do,' he said. 'Come on, old shaggy.'

And they started back towards the village.

PART TWO

THE QUEST

CHAPTER 11

THE LEAVING

The small expedition was ready to leave and the villagers had come out of their huts to bid them farewell. Sebastian, Cornelius and Max stood on the outskirts of the village with the other members of their party. Keera had come along, as promised, and Joseph's niece, Salah, was there too. To Sebastian's dismay, Cal had volunteered to accompany them, presumably to keep an eye on Keera; and he had brought along his best friend, Galt.

Many days had passed since the defeat of the Gograth – days that had been spent disposing of the dead, a task made even more irksome by the rain, which had continued to pour down for some time after the battle. Since there seemed to be nobody left to claim the bodies of the enemy, a mass grave had been dug in a jungle clearing and the fallen warriors had been piled up in the war wagon and ferried there by Max.

It had taken days to move them all but nobody had complained about the work. It was only now the Gograth had been all but obliterated that it dawned on the Jilith what they had achieved – their ancestral enemies had been defeated for ever and the villagers would never live in fear of them again.

They also had some mourning of their own to do: the victory had been achieved at a cost. Eight of their own warriors had died in the battle and scores of others had been injured.

Nobody seemed to feel the guilt of it more than Cornelius. The once happy-go-lucky warrior had become quiet and brooding. He took to sitting in the entrance to his hut, staring blankly out at the rain; and whenever Sebastian tried to talk about what was troubling him, he quickly changed the subject.

Finally the rain had stopped and the Jilith had held a celebration to mark their great victory, but it had been a curiously muted affair, as though everybody was simply going through the motions. Sitting in the place of honour, wearing his feathered headdress, Sebastian had been aware of Maccan looking at him expectantly, as though waiting for him to announce his intention to take Keera as his bride. But he didn't say anything and the party had wound down a good deal earlier than the last one they had attended.

Now a small expedition was setting out to retrace Joseph's

childhood journey, which they hoped would lead them to the legendary lost city of Mendip. A couple of Joseph's brawny neighbours had carried the old man outside on an improvised stretcher so he could bid farewell to Salah.

'Be obedient,' he told her. 'Take care at all times and make sure you come safely back to us.'

Salah nodded and gesticulated excitedly with her hands. Sebastian assumed that she was saying he was not to worry about her. At any rate, Joseph seemed content with her reply.

'Bless you, child,' he said.

Then a silence fell and the crowd parted as Maccan strode towards them, dressed in his finest regalia.

'May Okrin smile on your quest,' he told Cornelius.

'Thank you, your majesty,' said Cornelius. But his voice was flat and unresponsive, as though he no longer cared about his mission.

'You have performed a great service for my people,' Maccan told Sebastian. 'The bravery of the Chosen One will be spoken of. Your deeds will become legend. And now, as I promised you, I send my own daughter and my two best warriors to attend you in your quest. I shall pray that Okrin brings you all safely back to us.'

Sebastian bowed his head. 'Thank you, Great Chief,' he said respectfully.

Now Maccan turned to Keera. 'Daughter, may Okrin protect you,' he said.

Cal stepped forward. 'Have no worries, your majesty,' he said. 'My sword and spear shall afford her all the protection she needs.'

'Er . . . yes, and so will mine,' added Sebastian quickly.

Keera rolled her eyes. 'Don't worry, Father. I can look after myself,' she assured him.

'I know this,' said Maccan, smiling. 'I have taught you well. You are the equal of any warrior and your conduct during the final battle will also be spoken of.' They embraced for a moment and then Maccan stepped back. He looked meaningfully at Sebastian. 'And I hope that when you return, you and Keera will have some good news for me.'

There was a long, awkward silence and everybody stood there looking at each other.

'Er . . . well,' said Max. 'We'll . . . get going, shall we?'

'Yes,' said Sebastian hastily. 'Yes. Of course.' He looked at the others. 'Umm . . . which way is it?' he asked.

'This way,' said Cal, shaking his head and striding off towards an opening in the trees. 'For a Chosen One, you're not all that knowledgeable, are you?'

'I'm *very* knowledgeable, actually,' protested Sebastian. 'About some things. I tell you what, I know more jokes than you could shake a stick at.'

'Jokes?' Cal looked at him like he was mad. 'Jokes won't help you to survive in the jungle.'

'Well, no. But if we had to put on entertainment for

somebody out there, it wouldn't be much use coming to you, would it?'

'I don't think that's a very likely eventuality,' said Max.

'You keep out of it! Anyway, to be fair, I'm not even from these parts, so how *could* I know which way to go?'

'I thought Chosen Ones were supposed to be all-knowing,' said Galt.

'Yes,' said Max. 'Or at least reasonably brainy.' He glanced at Sebastian. 'Of course, there's always the occasional exception to the rule.'

'I'm very knowledgeable,' repeated Sebastian defensively. 'Anyway, look, I didn't ask to be chosen, did I? It just sort of happened.'

'Stop getting at Sebastian,' snapped Keera.

'Oh, excuse me,' said Cal. 'I forgot who I was talking to for a moment.' He gave a mocking bow. 'Please forgive me, o Splendid One. Perhaps you'd like me to carry your pack for you?'

Max rolled his eyes. 'This is a promising start,' he observed to nobody in particular. 'Not even out of sight of the village and you're bickering already.'

Sebastian had to agree. It didn't augur well for their expedition. He glanced back over his shoulder and saw that the Jilith were turning away and wandering back to their huts. A sense of foreboding took him. The village had been his haven in one of the darkest moments of his life. For a while it had felt like home to him.

He wondered how long it would be before he saw it again.

All that day they followed a jungle trail, the path so narrow they were obliged to walk in single file. Cal insisted on leading the way, swinging a machete to cut through any overhanging vegetation and only allowing Galt to take over from him. Keera walked behind them, followed by Sebastian. Every time he looked behind him, he found Salah trotting along in his wake, staring at him in apparent adoration. Cornelius came next, head bowed as if in defeat; Max trudged along at the rear, his huge back piled high with equipment.

In the end Sebastian dropped back down the line to walk in front of Cornelius so the two of them could talk.

'Cornelius, what's wrong?' he asked. 'You've been like this ever since the day of the battle.'

'I'm all right,' came the reply.

'No you're not; and don't think I haven't heard you crying out in your sleep the last few nights. It's not like you to have nightmares.'

'Can you wonder that I do,' said the little warrior dismally, 'after everything that's happened? I close my eyes and I still see the dead and the wounded lying there in front of me. It haunts me.'

'But . . . I don't understand.' Sebastian spread out his arms in a gesture of helplessness. 'You *planned* it that way. You were the general and everything went as it was meant to. And, forgive me, but you're no stranger to killing men in battle.'

'Aye. But always before it was in a fair fight, where my opponents had every chance of defeating me. I still had my honour. But that . . . *massacre* – that was nothing to do with warfare. I tricked those warriors into a killing circle and made sure they had no chance of escape. And why? Because I was intent on finding the lost city and claiming whatever treasure might be there. I sacrificed my honour in the name of greed and that knowledge will stay with me for ever.'

Sebastian sighed. 'You said yourself the Gograth were savage: they'd have shown you no mercy if it had been the other way round.'

'Yes. And you spoke of teaching them a stern lesson, show-ing them that if they didn't mend their ways, retribution would follow. I laughed at you, Sebastian, but now I see yours was the better way.'

Max's voice piped up from behind them. 'If you'd done that, they'd have come back and massacred everybody in the village. The young master is right, for once. You did what you had to do. Stop beating yourself up over it.'

'Keep out of this, you great windbag,' snarled Cornelius.

'Oh, that's nice,' said Max. 'Young master, are you going to allow him to talk to me like that?'

Sebastian sighed and, not wanting another row, quickened his pace to move back up the line.

'Now where are you going?' muttered Max.

'Somewhere the company is more agreeable,' said Sebastian. He overtook Salah and dropped back into position behind Keera. 'How much further do you think it is to the river?' he asked her. 'When Joseph told us the story, it didn't sound as if it took him long to reach it.'

Keera shrugged her shoulders. 'The memories of childhood can be misleading,' she said. 'Some of those hunts go on for days and nights at a time.' She lifted her head and called out to Cal, 'How far to the river?'

He glanced back over his shoulder. 'What's the matter?' he asked slyly. 'Are the Chosen One's delicate feet aching already?'

'Of course not,' said Sebastian. 'I was just wondering.'

'We'll be there in two days' time,' said Cal. 'Late afternoon if we keep up this pace. Of course, we'll have to stop to hunt at some point. We've no real food with us.' He glanced back down the line. 'I remember you said that you'd like to come hunting with me sometime. This will be your chance.'

Sebastian frowned. 'Great,' he said.

They walked on through the rising heat of the day. The narrow trail just seemed to lead deeper and deeper into dense jungle, the thick canopy overhead screening out all but the occasional shaft of sunlight. The green depths were full of strange noises: the chattering of boobahs, the screeches of strange multicoloured birds flapping around in the canopy, and occasionally the deep roars of creatures that Sebastian could not put a name to.

It was late afternoon when Cal stopped suddenly and lifted a hand in the air, a signal for everyone to halt. He looked back down the line and motioned for Sebastian to come forward. Sebastian moved up to the head of the column and Cal indicated something on the trail ahead of them: a large heap of dung.

'Rusa!' he whispered. He walked forward and crouched over the dung. Sebastian did likewise. Cal sniffed the air above it. Then he took hold of Sebastian's wrist and thrust his fingers into the pile of droppings.

'Ewww,' said Sebastian. 'Do you mind?'

'Shush!' hissed Cal. 'Feel the warmth? They're close.'

'That's lovely. Now perhaps you'd like to find a stream so I can wash my hand?'

Cal ignored him. He stood up again and stared thoughtfully off into the jungle. Sebastian wiped his hand surreptitiously on some leaves. Cal seemed to reach a decision. He turned back and thrust his spear into Sebastian's hands, then motioned to Sebastian and Galt to follow him. He left the trail and set off into the bushes.

Sebastian followed dutifully, but the last thing he felt like doing right now was hunting for rusa. He didn't really have the first idea how to go about it. He watched how the other two placed their feet carefully in the damp undergrowth to ensure they made no sound and tried to follow suit, but his boots crunched and crashed around as if they had a life of their own. Cal kept throwing him indignant looks, which he tried to ignore. When he glanced back, he could see that he was already some considerable distance from the trail, and it occurred to him that if he were somehow left on his own, he would struggle to find his way back to the others.

Cal paused again and signalled to Galt to circle round to his left. Then he looked at Sebastian and indicated that he should go right. Sebastian had no option but to do as he was told. He moved forward, holding the spear out in front of him, feeling vaguely foolish. Within a few moments Cal and Galt were lost to view and he found himself pushing his way through thick screens of fern and hanging vines. It was so dark here that he had to peer carefully at the ground ahead; the infernal background noise, myriad twitterings, shrieks and hoots, set his nerves on edge. The smell of rusa dung from his hand assailed his nostrils and sweat trickled down his back.

Sebastian was just telling himself that this was a complete waste of time when he detected movement up ahead and froze in his tracks. He tried to focus: a dark shape moved past the tree trunks in front of him, a splash of dappled light playing across a furry back . . .

Furry? Shouldn't that be *hairy*? The thought flashed through his mind an instant before he registered that the creature he was looking at wasn't a rusa at all, but something a good deal bigger. A low, rumbling growl seemed to resonate through the undergrowth. As he stared in mute terror, the huge shape suddenly reared up on its hind legs and bared its teeth, which glinted dangerously in the gloom.

Now Sebastian could see it in more detail: a huge beast with vicious-looking teeth and massive paws that ended in curved claws. He said something colourful under his breath and thought about beating a hasty retreat, but a great blasting roar from the creature seemed to fix him to the spot.

'Oh, great,' he murmured.

The beast dropped back onto all fours and started clawing the ground, flinging up clods of earth and shredded vegetation – a great bristling monster that looked powerful enough to tear the strongest man limb from limb. Its tiny black eyes glittered with feral rage, its open jaws dripped saliva – and it was preparing to charge. It didn't take an expert to see that.

In the brief time he had, Sebastian reviewed his options. He could run for his life; he could yell for Cal to come and help him; or he could stand and make a fight of it. He doubted whether he had time for the first option; the second would mean total humiliation; and so there was nothing for it but to

take a firm grip on his spear and brace himself for the onslaught.

He didn't have long to wait. The beast surged forward and came for him, head lowered, teeth bared. Sebastian gritted his teeth and tried to keep the spearhead pointed at the creature's chest but his hands were trembling violently. There was a sudden impact that jarred every bone in his body and the wooden shaft of the spear bent as though it had no more substance than a blade of grass.

For an instant it seemed it would splinter; but then the spearhead sank into the creature's chest and, as the shaft snapped straight again, Sebastian felt himself being lifted from his feet and carried backwards. He remembered Joseph's story about his encounter with a rusa boar but didn't have time to dwell on it, because now he was crashing through bushes and ferns and leaves and he could do nothing but hang on grimly and hope that he didn't get pushed back into anything more solid.

And just as this thought occurred to him, there was another impact and his backward motion was suddenly halted. He lost his grip on the spear and dropped into a sitting position. The beast kept on coming, its front legs extended towards Sebastian's face. As he watched in rigid terror, he saw that the spear was sinking deeper and deeper into the beast's body and that its progress was finally slowing . . .

Glancing back, he saw what had happened. The butt of the

spear had jammed into an opening in the broad trunk of a tree and the beast's own momentum had plunged the sharp spearhead deep into its guts. Finally it came to a halt, its legs quivering, its dripping snout a hair's breadth away from Sebastian's face. It gave a last convulsive roar, blasting out a great gust of raw-meat breath. Then its eyes flickered and clouded over, and the extended front paws swung downwards, the razor-sharp claws raking Sebastian's shoulders and tearing the fabric of his jacket.

For a moment Sebastian stared into those vacant eyes and then he remembered to breathe. He became aware of two sets of running feet approaching him through the undergrowth. Quick as a flash, he scrambled up, swung the end of the spear away from the tree, rolled the beast's carcass over onto its side and then took a seat on its lifeless body. When Cal and Galt burst into view from two different directions, Sebastian glanced up and affected a look of mild surprise.

'Oh, there you are,' he said. 'I wondered what had happened to you two.'

The warriors approached slowly, staring down in apparent disbelief at the great furry carcass.

'It's a gruntag!' exclaimed Galt. 'Biggest one I ever saw.'

'Oh, is that what it's called?' said Sebastian, trying to sound casual, though in truth his heart was still hammering fit to burst.

'What happened?' asked Cal suspiciously.

'What does it look like?' retorted Sebastian. 'This big lad decided he didn't like the look of me and charged. I had to take care of him. Well, I couldn't wait all day for help to turn up, could I? To be honest, I thought you two had given up and gone back to the others.'

Galt went down on his knees beside the carcass and examined the place where the spear had gone in. He let out a low whistle. 'How did you get it in so deep?' he asked.

Sebastian shrugged. 'I just threw it,' he said.

'You . . . threw it?' Galt looked astonished.

'Yes, the . . . what did you call it? The grunter?'

'Gruntag!'

'Yes, well it started towards me – it was still a good twenty spear-lengths away – and I thought, why not just throw the spear at it? Give it a sporting chance. Anyway, my aim was true, as you can see.'

Cal snorted derisively. 'There's not a man alive could throw a spear such a distance with *that* kind of force,' he said.

'True enough.' Sebastian got up from his seat on the gruntag's flank. 'But then, we Chosen Ones aren't exactly ordinary men, are we?' He started to walk away. 'I'll go and make sure the others are all right,' he said.

'Just a moment,' said Galt. 'If you're so strong, perhaps you'd like to throw this thing over your shoulder and carry it back to the trail for us?'

Sebastian rolled his eyes. 'Oh, come on,' he said. 'You can't

135

expect me to take care of *everything*. I've done the hard bit.' He looked around. 'Besides, this place is as good as any to make camp for the night.'

Cal sneered. 'Oh, so now you're an expert on campsites, are you?' he said.

'How hard can it be? Now you two get that thing skinned, gutted and ready to cook.' He thought for a moment. 'I suppose it *is* edible?' he asked.

Galt laughed. 'This is the jungle,' he said matter-of-factly. 'Anything that moves is edible.'

'Good. I'll go and fetch the others.' Sebastian smiled. 'I don't know about you lads, but I've worked up quite an appetite.' He began to walk away.

'Er . . . Chosen One?' said Galt, and Sebastian thought he deducted a new humility in his tone.

'Yes?' he said.

'You *do* realize you're walking in the wrong direction?'

'Of course.' He looked at Galt. 'A little test I devised,' he said. 'To . . . make sure you were staying alert. Yes, of course, I should *really* be going . . .'

'That way,' said Galt, pointing.

'Excellent.' Sebastian looked slyly at Cal. 'If only everyone was as clued up as Galt, we'd be laughing,' he said. He turned and walked in the direction Galt had indicated, hoping against hope that he wouldn't get lost.

CHAPTER 12

A FRANK EXCHANGE OF VIEWS

Sebastian sucked the last meat juices from a large bone and threw it into the fire, over which hunks of gruntag flesh were still sizzling enticingly. He gave a long sigh of content.

'Now, that's what I call dinner,' he said.

Everybody was seated around the flames – except for Max, who stood a short distance off, browsing through the lush undergrowth in search of something more suited to a vegetarian diet.

Keera, who was sitting on a fallen tree trunk beside Sebastian, nodded and let out a long belch, a popular custom among the Jilith. 'Yes, there's nothing like a hunk of fresh meat,' she agreed.

'Bit tough, if you ask me,' muttered Cal, who seemed thoroughly out of sorts. 'Not like a nice tender rusa. Now that's what I call tasty.'

'Nonsense!' said Sebastian. He looked down at Salah, who was sitting cross-legged by his feet, happily tucking into a hunk of meat that was nearly as big as she was. 'What do you think?' he asked her. 'Gruntag a bit tough?'

Salah grinned, shook her head, and gave him a thumbs up.

'No complaints there,' observed Sebastian. He was aware that he was laying it on a bit thick, but it was such a pleasure to get one over on Cal, he simply couldn't resist it.

'The Chosen One's right,' said Galt, through a mouthful of food. His mouth and beard glistened with grease. 'If you take the meat from the haunches, it's as tender as anything in the jungle.'

Now all eyes turned to Cornelius, as though his opinion might decide matters. He was eating all right, but without enthusiasm.

'It's fine,' he muttered dismissively. 'I'm just not that hungry.'

Sebastian frowned. He didn't like this new version of his old friend – somebody who seemed to have lost all appetite for life. It was not like him at all and Sebastian could only hope that something would return him to his usual good humour.

From a short distance away there was a sudden blast of expelled air.

''Scuse me,' said Max, still browsing. 'Some of this greenery is a bit rich on the old system.'

'Oh, don't worry,' said Keera. 'Amongst the Jilith, that is considered the height of good manners.'

'Don't tell him that,' muttered Sebastian. 'None of us will get a wink of sleep tonight.'

'I heard that,' said Max primly; and Sebastian and Keera shared a mischievous laugh.

'So,' said Cal, a little louder than seemed absolutely necessary, 'what's in this mysterious lost city we're seeking?'

Sebastian glanced up in surprise, the spell broken. He shrugged. 'Blessed if any of us know,' he said. 'It's just that Thaddeus Peel asked us to find it.'

Cal's eyes narrowed suspiciously. 'Who's Thaddeus Peel?' he asked.

'He's . . . the man who sent us on this mission. A powerful man in Ramalat. He wants to know all about the lost city.'

'Well, why doesn't this Thaddeus Peel come and find it for himself?'

'He was . . . well, he's just not the adventuring sort. He asked us to come and look for it – and bring back proof of its existence.'

'Why would he want you to do that?' asked Galt, mystified.

'Well, he's heard people talking about it since he was a small boy. So he put together this expedition. You see, he thinks it could be worth his while.' He lowered his voice as though somebody might be listening in. 'There could be treasure,' he said.

The warriors looked back at him blankly.

'What's that?' asked Galt.

'You know – gold . . . silver . . . precious jewels?'

They still looked bemused.

'What use would they be?' asked Cal.

It suddenly struck Sebastian what nonsense he was talking. The Jilith had no currency and therefore no use for any of the treasures that most of the world held in such high esteem. Give a Jilith man a handful of diamonds and he'd most likely use them as decorations to braid his hair. Hand him a bag of gold coins and he'd probably use them as ammunition in his slingshot. He certainly wouldn't have any other use for them. Sebastian considered what they might prefer.

'There might be other things,' he said. 'You know, like Joseph found? The globe with the little houses inside?'

Galt smiled. 'Oh yeah, now you're talking!' he said. 'I wouldn't mind one of those. I once asked Joseph if I could borrow his for a bit, but he just said no. He's very mean with it. We *could* find a really big one' – he extended his huge arms as wide as they would go – 'with *big* houses inside it. Then if he asked me if he could borrow mine, I'd just say no!'

Cal looked at him in a pitying sort of way. 'And if we found one like that, how do you suppose we'd get it back?'

'Hmm . . .' Galt lapsed into a thoughtful silence.

Sebastian leaned back and then noticed that Keera was looking at him with interest.

'The world you come from,' she said. 'It must be very different to ours.'

Sebastian considered for a moment. 'Yes, I suppose it is,' he agreed.

'These . . . *treasures* you speak of. They mean something in your world?'

He nodded. 'Where I come from, a man's importance is measured by the amount of treasure he has,' he explained. 'If he has enough gold and jewels, he can have whatever he wants. A fine palace, land, slaves . . .'

'Slaves?'

'People who must do his bidding, bring his food, clean his house. That sort of thing.'

'Take my word for it,' said Max wearily, 'you've already got one of those.'

'But you are a slave too,' Keera told Sebastian.

'I am?'

'Yes, because you must do the bidding of this Thaddeus Peel.'

'Er . . . well, he *is* paying us to do this.'

'Paying you . . . how?'

'With money. Gold coins.' Sebastian studied her baffled face for a moment. 'It's hard to explain,' he said.

'And you have a lot of this . . . money?'

'Oh no, hardly any. But of course some people have money beyond imagination. In a place called Keladon there was a king – Septimus – the richest man in the known world. He had vast palaces, armies, stables, gold, jewels, you name it . . . He was a mighty man indeed.'

'Until you killed him, young master,' said Max, from behind a bush.

Keera's eyes narrowed. 'You killed this king? Why?'

Sebastian frowned. 'It's complicated. He shouldn't really have been king. He was supposed to be minding the throne for his niece, a young woman called Princess Kerin, until she came of age. But he plotted to have her killed. And I . . . I wished to protect her. So I helped lead an uprising against him.'

Keera looked at him and her eyes seemed to burn, such was their intensity. 'You loved this Kerin,' she said. 'I can tell from your voice.'

Sebastian felt himself reddening. 'Oh no, not really – though I was quite fond of her—' he said.

'You were mad about her,' said Max. 'You were like a great lovesick ninny wandering about the place!'

'I was not!' protested Sebastian. 'He's exaggerating,' he told Keera.

'Hardly. You were like a big moon-faced twerp. When she threw you over, you acted as though you were mortally wounded. I almost expected you to start writing poetry about her.'

'Will you belt up?' snarled Sebastian. 'Just get on with your supper and keep your snout out of this.' He turned back to Keera, aware that, by his feet, Salah was shaking with silent laughter. 'You'll have to forgive him,' he said. 'He's always lived in a fantasy world – you can't trust a thing he says.'

'I think he speaks the truth,' said Keera; and she could not conceal the disappointment in her voice.

'It's all in the past,' Sebastian assured her. 'I don't even think about her now.'

Galt suddenly clapped his hands together. 'You'd roll it,' he said.

Everybody looked at him.

'What are you blathering about?' snarled Cal, who couldn't seem to take his gaze off Keera and Sebastian.

'The big globe. You'd just roll it along the ground. You'd have to be careful it didn't smash on rocks or anything, but—'

'Joseph's globe has a flat bottom,' said Cal. 'It wouldn't work.'

'Oh, yes.' Galt frowned and thought for a moment. 'A raft,' he said. 'We could build a raft and float it downriver.'

'But we'd be heading *up*river,' said Cal flatly.

'Huh?'

'If we were going back to the village, we'd be heading upriver, wouldn't we? How would we get a raft to go upriver?'

'Couldn't we paddle really, really hard?' suggested Galt.

Meanwhile Keera hadn't quite finished questioning Sebastian. 'So even a Chosen One can be unlucky in love,' she observed. 'Was this Princess Kerin the only one you loved, or were there others?'

'Umm . . . well . . .' began Sebastian. 'I suppose . . .'

She took hold of his hand. 'And do you think you could ever feel the same way about another woman?'

'Oh, I already do,' he assured her.

'Really?' She looked delighted.

'Yes, her name is—'

'I think you can safely let go of her hand now,' said Cal, staring across the fire at Sebastian.

Sebastian looked down in surprise. 'Oh, but . . . she was holding *my* hand,' he assured Cal.

'I don't see much of a difference. It seems to me that you need to learn your place, and not go chasing after Jilith women!'

'What?' Sebastian stared at him. 'I'm not chasing after anyone! I was just trying to—'

'I can see what you were trying to do. But you need to remember that Keera belongs to me!'

Now it was Keera's turn to look indignant. 'Is that so?' she said. 'Well, it's the first I've heard about it.'

'Oh, come on, you know how I feel about you.'

'I am aware of that, yes. But you must also understand that I have never felt the same way about you. To me, you're a good friend, nothing more.'

'Oh, you say that *now*! But everything was different before this . . . this jumped-up fancy pants arrived in the village.'

'Jumped-up fancy pants?' cried Sebastian. 'Well, I've been called a few things in my time, but—'

'Cal, you know the prophecy,' said Keera, her voice as cold as a field of Golmiran snow. 'Sebastian was sent by Okrin to help us. He and his companions have rid us of our greatest enemies.'

'Yes – with the help of the entire tribe. And at the cost of eight lives.'

'That doesn't matter. He fulfilled his part of the prophecy and it's up to me to fulfil mine. After everything he's done for our village, how can I not give him whatever he asks of me?'

'Yes, but hold on,' said Sebastian. 'I wasn't—'

'You shall never marry him!' roared Cal.

'Look,' reasoned Sebastian, 'I don't even want to—'

'My father has said that we *must* marry!' said Keera. 'Would you have me defy Maccan as well?'

'You will wed this preening fool over my dead body!' yelled Cal and he got to his feet, reaching for his sword.

'Preening fool?' gasped Sebastian. 'Well, that's just—' He broke off as something occurred to him – something so obvious he was amazed it hadn't come to him before. He pointed at Cal.

'You . . . snake in the grass!' he cried. 'That's why you sent me into the jungle on my own. You knew it wasn't a rusa I'd be going up against. You knew it was a gruntag. You hoped I'd be killed and then you'd no longer have a rival!'

'Nonsense,' said Cal; but he didn't sound too convincing.

'You expect me to believe a seasoned hunter like you could mistake gruntag poo for rusa droppings? You knew exactly what you were doing. Oh yes, you thought I'd wander in there and be torn limb from limb.' Now Sebastian got up from his seat and reached for his own sword. 'I ought to teach you a lesson you'll never forget.'

'You're welcome to try, elfling,' snarled Cal, stepping forward. Behind him, Galt threw aside what was left of his food and started up. Max came trotting back to stand by Sebastian. Keera and Salah sat regarding the scene in silent horror. In the brief silence that followed, the crackling of the fire seemed very loud.

And then there was a sudden blur of motion whirling through the air from one side of the fire to the other. Sebastian received a powerful punch in the face that tipped him back over the tree trunk he'd been sitting on and left him lying with his skinny legs sticking up in the air. A fraction of a second later, Cal received a kick in the stomach that sent him sprawling into Galt and the two of them went down in a tangle of arms and legs.

The blur came back to earth and into focus. Cornelius stood there, hands on hips, glowering around at his fallen companions.

'What was that for?' gasped Sebastian. He was trying to get himself upright, but in his current undignified position it wasn't easy. In the end, Keera and Salah pulled him back up so he was sitting. 'What . . . what do you think you're doing?' he spluttered.

'What are *you* doing, more's the point?' growled Cornelius. 'Shadlog's teeth, we've only been on this expedition one day and you're all at each other's throats. What chance of success do you suppose we have if that carries on?'

'But' – Sebastian pointed at Cal, who was now being helped to his feet by Galt – 'he sent me in against that gruntag to get me killed.'

'That's not true!' protested Cal. 'The droppings I found were from a rusa; I wouldn't send anybody to do a job I wouldn't do myself. Even *him*.' He somehow managed to make the last word sound like the worst kind of oath. He pointed back at Sebastian. 'Just tell him to stay away from my girlfriend.'

'Your *girlfriend*?' cried Keera. She looked at Cornelius. 'You tell Cal that I'm not his girlfriend and never have been!'

'Yes,' added Max, 'and you can also tell him to stop threatening my young master or I'll butt him from one side of this jungle to the other.'

'PLEASE!' Cornelius lifted his hands to his ears and affected a tortured look. 'I can't listen to any more of this nonsense. Sebastian . . . Cal . . . I want you to shake hands and apologize to each other.'

'You are joking, I hope,' protested Sebastian.

'No I'm not. It's either that or I send Cal and Galt back to their village and we carry on without them. And as they're the only ones who have a clue how to find their way through this jungle, I don't think that's the best idea.'

There was a very long silence. Sebastian and Cal glared at each other across the campfire. Finally Sebastian gave a sigh. He got up from his seat and approached Cal. At first it looked as though Cal wasn't going to follow suit but Galt pushed him forward and finally the two of them stood face to face.

Sebastian extended a hand. 'I'm sorry,' he whispered.

'Louder!' insisted Cornelius. 'And sound like you mean it.'

'I'm sorry,' repeated Sebastian. 'And for what it's worth, I'm not after Keera. I mean, I like her of course, she's a very nice person. But . . . I have a sweetheart back in Ramalat.'

'Oh,' said Keera flatly. She stood up. 'I'm going for a walk,' she announced.

'Wait, I'll go with you,' suggested Cal. 'It's a jungle out there.'

'I don't want any company, thank you,' she told him. 'And I can look after myself.' She walked away into the shadows.

'Oh, well done, young master,' said Max, gazing after her. 'You handled that with your usual sensitivity. Like a blind rusa in a pottery shop.'

'Shut up!' said Sebastian. He turned back to Cal. 'I don't want there to be bad blood between us. If you can honestly assure me that you didn't know there was a gruntag waiting for me, then I'm willing to accept that. Now, will you shake my hand?'

Cal scowled, but after a moment's hesitation he put out his own hand and they shook.

'Good,' said Cornelius. 'I'm glad that's settled. I can see that I've taken my eye off the ball for far too long. I've let my own worries cloud my judgement. But there's no sense in dwelling on past mistakes. What's done is done, and if we don't try our very best to carry out this mission, then we may as well just pack up and head back where we came from. From here on in, we're all going to pull together as a team. Understood?'

There was a long silence and everybody nodded. One thing was clear. Cornelius was back in control.

*C*HAPTER *13*

THE RIVER

They set off again at first light, moving in single file along the narrow trail. Whatever had happened the previous night, it seemed to have revitalized Cornelius, and he was more like his old self, marching along briskly, shouting orders to whoever was leading the way and always ready with a solution to any problem. It was Keera who had gone all quiet. She trudged along at the rear of the column, her head bowed, looking sad beyond belief.

'That poor girl,' whispered Max when Sebastian was walking just ahead of him. 'You've cut her to the quick, you know. She obviously had her heart set on marrying you. I thought she was going to burst into tears when you said those hurtful things last night.'

'Well, what was I supposed to say?' hissed Sebastian. 'I didn't want to get her hopes up, did I?'

'Oh, is that why you sat there holding her hand? No wonder she's confused.'

'For the last time, I wasn't holding her hand; *she* was holding *mine*.'

'Well, you weren't exactly fighting it, were you?'

'How could I?' argued Sebastian. 'I didn't want to insult her. It's all because of this daft prophecy thing. I'm sorry now that I went along with it. She thinks she *has* to marry me to keep Okrin happy. That's the only reason she brought up the subject.'

But Max shook his head. 'It's nothing to do with the prophecy, young master, believe you me. That young lady has set her sights on you and she isn't going to settle for anything less.'

'Nonsense! She'll soon accept that it's not going to happen.'

'I wouldn't bet on it. If I was you, I'd try to—'

He broke off as Sebastian quickened his pace and moved up along the column.

'Now where are you going?' complained Max.

'I'm sorry,' said Sebastian, 'but I absolutely refuse to take romantic advice from somebody whose first and only love is a big bucket of food.'

He slotted himself in behind Cornelius. 'We're making good progress today,' he observed.

Cornelius glanced back and nodded. 'I want to be at the river before nightfall,' he said. 'If we keep up this pace, we should be fine.'

Sebastian studied the little warrior for a moment as he marched along. 'So what snapped you out of your mood?' he asked.

'Listening to you lot arguing,' replied Cornelius without hesitation. 'It made me realize that what's done is done and there's not a blessed thing I can do to change it. I shall always have the blood of the Gograth on my hands, but now we have to get on and do the best we can to achieve what we set out to do. We must find the lost city and the evidence we need to prove its existence.' He was silent for a moment, and when he spoke again, it was in a quieter tone. 'I felt very sorry for Keera last night,' he murmured. 'Did you see the poor girl's face when you said you had no intention of marrying her?'

'Don't you start!' snapped Sebastian. 'I've already heard all this from Max. What would you have me do?'

'I don't suppose there's anything you *can* do. It's just unfortunate, that's all. The thing is, Maccan expects you to marry her. I wouldn't like to be the man who has to tell him you're not interested.'

'Let's cross that bridge when we come to it,' said Sebastian. 'I'll tell you something. That lost city had better be where Joseph said it was. If all this turns out to be a pointless exercise, I am never embarking on one of your mad missions ever again.'

'That makes two of us,' agreed Cornelius.

* * *

They marched all that day, taking only a short break to wolf down some chunks of gruntag they had brought along with them, wrapped in fragrant leaves to keep it fresh. After a quick gulp from their water canteens, they set off again, walking till every muscle ached.

Towards late afternoon, just when Sebastian was telling himself he could go no further, he heard an excited shout from up ahead. It was Galt announcing that he could 'smell water'. Sebastian tried sniffing the air but was aware of nothing except the odour of his own sweat; however the idea of being close gave a little extra spring to his step. Everyone quickened their pace, eyes fixed on the way ahead; soon they were aware of a distant roar, and then, quite unexpectedly, the trail widened out to reveal that they were standing on the bank of a mighty river. Sebastian gave a gasp of astonishment. When Joseph had told his story, he had pictured a fast-flowing stream, but this was on a scale he couldn't have imagined – a vast stretch of dark water, the other bank so far away it would be impossible for even the strongest of archers to fire an arrow across it.

Sebastian was just wondering if they had got the right river when Cornelius pointed out a huge tree some distance down-stream, the roots forming a series of hollows in the ground.

'Just as Joseph described it!' he cried. 'That must be where the herd of rusa were resting.'

Everybody threw down their packs and took the opportunity to grab a few minutes' rest. Sebastian pulled off his
boots and allowed his feet to enjoy a little fresh air. Cornelius
sank down beside him, removing his helmet and unbuckling
his breastplate. Max looked hopefully around at his
companions, no doubt waiting for somebody to come and
untie the equipment weighing him down, but for the time
being at least, nobody made a move to help him. Cal and Galt
sat together as always, their eyes darting this way and that,
always on the lookout for trouble. Salah, who never seemed
to tire, started collecting bits of dry timber to make a fire.
Keera, meanwhile, sat a short distance away, her pretty face
marred by a sullen look.

Cornelius glanced at the group for a moment, as though
gauging their strength. 'Tonight we rest,' he told them. 'First
thing tomorrow morning, we start building the raft.'

Everyone stared at him.

'What raft?' asked Cal. 'Nobody said anything about a raft.'

'That's because I only thought of it last night,' said
Cornelius. 'Actually, it was Galt who gave me the idea.'

'Really?' Galt looked around proudly. 'Hear that? The little
warrior wants to use *my* idea.'

Cal seemed decidedly unimpressed by this news. 'We'll
spend two days building a raft,' he said.

'Yes, we will,' agreed Cornelius. 'But think for a moment.
To find the lost city we have to follow the course of the river.

Those are the only directions we have.' He pointed towards the dense undergrowth that crowded both banks. 'Imagine how long it would take us to hack our way through that lot! Yes, we'll lose a couple of days, but we'll make it up in no time – and we'll be doing exactly what Joseph did, heading straight down the river. That way we can be there in double-quick time.'

'And back again,' said Galt, who still didn't seem to understand that you couldn't sail a raft upriver.

Sebastian considered explaining this to him but decided that after all that walking, it was simply too much effort. He gave Cornelius a questioning look. 'You know how to build a raft, do you?'

Cornelius shrugged. 'How hard can it be?' he asked. 'We've brought axes with us and there's no shortage of wood around here. We'll use lengths of vine to tie it all together. You'll see, it's going to save us weeks.'

Max snorted. 'After our last adventure, I said I'd never travel on water again,' he said.

'No,' said Cornelius. 'You said you'd never go on the *ocean*. This is just a river – it's not the same thing.'

'It looks deep enough,' said Max. 'And I'll wager the water's just as wet.'

'You needn't have any worries on that score,' said Cal dismissively. 'We won't be taking you with us anyway.'

Now all eyes turned in his direction.

'What do you mean?' asked Sebastian.

'Well, we're not going to put a great fat brute like that onto a raft, are we?' reasoned Cal. 'He'll just capsize us.'

'Don't spare my feelings,' said Max.

'Of course we're taking him,' retorted Sebastian. 'He's a valuable member of the team.'

'What, *him*?' Cal sneered. 'All he does is moan and fart. How is that valuable?'

'If I started to list the reasons why I'm valuable, we'd be here all day,' said Max. 'And I'll thank you to keep a civil tongue in your head. Don't forget, my best mates are the Chosen One and the little warrior. One word from me and they'll smite you; and you won't like being smitten!'

'If you knew anything about rafts,' Cornelius told Cal, 'you'd realize that Max is the best thing we could ask for.'

'Yes!' said Max, then looked at Cornelius. 'And that would be because . . . ?'

'He'll provide *ballast*. A great big heavy lump right in the middle of the raft – that's just what we need.'

'Thanks,' said Max. 'I think.'

'But he must weigh *tons*!' protested Cal.

'Yes, but that's good. A huge hulking lump like that is exactly what will *prevent* us from tipping up.'

'Did you have to use the word "hulking"?' asked Max.

Cal scowled. 'Well, I don't know,' he said. 'I've made

canoes before, but never rafts.' He looked at Galt. 'What do you think?'

Galt just beamed. 'A raft,' he said. 'That was *my* idea!'

'So we're agreed then?' said Cornelius, clapping his hands together. 'Tomorrow we start building the raft and Max comes with us.'

Everybody exchanged glances and most nodded, though Cal was clearly unhappy with the decision.

'Tonight we'll rest, get our strength back,' Cornelius told them. 'I see Salah has already got a fire going. What about dinner? Perhaps our hunters would like to go out and rustle up something tasty?'

'No need,' said Galt, producing a length of line and some hooks from his pack. 'Let's have a nice fish supper for a change!' He shambled down to the riverbank to find a good spot to cast his line.

Sebastian started to massage his aching feet but suddenly became aware of a pair of eyes glaring at him. He glanced up to see Max's mournful face.

'Comfortable, are we?' asked the buffalope.

'Yeah, not bad,' said Sebastian.

'Well, it's all right for some, isn't it?' Max twitched his flanks, making the various cooking utensils and tools rattle.

'Oh, right.' Sebastian got up and went over to him. 'I suppose you'd like me to untie all this equipment.'

'If it's not too much trouble,' muttered Max, then, as

Sebastian approached, inclined his head to whisper, 'After you've done this, you can go and chat to Keera.'

Sebastian shook his head. 'I'm not sure that's a good idea,' he said. 'Right now all I feel like is having a good soak in the river.'

'You've plenty of time for that,' hissed Max. 'Look at her! Have you ever seen such a miserable face?'

'Many times, but it usually has a big horn on either side of it.'

'Oh, very droll!'

Sebastian undid the last strap and lowered the jumble of equipment to the ground. Max gave a long sigh and shrugged his shoulders. 'Ah, that's better,' he said. 'I thought we'd never get to this blooming river.' He nudged Sebastian with his snout. 'Now go on – have a word with Keera.'

'But—'

'Just go!' Max lowered his head and gave Sebastian what was probably intended to be a gentle shove in the back, but Sebastian's lanky frame was catapulted forward across the clearing. He caught one foot in a discarded pack, tripped, performed an ungainly somersault, and came crashing down a short distance from a rather startled Keera.

She gazed down at him for a minute and then did something she hadn't done all day. She laughed. 'You're so funny!' she cried.

Sebastian sat up and directed a withering glare in Max's

direction. 'Just trying to cheer you up,' he said. 'You know, I . . . I used to be a professional jester.'

'What's that?' asked Keera.

He shuffled round to sit beside her. 'I used to make people laugh for a living,' he said. He thought for a moment. 'Well, I used to *try* to, anyway. Didn't have all that much success, now that I think about it.'

'You should have. You're good at making people laugh.'

'Only when I'm not trying to,' Sebastian assured her. He glanced nervously across at Cal, who didn't seem to be at all amused by his antics. 'Look, Keera,' he said. 'About what I said last night . . . I understand that you were expecting me to fulfil the prophecy and everything, but as I said, there *is* somebody else . . .'

'Yes, this sweetheart you spoke of – tell me about her.'

'Umm . . . well, her name's Jenna and she's a sea captain . . . You remember – the boats I spoke of that travel on the wide stretch of water?'

'Yes, like this water,' said Keera, pointing.

'Oh no, that's nothing compared to the ocean. I mean, you can see the far side of a river, but on the ocean you could travel for many moons and never have sight of land.'

Keera nodded. 'So where is this . . . Jenna?'

Sebastian laughed. 'That's a good question. She's on a long voyage. Right now she'll be somewhere south of here.'

'A dangerous voyage?'

'Er . . . yes, I suppose *all* voyages can be dangerous.'

'And you will marry this sweetheart one day?'

Sebastian shrugged. 'I don't really know. I . . . expect so. But we're both still very young; there's plenty of time for that. But look, Keera, just because there's somebody else in my life, it doesn't mean we can't be mates . . . does it?'

She seemed to brighten considerably. 'Really?' she cried. 'Oh, well, that's wonderful!'

He was somewhat taken aback by her reaction. 'Is it?' he said.

'Yes. I won't have to be sad any more. And I will try not to hate this . . . Jenna. But if one day we meet, perhaps we will fight each other.'

Sebastian looked at her, startled. 'I don't think there's any need for that,' he protested.

'Well, that's how we settle things in the jungle,' said Keera. 'Not with weapons; just our fists. Would she not be willing to fight for you?'

'I really couldn't say.' He glanced around nervously. Across the clearing, Cal was gazing at him intently and sharpening a vicious-looking knife on a stone. 'You know what? I think I'm going to find a quiet spot in the river and have a good bath. Wash some of the sweat off.'

'Great,' said Keera. 'I'll come with you.'

'What?' He stared at her. 'Oh no, I don't think that's a good idea.'

'But we're *mates*, aren't we? Mates wash together.'

'Do they? Not where I come from, they don't.' Sebastian got hastily to his feet. 'No, you . . . you stay here and talk to Cal. I'm sure he'd like to sort things out with you.'

'There's nothing to sort out,' said Keera irritably, shooting an indignant glare in the warrior's direction. 'Cal thinks he has some kind of claim over me, but he doesn't.'

'Yes, but he's your mate too, right?'

Now Keera looked positively horrified. 'No he is not!' she cried. 'What sort of girl do you think I am? You can't have more than one mate at a time!'

'You can't? But . . . I have lots of mates.'

She stared at him. 'Then the ways of your people are strange indeed,' she said.

Sebastian was beginning to get the impression that something was very wrong. 'Umm . . . l-look,' he stammered. 'I . . . I'm going to go and get cleaned up.' Keera started to get up too but he waved her back down again. 'No, you stay here, I'll . . . see you later . . .' He walked quickly towards the river, giving Max another accusing glance as he went by.

He came upon Galt, who was crouched by the bank, staring intently down at a float he had made out of a piece of twig. Sebastian saw that he already had a good-sized fish lying beside him on the riverbank.

'How's the fishing?' he asked.

'Great,' said Galt without looking up. 'These waters are teeming with fish.'

'And those things are edible, are they?'

'I told you before. This is the jungle – everything—'

'. . . is edible. Yes. Er . . . sorry to interrupt. Can I ask you a question?'

'Ask away,' said Galt, his gaze still fixed on the float.

'Right. If I said to you that you were my mate, what would you think?'

Galt glanced up in alarm. He stared at Sebastian for a moment and then burst out laughing.

'What's so funny?' asked Sebastian.

'If you said that, I'd be very worried,' Galt told him. 'You see, in the Jilith tribe, a man can take a wife but he can also have a *mate*.' He raised his eyebrows. 'That's somebody who is very close to him, almost like a second wife; but they don't have to actually get married.'

'Oh,' said Sebastian. 'I see.'

'It's an old custom. Not too many do it these days, because of the trouble it causes.'

'Trouble?'

'Between the wife and the mate, usually. There's been all kinds of ructions in the past. Some of 'em have even been known to fight to the death.' He pulled a face. 'They're supposed to just use their fists, but I've heard of them using clubs, knives, axes, all sorts.'

Sebastian groaned and slapped a hand to his forehead. His attempt to let Keera down gently had misfired horribly. And what had he just said to her? That he had lots of mates? 'Perfect,' he muttered.

Galt grinned. 'So . . . still like to be my mate?' he asked mockingly.

'Er . . . no, that's . . . OK. I'll, um . . . see you later.' Sebastian hurried away along the riverbank to find a secluded spot, then stripped off his clothes, gave them a good wash in the shallows and hung them from a branch to dry before wading out until he was chest-deep in the water. The shock of it against his bare flesh felt delicious and with a sigh of contentment he let himself sink right beneath the surface; he stayed under as long as he could – at least down here, he thought, he was unlikely to get into any trouble.

Which was when a large crab took his big toe in its pincers and squeezed hard; he rose up from the depths with a bellow of agony.

'Do you mind?' yelled Galt from upstream. 'You're frightening the fish!'

CHAPTER 14

THE BIGGEST CUP

At dawn the following day, Sebastian was shaken roughly
awake by Cornelius.

'Come on,' said the little warrior. 'You can't lie there all day
– there's work to be done!'

Sebastian cast a bleary eye around the camp and saw that
everybody else was up and moving around. Salah already
had a pot of chai bubbling over one fire while Cal and his
team were cooking fish over another. The smell of them made
Sebastian's stomach rumble but he was too exhausted to care.

'Just a bit longer,' he pleaded, pulling the animal-hide
blanket over himself. 'I was having a nice dream.'

But Cornelius was not to be denied. 'Stir yourself – we have
to get on with building the raft,' he growled. 'I've allotted
tasks to everybody, including you.'

Sebastian scowled. 'I think I preferred you when you

weren't talking to anybody,' he said. He managed to get himself upright and, yawning and scratching, stumbled across to the fire. Before he even reached it, Keera was there, putting a big steaming cup of chai into his hands.

'Good morning, *mate*,' she said, favouring him with a dazzling smile, and he had to resist the impulse to groan. 'I saved you the biggest cup.'

'Er . . . thanks,' he said. 'Keera, this "mates" business . . . we really need to talk about it.'

'There's nothing to say,' she assured him. 'You have made me very happy.' She moved off to help Salah with the fish. Sebastian couldn't help noticing that the younger girl was grinning in his direction. Evidently Keera had shared the news with her.

'Oh, that's perfect,' he muttered under his breath.

He turned away, aware that Cal was giving him the evil eye from across the clearing but unwilling to face an argument so early in the day. He sat down on a log at the edge of the clearing and sipped his chai, feeling its warm sweetness reviving him.

There was a rustling in the bushes and Max's head appeared. He looked a little bashful and Sebastian surmised that the buffalope had been relieving himself.

'Good morning, young master,' he said. 'I trust you slept well?'

'I slept like a baby,' said Sebastian, recalling one of his

father's old jokes. 'I woke up screaming every few moments.'

Max looked at him blankly. 'I didn't hear anything,' he muttered, missing the point entirely. He looked over at Keera. 'She's in good spirits now. Whatever you said to her, master, it seems to have done the trick,'

Sebastian sighed. 'It has not done the trick,' he said. 'It has dropped me right in the brown stuff. Now she thinks I want her as a *mate*.'

Max was puzzled. 'What's wrong with that?' he asked.

'Nothing, unless you happen to be a Jilith; and then it makes a big, big difference. She thinks I—'

He broke off as Keera came towards him carrying a whole cooked fish laid out on a flat green leaf.

'I picked the nicest one for you,' she said, placing it in his lap. 'Now be sure and eat up every scrap – you're going to need all your energy today.' She took the opportunity to stroke Sebastian's hair. 'You washed it,' she observed. 'It's all shiny.'

Across the clearing there was a crash as Cal set a metal cauldron down with more force than was strictly necessary.

Sebastian flinched. 'That's, er . . . just the river water,' he said. 'Good for your hair, they say.' He gestured at the fish. 'Thanks for this. Looks great. Now . . . why don't you, er . . . run along and get some breakfast for yourself?'

Keera bowed her head obediently. 'If that's what you want,' she said; and she returned to the fire.

167

'Young master,' murmured Max, 'she seems a bit *too* friendly, if you catch my drift.'

'Oh, you noticed?' Sebastian tore off a mouthful of fish and started eating. 'It's all your fault – you're the one who made me go and speak to her.'

'Yes, but I didn't think you were going to sweet-talk her.'

'I didn't! The whole thing's a misunderstanding. You see, to the Jilith, a mate is—'

The sound of Cornelius clearing his throat made everybody sit up and take notice. Sebastian saw that he had climbed onto a tree stump so that everybody could have a clear view of him.

'All right, everybody, you need to finish up your breakfasts quickly,' he said. 'I want to have the raft ready to leave here by the day after tomorrow.' He gazed around at his companions. 'I know it's a tall order . . .'

'From a short chief,' murmured Max, under his breath.

'. . . but I feel sure we can do it. While you lot were resting yesterday afternoon, I went out and marked the trees we need to cut down with an X. I've chosen jibara trees. The wood's incredibly light, which means it will be easy to cut down and manoeuvre and it should float well. The wood also exudes a sticky sap which will stop the water from soaking into it.'

'Oh, so now he's an expert on trees,' said Max. 'Is there anything that man doesn't know?'

Cornelius glared at him. 'I was told about jibara trees when I was researching a source of wood to make the battle chariot,' he explained. 'The Jilith have made canoes out of jibaras for generations – isn't that so, Cal?'

Cal nodded. 'It's good for canoes right enough, but I've never seen it used to make a raft before.'

'There's a first time for everything,' said Cornelius. 'Now, you and Galt will be our logging team. You'll be cutting down the trees and removing all the branches. It's hard work but I know you're up to it.'

'Lead us to it!' said Galt, lifting a stone axe, which in his huge hand looked like a child's plaything.

'Max, you'll be dragging the stripped trunks back here one by one, then Sebastian and I will assemble the raft.'

Max sighed. 'I knew I'd end up doing all the hard work,' he muttered.

Cornelius ignored him. 'Keera, Salah, you'll have one of the most important jobs. You'll be collecting the vines and then plaiting strong ropes from them. That's a skilled task, but I can't think of anybody better to handle the job. What do you say?'

Keera nodded and Salah gave an exuberant thumbs up.

Cornelius looked around. 'Any questions?'

'Yes,' said Max. 'Isn't there something more challenging I could do?'

'Challenging?' Cornelius muttered.

'Yes. I mean, I'm not being funny, but all I ever do is drag stuff around. Haven't you got something that requires a little more . . . brain power?'

Cornelius studied him for a moment. 'There's nothing particularly brainy about making a raft,' he said. 'It's all common sense. Let me see now . . . could you cut down a tree with an axe?'

'Well . . . no, but—'

'Could you plait a rope?'

'Obviously not, but—'

'Or perhaps you think *we* could drag the trees to the clearing and you could just lie there, eating fruit and having the occasional nap.'

Max looked thoughtful. 'I didn't realize that was an option,' he said.

'It's not. You'll do the dragging. End of story. Now, everyone, finish up your grub and we'll get this show on the road.' Cornelius climbed down from his perch and Max snorted.

'Well, it didn't take him long to get back on his soapbox,' he observed. 'We'll be promoting him to King Cornelius next.' He looked at Sebastian. 'What do you think about this raft idea?'

'I suppose it makes sense,' admitted Sebastian. 'There's a strong current out there – I could feel it yesterday when I was bathing in the shallows. And it's true – it could take us many moons to cut our way through all that jungle. So long as the raft doesn't collapse under our weight, we should be fine.'

Max gave him a look. 'A proper little ray of sunshine, you are,' he said. 'Oh well, I suppose I'd better report for duty. Don't want anybody to accuse me of slacking.' And he lumbered off towards Cornelius.

Sebastian hastily ate the rest of his fish, aware as he did so that Keera was regarding him in silent adoration and that, on the other side of the clearing, Cal had gone back to sharpening his knife.

They worked all through the day. The jungle rang to the sound of stone axes thudding into tree trunks. Every so often there came a cry of 'Timber!' followed by the rending and crashing of vegetation as a tall tree fell to the ground. Meanwhile Cornelius and Sebastian accompanied the two girls into the jungle to collect as many vines as they could harvest. Luckily they were plentiful and they soon had a large heap waiting to be converted into ropes.

As the day progressed, Max started lumbering out of the jungle dragging a series of huge tree trunks behind him, and Cornelius and Sebastian rolled them into position to form a platform. Keera and Salah set to work plaiting the vines into stout ropes, and as each successive length appeared, Sebastian and Cornelius lashed it securely to its neighbour, bracing the whole structure with stout cross-pieces.

'What I wouldn't give for a hammer and some nails,' said Sebastian at one point.

'No need for them,' Cornelius assured them. 'The people of this jungle have been making canoes and rafts for generations without tools like that.'

The raft soon began to take shape. Cornelius had kept things simple. All that was required was a large floating platform that could be pushed along by a series of wooden poles; but he ensured that loops of vine rope were attached so that the travellers could lash themselves down should the water become turbulent; and he insisted that deep grooves be cut into the end of every log – the ropes would then sink in and stay in place.

They worked all through the first day, stopping only for a brief lunch of chai and the inevitable fish. Sebastian was already beginning to long for some roasted meat, but he knew there was no time to go hunting, and he was so ravenous, he wasn't about to complain. Once again, rather embarrassingly, Keera snatched up the biggest of the fish and hurried across to him with it. This time he felt that it wasn't just Cal who was glaring at him, but Galt too, who after all had been working much harder than he had. But it was pointless to try and stop her. She insisted on bringing her own lunch over so she could sit close to him.

'What will you do when we have found the lost city?' she asked Sebastian.

He looked at her in dismay. 'I suppose I'll be going back to my own world,' he said. He'd expected her to express disappointment at this but she just smiled.

'I am looking forward to seeing it,' she said. 'And to meeting your Jenna.'

He nearly choked on a mouthful of fish. 'Oh, but . . . I wouldn't expect you to leave your tribe,' he said. 'Your place is with them – and with your father.'

'He'll understand,' she assured him. 'Obviously we'll come back and visit from time to time. But I'm your *mate* now; my place is with you.'

Sebastian opened his mouth to say something, but at that moment Cornelius called everybody back to work and he was almost grateful for the excuse to get away.

As the afternoon wore on, the raft began to look as though it might actually function. By the time darkness fell they had what looked like a serviceable platform. After supper they fell exhausted onto their bedrolls and slept like the dead. But the following morning, at first light, Cornelius was shouting to them to get up and, after a quick breakfast, they went straight back to work.

The final parts of the deck had now been roped together. Cornelius subjected it to as much rough treatment as he could devise, kicking it, hitting it with stout cudgels, making sure that the ropes were strong enough; but Keera and Salah's blistered hands were proof of the hard work they had put into making them and they held fast. One of the last jobs was to find a different wood to make the long poles that would propel the raft along. Late that afternoon, Galt showed Cornelius a grove of maluba canes – slender sticks of hardwood that grew straight up out of the earth to an incredible height. Cornelius cut down a length and Sebastian tried to break it across his knee, but found that although he could bend it, he could not make it snap.

'It's like flexible iron,' he observed, and Cornelius nodded, clearly satisfied with the choice. They cut six poles, wanting to have some spares just in case.

Finally, as the sun declined on the horizon, it was time for the final test. Using a series of slim logs as rollers, they all helped to push, pull and prod the raft down to the river's edge and launched it into the shallows. The foremost logs hit the water with a splash and dipped alarmingly beneath the surface. Everybody held their breath; but then it rose again and floated easily. There was a collective sigh of relief and Galt lashed the raft to a stout tree trunk on the riverbank. The raft seemed to be eager to set off, moving easily to the end of its rope and rocking gently on the water.

Everybody stood looking at it.

'It looks OK,' said Cal at last. 'Mind you, it hasn't got that great fat buffalope on it yet.'

Max glared at him. 'Have you ever considered a career in

diplomacy?' he asked. 'Because if I were you, I wouldn't bother.'

Cornelius sighed. 'It's floating well enough,' he observed. 'We'll see if it's still floating tomorrow morning.'

Sebastian stared at him. 'But . . . we used jibara wood,' he said. 'Didn't you say it had a resin that would stop it from becoming waterlogged?'

'I *said* that,' agreed Cornelius, 'but it's only an educated guess. If it *does* sink, we'll have to build another one with a different kind of wood.'

The silence that followed this remark spoke volumes and Sebastian reflected that if Cornelius had to ask people to repeat the kind of work they'd done today, he'd probably have a mutiny on his hands. But he was too tired to worry about it now. The exhausted group staggered back to their places around the fire and wolfed down more chai and fish before settling themselves down for the night.

They stretched themselves out on their bedrolls and were asleep in moments.

CHAPTER 15

DOWN RIVER

Everybody held their breath as Max inched his vast bulk down the riverbank towards the raft.

They had awoken that morning to find to their collective relief that the log platform was still floating, and after a final meal they had packed up all their equipment. Now everybody stood in the shallows, steadying the sides of the raft as best they could.

'Right,' said Max. 'Here goes.' He put one hoof onto the wooden platform and then followed it with another. The raft tipped alarmingly in the water. 'Oops!' he said, but Cornelius waved at him to keep moving.

'Go to the middle!' he ordered, and Max performed an ungainly scramble, his back legs kicking water into Cornelius's face as he lunged forward across the wooden platform. As he reached the centre, the raft righted itself, the leading edge coming down with a splash that swamped Cal and Galt, who had been attempting to steady it. For a moment it looked as though the logs were simply going to sink beneath the water, but then the platform rose again, leaving Max standing in the middle, looking decidedly nervous, his legs quivering.

'I don't like this,' he said loudly. 'I don't like this at all.'

'Never mind that,' Cornelius told him. 'You don't have to like it. Just settle yourself down and don't move a muscle.'

'Yes, Chief,' said Max, and did as he was told, lowering himself with exaggerated care. He thought for a moment. 'What happens about my ablutions?' he asked.

'Your what?' asked Sebastian.

'You know, when I have to . . . do my *business*.'

'We'll cross that bridge when we come to it,' Cornelius told him unhelpfully. He looked around at the others. 'Right,' he said, 'let's get the equipment aboard. Don't worry, it's not going to tip up now that we've got that prodigious weight as ballast.'

'Are you deliberately trying to upset me?' asked Max, but his question was lost in the general scramble as everybody threw the packs aboard. Finally, one by one, they clambered onto the raft. Keera and Salah settled themselves beside Max, and Sebastian, Cal and Galt took up their positions at three corners of the rectangular platform, each holding a long maluba cane. Then Cornelius cast off and jumped aboard, his light frame making hardly any impact. He grabbed a cane and went to stand at the fourth corner. Poles were dipped into the river, and with a couple of pushes the raft began to drift smoothly out towards midstream.

Once there, the powerful current took it and it began to move forward at a surprising speed, needing only the occasional thrust of a pole to keep it pointing straight ahead.

Cornelius clapped his hands delightedly. 'What did I tell you?' he cried. 'This is going to save us so much time!'

'I wish people wouldn't say things like that,' muttered Max. 'It's just asking for trouble.'

Salah started making a series of energetic gestures at Max. 'What's she saying?' he asked Keera.

'She's telling you not to worry. She's a strong swimmer – if you fall into the water, she'll rescue you.'

'Oh, well, that's a weight off my mind,' said Max. But he bowed at Salah. 'Thank you,' he said politely. 'At least it shows that one person on this raft cares what happens to me.'

Salah smiled and gave him a hug.

Standing at the front starboard corner, Sebastian lifted a hand to shade his eyes from the sun and squinted down the great wide waterway ahead of them. It looked clear enough for as far as he could see; though they had all endured two horrific days building the raft, this form of travel certainly beat hacking their way through mile after mile of dense vegetation. He was even more delighted when, after a couple of hours of uneventful travel, Cornelius announced that two of the pole handlers could stand down and take a rest.

'We'll change over every hour or so,' he said. 'For the moment two people can do the job without any problem.'

He and Galt elected to take the first shift. Sebastian and Cal moved to the centre of the raft, and sat down beside the others gratefully.

'You must be tired,' said Keera, looking at Sebastian.

'I am,' he said.

'Not as tired as me,' snapped Cal. 'Don't forget, I've been felling trees for the last two days.'

Keera regarded him haughtily. 'You are well used to such work,' she said. 'The Chosen One is not.'

Cal rolled his eyes. 'What else is new?' he sneered.

'I wasn't exactly idle,' Sebastian told him. 'Cornelius and I had the task of putting this raft together.'

'Yes, well, we'll soon see how good a job you made of it,' said Cal. 'I for one don't have the greatest expectations.'

'Oh, there's nothing wrong with our workmanship,' said Sebastian, slamming one foot down on the trunks beneath him.

'I'd really rather you didn't do that,' said Max nervously.

'Relax – we've built this baby to take some hard knocks,' said Sebastian. 'She's not going to fall apart.'

'There you go again,' said Max. 'Inviting trouble.'

Salah started making her frenzied gesticulations and Keera translated.

'She's saying that this is a fine raft and that the Chosen One and the little warrior are very clever indeed to have built it.'

'Oh, for Okrin's sake,' growled Cal. He turned his back on the others and lay down on the wooden platform. 'I'm going to get some sleep,' he announced.

'You do that,' said Keera dismissively. She smiled at Sebastian. 'Perhaps you would like me to massage your shoulders?' she suggested.

'Er . . . no, that's all right,' he assured her. He glanced at Salah and saw that once again her hands were over her mouth, suppressing silent giggles. He turned his attention to Cornelius, who had set aside his cane for a moment and was scanning the banks on either side of the river with his ancient spyglass. 'What are you looking for?' he asked.

'Always a good idea to keep an eye out for trouble,' Cornelius told him. 'This is uncharted territory – who knows what monsters might lurk in these regions?'

'Monsters?' murmured Max. 'Oh, great.'

'How long do you suppose it will take us to get to the lost city?' asked Sebastian.

Cornelius frowned. 'Well, if Joseph's memory is correct, he was in the water for the best part of a day and a night. But I have to say, I'm puzzled.'

'Why's that?' asked Keera.

'The river that he described sounded like a hazardous, fast-flowing one. There's a strong current here, but I'd expected to see rocks and rapids.'

'But we found the big tree with all the hollows in its roots,' Sebastian reminded him. 'It must be the right river.'

'I suppose it was a very long time ago,' said Cornelius. 'Perhaps the river has changed in all those years. Or perhaps his childish imagination simply got the better of him.'

'I'm not so sure about that,' shouted Galt from the front of the raft as he pointed up ahead.

Sebastian and Cornelius went over to stand beside him and Cornelius lifted his spyglass to get a better look.

'Yes, now *that's* more the kind of thing I was expecting,' he said calmly. He handed the spyglass to Sebastian, who lifted it to his eye. Ahead he could see that the river narrowed somewhat and several jagged grey rocks stuck up from the shallows, forming a perilous opening. Around the rocks, white water foamed angrily.

Sebastian looked at Cornelius. 'Perhaps we should put in to the bank,' he said.

'Are you kidding?' Cornelius looked indignant. 'We've only just got going. Don't worry, this raft is strong enough to ride out a few rapids. Grab your pole – and wake Cal up.'

As Sebastian made his way back, he was aware that the raft was already moving faster, being pulled along by the strong currents that led to the rapids. He stooped and shook Cal awake. The warrior looked irritated, but quickly realized that something was wrong. He jumped to his feet and, taking up his pole, went to stand at the vacant front corner, opposite Galt. Sebastian glanced at Keera and Salah and indicated some loops of rope sticking up from the logs beside them. 'You'd better wrap those around yourselves,' he advised them.

'What about me?' asked Max anxiously. 'What do I hang on to?'

Sebastian frowned as he realized that they had neglected to install any Max-sized loops. 'Er . . . you'll be fine,' he told the buffalope. 'Just . . . hang onto yourself.'

He picked up his pole and went to stand at the rear port side, opposite Cornelius, aware as he did so of a roar from up ahead. He located his own loop of rope, pulled it up around his waist and drew it tight. Looking over the heads of Galt and Cal, he saw that the first rocks were rapidly approaching; beyond them, the river descended a series of levels as it thundered down into a valley.

'It's going to be quite a ride,' said Cornelius, as if he was looking forward to it. 'Everybody brace themselves!'

The first rock reared up at them from the port side and Galt lifted his pole and fended the raft away from it. They swung wildly to starboard and Cal managed to keep clear of the next rock only by pushing with all his strength. The raft swung back to port and went over the first drop; Sebastian felt his stomach lurch. They smacked down onto the water, a great wave swamping them, and then the raft began to turn wildly to starboard as it raced along the river again. Sebastian suddenly found himself standing on the leading side and had to turn round as they hurtled towards the next obstacle, a tall grey rock with razor-sharp edges. He pushed against it as hard as he could, feeling his pole bend as he did so. But the maluba cane, though pliable, refused to snap. The raft began to spin in a dizzying circle. Now it was Cornelius who had to manoeuvre it away from a low-hanging ledge that threatened to slam into the side of them.

Stinging spray lashed into Sebastian's face and he felt the raft shoot out over another sudden drop. It seemed to hang suspended in the air for a moment and then ploughed down into water. For an instant he was completely submerged and he realized how wise it had been to install the grab ropes. His feet came free of the planks and he had to resist the impulse to let go of the pole; but then the front of the raft was buoyed upwards and the rough wooden trunks slammed into his backside.

He sat there for a moment, spluttering and spitting out river water; then he heard Cornelius yell something and felt a sudden impact that jarred every bone in his body. The raft spun round to port; he was now at the back again and it was Galt and Cal who were doing all the work. He glanced around quickly to make sure everybody was still aboard.

Keera and Salah were hanging onto a very wet and frightened-looking Max. Cornelius stood just behind them, clinging to a rope and grinning like a demon.

'Isn't this great?' he yelled over the roar of the water. 'I haven't had this much fun since I went white-water rafting in Golmira!'

'*Fun?*' cried Max. 'You call this fun?'

The raft shuddered like a kicking mule as it glanced off a rock and plunged on its way. There was a last stomach-churning drop, a mighty splash and then, surprisingly, inexplicably, everything was quiet again and they were sailing along without a care in the world. Sebastian looked around in amazement. The river was as it had been before, wide and smooth with not an obstacle in sight. Glancing back over his shoulder, he could see the hellish waters through which they had just passed. He turned back to look at Cornelius.

'Do you think that was the last of the rapids?' he asked hopefully.

'Perhaps,' said Cornelius.

But of course it wasn't. The day became a bewildering mix of experiences. They would cruise along happily for a while; then there was a sudden shout of alarm and everybody scrambled for the poles, roped themselves down and the battle to stay in one piece began again.

The sun went down and night fell quickly. Now the task

became even more difficult: the two men at the front of the raft peered into the darkness ahead, looking for rocks and churning water. Luckily, a full moon soon rose, illuminating the surface of the river. At one point Salah brought a cup of river water to each person, together with a small portion of cold fish wrapped in a leaf.

'If I eat any more of this stuff I'll turn into a ruddy fish,' complained Galt.

'That could be useful,' said Cal, staring ahead.

'I don't know what you're complaining about,' said Max. 'At least you've had something to eat. I don't suppose anybody thought to bring anything for me?'

In answer, Salah reached into a pack and pulled out a couple of handfuls of succulent green leaves, which she placed in front of the buffalope like a sacrificial offering.

Max was clearly touched by the gesture. 'Bless you, child. How kind of you to take the trouble.' He looked accusingly at the others. 'See that?' he asked them. 'At least somebody is thinking on their feet.' And then he chomped down the food in three big mouthfuls. 'Very tasty,' he said. 'Now, what's for the main course?'

At last the sun rose in the sky again. The powerful current continued to carry them onwards, but they saw nothing that resembled the place where Joseph had finally come ashore. Sebastian was decidedly groggy after a series of very short naps. Max, on the other hand, was feeling downright uncomfortable and wanted everyone to know about it.

'Can't we stop for a moment?' he complained. 'I need to go.'

'Go where?' asked Cornelius unhelpfully.

'You know perfectly well what I mean. It's been ages. I need to . . . you know . . . have a wee!'

'We're not stopping for that,' Cornelius told him. 'You'll have to do what the rest of us have been doing. Go over the side.'

This was true enough. Mostly under cover of darkness, the human occupants of the raft had taken the opportunity to go to the rear of the raft and empty their bladders into the river. Sebastian had only done so with great reluctance but the Jilith didn't seem to turn a hair over something they saw as perfectly natural. For Max, though, it wouldn't be quite so simple.

'If I move to the edge, I'll tip up the raft,' protested Max.

'He's right,' said Sebastian, looking at Cornelius. 'Perhaps we could pull in to the side and let him off for a few moments?'

'No way!' said Cornelius. 'We're pressing on. There's no need for you to move a muscle,' he told Max. 'Just do it where you're lying and it'll trickle down into the water.'

'Do it where I'm . . . ?' Max was horrified. 'I'm not doing that – there are ladies present! Surely we could put in to the riverbank so I can find somewhere a bit more private.'

'We're not stopping,' Cornelius insisted. 'And you're getting a bit too sensitive in your old age.'

Salah started making her complicated hand signals and Keera supplied the translation.

'She says if you like we will all close our eyes while you take care of business.'

Max snorted. 'Don't worry about me,' he said. 'I'll try to hang on for a while. Surely it can't be much further.'

Sebastian felt really sorry for the buffalope. He understood his acute embarrassment, but it was clear that Cornelius was not about to change his mind.

The raft moved on through the rising heat of the day. Sebastian was scanning a sandbank beside the river when he noticed a series of greenish-brown tree trunks lying by the water's edge. His curiosity aroused, he asked to borrow Cornelius's spyglass, but when he turned it to the same spot, the sandbank was empty; however, the water nearby was rippling as though something large had just entered it.

He frowned. 'Cornelius,' he said quietly.

'Yes?'

Sebastian leaned down to whisper. 'Don't make a big fuss about this but I think something's in the water with us. Something big.'

'Really? What kind of thing?'

'Well,' said Sebastian, 'they looked sort of like—'

He broke off in surprise as something bumped hard against

the underside of the raft, then looked down in horror as a long dark shape cut through the water a few feet below the surface. He caught a glimpse of a rough, scaly back and a long sinuous tail.

'Sort of like that,' he finished flatly.

'What was it?' he heard Max wail. 'Something bumped into us!'

'Probably just a rock,' said Cornelius automatically; but Sebastian saw that he was assembling his miniature crossbow.

'That was no rock,' said Cal flatly; Sebastian could gleefully have throttled him. 'It was some kind of water dragon.'

'A water dragon?' Max was craning his head this way and that. 'What's a water dragon?'

'Don't worry,' Cornelius advised him, pulling a length of bowstring from his belt. 'That's just a fanciful name for some kind of . . . amphibious lizard.'

'Oh, and that's supposed to reassure me, is it?' said the buffalope. 'I don't like lizards. Remember those yarkle things we encountered on the pirate island? They were terrifying.'

'Relax,' said Cornelius. 'There's no need to—' He broke off as another bump shook the wooden platform.

Sebastian spotted a second creature knifing through the water; this time he saw the long pointed jaws, the huge mouth crowded with jagged teeth. An instant later, Galt thrust his wooden pole down into the water and there was a big splash as a long brown tail lashed the surface into foam.

'They're after us!' cried Max. 'We need to put in to the bank, NOW!'

'I don't think we can,' shouted Galt. He pointed ahead. 'More rapids.'

Cornelius slotted a bolt into the crossbow. 'I doubt they'll follow us over those,' he reasoned. 'We just need to hold them off until we reach them.'

Sebastian spotted a dark shape speeding towards them. 'There!' he cried.

Cornelius nodded and lifted the crossbow to take aim. He squeezed the trigger and the bolt shot straight towards its target, but then careened off and spun uselessly away across the water. 'Ruddy things must be armour-plated!' he yelled.

'Oh, good,' said Max. 'Armour-plated water lizards. Nothing to worry about there, then!'

An instant later, something slammed directly into the raft, lifting the back end clear of the water. Cornelius lost his balance and started to fall, but Sebastian grabbed his arm and pulled him back. The little warrior's kicking heels hung in the air for an instant and a great set of jaws opened beneath them, then slammed shut with a dull clunk.

The raft levelled out again and Cornelius looked at Sebastian. 'That's another one I owe you,' he said. He looked ahead but the rapids were still some distance away, and now Sebastian was aware of several dark shapes closing in on the raft. He hefted his wooden pole and went to stand at the edge of the deck.

'Sebastian, be careful!' shouted Keera.

Sebastian nodded. He studied the nearest of the approaching shapes and saw that its eyes were on top of its head so that it could see above the water when its body was submerged. They appeared to be the only part of the creature that wasn't swathed in thick leathery armour.

'The eyes!' he shouted. 'Aim for the eyes!'

Then the creature was moving within range. He braced himself, lifted the wooden pole, pointed the tip at one of the creature's eyes and, as it sped closer, drove down with all his strength. The pole struck home and there was a sudden commotion as the water dragon began to thrash and claw the water in agony.

Meanwhile Cornelius had trained his crossbow on a second beast. He fired and the bolt shot out and buried itself in its eye. It burst up from beneath the surface with a nerve-shattering shriek and then crashed down again, smashing the water to foam as it went into its death throes. As the raft moved on, Sebastian looked back and saw that the other creatures were homing in on the stricken beasts. In a few moments they had seized their dying comrades and were dragging them below the surface.

'That should hold them off for a while,' he said.

But Cornelius wasn't listening to him. He was staring

ahead, a grim expression on his face. Sebastian turned round and only then became aware of the rising roar of the water. He saw to his horror that a short distance away, the river ended in a straight line, then plunged over a sheer drop. The spray rising from below was so dense that it was impossible to tell how far down it was to the next level, but it was evidently a lot further than the rapids they had experienced so far.

'Joseph didn't said anything about a waterfall!' he gasped.

Galt and Cal were desperately trying to steer the raft out of the current and Sebastian took up his own pole, but to no avail. The raft was gripped as if by an invisible hand and wasn't about to be pushed off course. They could only stand and stare as disaster approached.

'Rope yourselves down!' shouted Cornelius.

The roar rose to an ear-splitting din and they began to gather speed. Sebastian watched in silent terror as the front of the raft shot out into empty space and then began to lose its fight with gravity. It tipped forward and tumbled head-long into the abyss.

CHAPTER 16

ALL WASHED UP

After that everything was confusion. Sebastian was falling, and people and things were falling into him and around him. He had a brief glimpse of a huge, hairy shape tumbling past and he thought he heard Max yelling, 'I told you this would happeeeeeeeeeeeen!'

Then, abruptly, there was nothing. The deepest calm that he had ever experienced settled over him; he felt like a dry leaf plucked from a tree branch by the wind and borne down, down . . .

He struck the water with an impact that drove the breath from his lungs and sank into icy depths. Panic came over him like a chilly cloak, snapping him out of his reverie and galvanizing him into action. He kicked his legs in a desperate attempt to head for the surface, but he didn't seem to be going anywhere. Then it occurred to him that the rope was still looped around his waist and that the end of it was attached to the logs which, driven down by their own impetus, were still sinking. He shrugged himself free of the loop, and began to power his way up towards the light.

But then a long hard shape came up from below and struck him a glancing blow on the back, knocking the air out of him in a stream of bubbles; he realized it was a tree trunk that had broken free from the raft and was now rising back to the surface. It pushed past him, flipping him over. He twisted and kicked his legs, and now he could see the ripples on the surface of the water, but it seemed such a long way off and his chest was aching because he hadn't thought to snatch a breath before he hit the water. A dizziness welled in his head and he felt as though his lungs were about to burst . . .

He broke the surface and floundered for a moment, gulping in air as he looked frantically around him. At first he saw nothing but empty water and he began to panic. Then somebody surfaced beside him with a loud gasp; he recognized Keera and saw that she had her arms wrapped around Salah, who appeared to be unconscious. Sebastian swam up to them, still looking this way and that for something to cling to. The tree trunk that had struck him was floating a short distance further on; he thrashed his way over, flung his arms across it and pushed it back towards the two women, urging Keera to cling on. He kept an arm around it himself and turned to stare down into the depths.

He felt a jolt of terror as he saw a huge dark shape rising steadily beneath him, but the feeling turned to relief when he saw that the shape was covered in shaggy hair. An instant later, Max's huge head emerged; he spluttered loudly and shook himself to get the water out of his eyes. He headed towards Sebastian in an ungainly doggy paddle.

'Well, at least there's one thing,' he said mournfully.

'What's that?' Sebastian asked him.

'I don't need to do a wee any more!'

Sebastian almost laughed but realized this was neither the time nor the place. He looked around again and saw that the waterfall had deposited them in a wide, slow-moving pool, one side of which was bordered by a steep bank of shingle. He kicked his legs to steer the tree trunk towards land, and Keera did likewise. Halfway across, Salah coughed, threw up a mouthful of water and looked around with fearful eyes.

'It's all right,' Keera assured her. 'You're safe – just hang on.'

A few moments later, Sebastian felt his boots crunching against gravel and, pushing aside the tree trunk, he helped Keera drag the girl up onto dry land. They lay her on her back. She was shivering and her face looked pale, but as far as Sebastian could tell, she was uninjured.

Max lumbered out of the water and up the bank, shaking the water out of his coat. Sebastian turned back, anxiously scanning the pool for other survivors. He saw Cal emerging on the far side of the pool and shouted to him. The warrior waved a hand and began to swim towards him. Soon Sebastian spotted Cornelius too, clinging onto another chunk of wood and kicking with his little legs. Sebastian hurried down to the water's edge and helped Cal out of the water.

'Where's Galt?' the warrior asked anxiously. 'Did you see him?'

Sebastian shook his head. 'Not yet,' he said. 'But I'm sure he'll turn up.'

Cal stumbled a short distance up the bank and collapsed onto the shingle, gasping for breath. Now Cornelius came within reach and Sebastian extended a hand to help him ashore. Something bumped against his foot as he did so and, looking down, he saw a piece of maluba cane, snapped to half its length during the fall. He picked it up and examined it.

'I thought this stuff was unbreakable,' he murmured, showing it to Cornelius. 'Must have been quite an impact when we hit the water.'

But the little warrior was gazing about excitedly. 'I think this is it!' he said.

'What are you talking about?' cried Sebastian.

'I think it's the place where Joseph found the city. Remember, he mentioned a big pool and a bank of shingle?'

Sebastian stared at Cornelius, amazed that he could think

of such a thing at a time like this. 'Yes, he did mention a shingle bank,' he agreed. 'A pity he didn't think to mention the waterfall.'

'Hmm.' Cornelius stared back as though he had forgotten about that part of it. From here they could see just how far they had fallen – Sebastian realized they had been extremely lucky to survive such a drop.

Cornelius looked at the others. 'Everyone accounted for?' he asked.

'Everyone except Galt,' Sebastian told him. They turned to survey the pool, where pieces of flotsam were still bobbing up from the deep. 'Do you think he's all right?'

Cornelius was about to answer when a familiar figure came thrashing to the surface, gasping for air and holding a dagger in his right hand. Galt looked around in bewilderment; but then he spotted his comrades on the bank and began to splash towards them.

'You all right?' Sebastian asked him, wading into the shallows to help him ashore. 'You were a long time down there.'

'Got tangled up in some weeds,' Galt told him. He waved the dagger. 'Had to cut myself free.'

'Thought you'd decided you preferred it down there,' shouted Cal, from further up the bank.

'Nice place to visit, but I wouldn't want to stay,' said Galt with a grin. He stood up in the shallows, slicked his long hair back out of his eyes and began to wade towards the bank. 'I tell you what, though: I thought I saw—'

His words were cut short as a huge greenish shape suddenly lunged up out of the water beside him. He froze in mute terror, staring into the water dragon's open jaws as they closed on him. Sebastian acted on pure instinct. He threw himself forward and thrust the maluba cane he was holding vertically into the creature's jaws. They attempted to snap shut but were stopped by the length of cane. Sebastian grabbed Galt's arm and pulled him away. They fell heavily into the shallows, while the water dragon, issuing strange choking sounds, thrashed wildly to and fro and crashed back into the deeper water, its jaws wedged open. There was just a flick of its tail to mark its passing.

Sebastian lay there, staring at the diminishing ripples on the surface of the pool. Behind him, he heard Keera cry out in disbelief and Cal uttered an oath. Then there was a silence so deep, the smallest noise would have sounded like a thunder-stick.

Galt turned his head and looked at Sebastian. He swallowed. 'You saved my life,' he said.

Sebastian could only nod. It was true enough, he decided, but it had been sheer luck that he had been holding the maluba cane. The only other thing he could have put into those open jaws was his own body. He let out a long exhalation of air.

'Well done, lad!' said Cornelius, slapping him on the shoulder. 'Now that's what I call reflexes.'

Cal came running down the bank and helped Galt to his feet. The big warrior looked at his friend and they embraced.

'I thought you were gone,' he said.

'So did I.' Galt pulled away. 'It was the Elf Lord. He—'

'I saw,' said Cal. He turned and extended a hand to help Sebastian back to his feet. 'You did good,' he said grudgingly and Sebastian smiled, thinking that this was high praise indeed, coming from Cal.

'It was . . . I just happened to be . . .' He gave up and shrugged his shoulders.

'I owe you one,' said Cal and threw an arm around Galt's shoulders.

Sebastian and Cornelius exchanged looks.

'Young master, that was positively heroic.' Max had observed the scene from a distance. 'It happened so quickly, otherwise I would have been there to back you up.'

Sebastian smiled. 'I know,' he said.

The three of them turned and followed the others up the shingle. Keera was sitting with her arms around Salah. They were both gazing at Sebastian so reverently that he began to feel a little uncomfortable.

'Now who can say you weren't sent to save us?' asked Keera. 'Okrin sent you to us, and once again we are in your debt.'

'Oh, please,' Sebastian insisted. 'I just did what anyone would have done.'

'Forgive me,' said Keera, 'but I know better.' She glanced at Cal, who was sitting with Galt a short distance away. 'Now do you accept that he is the Chosen One?' she asked him.

Cal grimaced. 'I accept that he's brave,' he said. 'I accept that he saved Galt's life. But that doesn't mean he's the one written about in the old stories.'

Keera was exasperated. 'I don't know what it would take to convince you!' she cried.

'Listen,' said Sebastian. 'It really doesn't matter. Let's just forget the whole thing, shall we?'

'Yes, let's,' said Max. 'We don't want the young master getting a big head, do we?'

'It was a brave thing he did though,' said Cornelius. 'And courage should be acknowledged.' He seemed to remember something and lifted his head to stare thoughtfully up into the trees beyond the shingle. 'Now, I was just saying before that water dragon popped up . . . this looks very much like the place that Joseph described.' He continued up the bank and Sebastian followed, his boots clunking on the loose stones.

Max trailed along in their wake. 'But the waterfall,' he reasoned. 'He would have mentioned that surely?'

'It was a long time ago,' said Cornelius. 'An old man's memories can play tricks on him. And I seem to remember that he was unconscious for the last part of his time in the water.'

'Yes, that's true,' said Sebastian. 'But he would only have had to glance upstream to see it.'

Cornelius shrugged. 'Nevertheless, it feels like the right place.' He came to the edge of the jungle and reached up on tiptoe to pull aside a screen of ferns. Beyond were more ferns, so he took out his sword and began to hack them aside.

'Oh, so now we're trusting everything to your instinct, are we?' asked Max. 'I said from the beginning, I wasn't even convinced we had the right river. What are we supposed to do now?'

'That rather depends,' said Cornelius, swinging the sword from side to side.

'On what?'

'On what we find in the next few moments.' Cornelius gave a particularly fierce swipe and a huge fern crashed to the ground in front of him. There was a long silence. 'There now,' he said quietly.

Sebastian stared. Rearing above the dense vegetation some distance ahead was the top of a gigantic stone building. It soared some thirty or forty storeys into the air, its many windows staring sightlessly down at the desolation around it.

'Is that what I think it is?' muttered Max, overcome with awe.

Cornelius nodded. He turned back and gave a theatrical bow. 'Ladies and gentlemen,' he said, 'I give you the lost city of Mendip!'

PART THREE

THE CITY

CHAPTER 17

INTO THE LIGHT

They walked slowly into the shadow of the buildings, gazing up at the dizzying heights that towered above them.

'What kind of a place *is* this?' whispered Galt fearfully.

'It's impressive,' admitted Cornelius. 'But at the end of the day it's just a city that men have built. Nothing more.'

Sebastian frowned. He tried to imagine it as it must once have been. He remembered the opulence of the king's palace in Keladon, with its towers and minarets and marble staircases – but the sheer scale of this place put that city to shame. However, it was clear that it must have been deserted for many years.

Here, at the edge, the jungle had made incursions: trees and ferns burst up through the surface of the road, jutted from broken windows, crowded up sheer walls as though trying to

205

obliterate them. But as the explorers moved deeper into the heart of the city, so they left the jungle behind and found themselves in a wasteland of smooth grey stone and broken glass. Even in Keladon, glass had been a precious commodity, fitted by only the wealthiest merchants. Here, it had once graced every window.

Sebastian stepped closer to one of the buildings and peered in through the empty window frame. Within he saw nothing but a litter of fallen stones, mouldering furnishings and torn and tattered fabrics – nothing that might hint at who had created this city and why they had left it to fall into ruin.

Max came up to stand beside Sebastian. 'I don't like it here,' he said flatly. 'It feels . . . bad.'

Sebastian stroked the buffalope's head fondly. 'Don't worry, old shaggy,' he said. 'There's nothing to hurt us here.'

No sooner had he said this than he heard a noise from within – a sudden clatter, as though something had fallen over. He and Max exchanged glances.

'What was that?' asked the buffalope nervously.

'Not sure,' said Sebastian. 'We'd better have a look inside.'

'You are joking, I hope!'

'There's definitely someone in there.'

'Someone or some*thing*,' hissed Max. 'I think we should ignore it and move on.'

But Sebastian was already heading for an open doorway. He gestured to the others, pointing through it.

Cornelius nodded and came hurrying back to him. 'What's wrong?' he whispered.

'I heard something,' Sebastian mouthed at him. He drew his sword and stepped through the doorway into the gloom, straining his eyes to see in the shadowy interior. Cornelius followed and Max would have gone too, but the doorway was too narrow to admit his huge body, so he had to content himself with staring fearfully into the darkness. The other two crept carefully across the rubbish-strewn floor. Every so often they stopped to listen. Now Sebastian heard another sound – a scraping. It seemed to be coming from beyond an open doorway up ahead. He gulped, took a deep breath and moved forward again, his sword held ready to meet any attack. As he approached the doorway, so the sound increased in volume and he knew with a cold and dreadful certainty that whatever was making the noise was just on the other side.

He paused a short distance away and looked down at Cornelius. The little warrior nodded grimly. Sebastian steeled himself and then stepped quickly through the opening.

There was a loud shriek and several ragged black things came swarming up from the floor, squawking and flapping their wings in his face. He gave a cry of terror and lifted his arms to shield his head, but they flew past him and out through the doorway, making for the exit.

'Birds!' laughed Cornelius. 'Pecking at something.' He gestured at a scattering of rodent bones on the floor. 'By Shadlog, they gave me quite a start!'

Sebastian nodded, then remembered to breathe. He returned his sword to its scabbard and glanced quickly around the room, reassuring himself that there was no other living thing in there. Then his gaze fell on the far wall. Words had been scrawled upon it in large black letters but in a language he had never seen before.

He glanced at Cornelius. 'What do you suppose that says?' he asked.

Cornelius shrugged. 'I haven't a clue,' he said, 'but that last bit means the same thing in any language.' He pointed to a picture beneath the words – a crude drawing of a skull, with empty black eye-sockets and grinning teeth.

'Charming,' observed Sebastian.

The two of them turned and headed back towards the exit. Max was still peering fearfully in through the doorway and had to step back to allow them out. The others were waiting just behind him.

'Well?' asked Max.

'Nothing,' said Sebastian. 'Just some birds.'

'Yes, I saw *them*! Nearly flew into my face. But nothing else? No . . . treasure or anything?'

Sebastian could only shake his head. They all stood in silence for a few moments, gazing at the maze of deserted streets.

'I had no idea it would be so big,' said Sebastian at last. 'It could take weeks to search it all.'

'What exactly are we looking for?' asked Galt.

Sebastian and Cornelius exchanged glances.

'We'll know when we find it,' said Cornelius.

Cal gave a snort of exasperation. 'I'm getting a bad feeling about this,' he announced. 'We've come all this way, all our equipment is at the bottom of the river and you two don't seem to have a clue why we're even here.'

'Cal, you don't question the Chosen One,' Keera told him.

He glared at her. 'I'll question whoever I like,' he exclaimed. 'I can't believe you still think there is something special about these people.'

'I know they are special,' she told him. 'They have saved the Jilith from the greatest threat they ever faced. And Galt wouldn't be with us now if it wasn't for Sebastian. Have you no gratitude?'

Sebastian felt shamed by her trust in him; part of him had begun to wonder about the prophecy. Supposing after all there was something in it? Could his journey here really have been foretold centuries ago? Was he just part of some great cosmic plan? The thought made him feel decidedly strange, so he shrugged his shoulders and turned away.

'Come on,' he said. 'Let's keep looking.'

And they went on into the heart of the city.

* * *

They walked around for hours and saw nothing of any value; just more empty buildings. From time to time they went inside to investigate a likely looking place, but found nothing but rubble, broken furniture and shards of pottery. It seemed as if the city had been systematically looted over the years until there was nothing of any value left; and the only signs of life were the ever-present black birds and the occasional rusa, wandering the deserted streets.

The sun began to descend in a splash of crimson and they decided it was high time they made camp somewhere; but that wasn't going to be easy. They had lost almost all their equipment when the raft turned over. Darkness was almost upon them and, as usual, they started squabbling.

'The next rusa we see, let's kill it and make camp in the nearest building,' said Cal.

'Kill it with what?' growled Cornelius. 'You lost your bow in the river, did you not? And I lost my crossbow. What are we going to use, harsh language?'

'I've got a knife,' said Galt. 'And we still have our swords. I could lie in wait somewhere and you lot could drive the rusa towards me. Then I'll jump out and give it what for.'

'But it's getting dark,' argued Sebastian. 'Even if we happened upon a rusa now, what are the chances of being able to drive it towards you?'

'If we found a straight piece of wood, we could tie Galt's

knife to it and make a spear,' suggested Keera. 'Then at least we could throw it at the rusa.'

'Oh yes, and have the thing run off with the knife stuck in it,' said Cal. 'Good idea! No, I think we'll just have to wait it out until morning and then see about breakfast.'

'But I'm starving,' complained Max. 'And what do you suppose *I'm* going to eat?'

'That's all you think about,' sneered Cal. 'All I've heard on this trip is you moaning. I don't know how those two put up with it.'

'We do because we have to,' snapped Cornelius. 'And watch what you're saying about our friend.'

'Yes,' said Max, 'you're too lippy altogether.'

The argument was interrupted by Salah, who suddenly jumped into their midst and started making frantic gestures.

'What's she saying?' muttered Cornelius.

'Probably telling Cal to pipe down,' said Max. 'Probably sick of the sound of his voice, like the rest of us.'

'Sick of *my* voice?' roared Cal. 'Oh, that's a good one!'

But now Salah was leaping about, trying to get their attention, and Sebastian saw that she was pointing along the street.

'What's wrong, Salah?' he asked. 'What have you seen?'

Salah pointed again, her eyes imploring him to look. He gazed in the direction she was indicating and drew in a sharp breath.

'Wait,' he said. 'Look. Look there!'

Now everybody turned to see.

A long way off, a light was burning in a window at the top of one of the tallest buildings.

'Shadlog's teeth!' said Cornelius. 'There must be somebody living here after all. That's an oil lamp or something.' He looked around at the others. 'We must go and investigate.'

'Yes,' said Sebastian. 'We should—'

He broke off in surprise. Something had just scuttled past behind him. He caught a glimpse of a ragged flapping cloak.

'What's wrong?' asked Cornelius.

'I'm not sure. There was something—'

He broke off again as another shape flew across a narrow opening to his right. This time Sebastian thought he saw a pale, staring face.

'What in Okrin's name was that?' muttered Galt.

'I don't know,' said Sebastian. 'But whatever it was, it was no rusa.' He glanced around at the others. 'I think we should make our way towards the light,' he said. 'Right now.'

Nobody disagreed with him.

They set off along the street, pulling out their swords as they went, looking to left and right.

Now Sebastian became aware of a strange sound – a sort of high-pitched giggle that might have been made by a child, except that there was no joy in this sound: it was cold and empty enough to chill the blood in his veins.

Something flapped overhead as one of the cloaked things jumped from roof to roof above them.

'What are they?' whispered Keera fearfully. 'They look like men.'

'Not like any men I've ever seen,' said Cornelius coolly. 'And whatever they are, I don't think they're here to offer us the keys to the city. Come on, let's pick up the pace a bit.'

Everybody did as he suggested. The light burned enticingly in that high, high window, but it was a long way off.

As they passed a narrow alleyway, something came towards them out of the darkness; something with a deathly white face and long claw-like fingers. Galt turned to meet the attack and swung his sword at the creature. There was a hideous shriek that seemed to fill the air around them. The thing leaped impossibly high and disappeared into the shadows again. Galt looked at his blade and showed it to Sebastian. It was slick with greenish-black liquid.

'What creature has blood that colour?' gasped Galt; Sebastian had no answer to give him.

Now the weird high-pitched sounds were coming from all around them. Sebastian glanced up and saw a couple of the creatures clinging to the sheer wall above him, their eyes shining in the dark. Quite suddenly one of them came hurtling down at him. He swept his sword blade above his head in a deadly arc and felt metal cleave through flesh and

bone. The creature flopped down, hitting the ground just behind him. He had expected it to lie still, but it rose up again, howling and gibbering, before disappearing back into the shadows.

'I don't like this!' protested Max. 'Those things don't want to die.'

Sebastian had to agree. A blow like the one he had just delivered should have killed anything that moved, but the creature had seemed merely angered by the blow. He looked ahead. The light was much closer now, and he began to think they might have a chance; but then one of the beasts swooped low over their heads, flung down an arm and grabbed Salah by the collar of her tunic, wrenching her away from Keera's side. It alighted in front of them and prepared to bound off with Salah still firmly in its grasp; but then Keera's arm lifted and fell and something bright and metallic flashed through the air. A dagger thudded into the creature's back. It gave a high-pitched squeal and rose up, leaving Salah slumped on the ground. Keera ran to her, yanked her to her feet and they ran on.

But there were more of the things now, emerging on either side as they approached the tall building. One spindly, gibbering creature came for Max and met a pair of mighty horns that hoisted it back into the air. Sebastian realized that the light was now their only hope. If it proved to be a false one, then they would be overrun in moments.

Looking up, he saw the light burning in a barred window high above. He ran up to a huge metal door and started hammering on it with the hilt of his sword while the others turned at bay, swords drawn as a semicircle of shrieking nightmares closed in on them.

'Hurry, Sebastian, we can't hold out for long!' cried Cornelius. 'There's too— Ugh!' He swung his sword, and an echoing scream told Sebastian that his blade had found its target. He continued to hammer on the door, the noise of metal upon metal ringing out into the night. Finally, after what seemed like an age, a small panel slid aside and a pair of blue eyes stared out at him.

'Who goes there?' cried a voice.

'Travellers,' yelled Sebastian. 'We're under attack – please help us!'

The panel slid shut and then he heard the rasp of bolts being withdrawn, one after the other. He turned back to see a hideous white vision closing in on him; he had a night-marish image of a long cadaverous face, the skin white as parchment, two lidless yellow eyes and an open mouth, the jaw hanging down at an impossible angle.

The thing screamed at him and a blast of foul breath gusted into his face with a hideous stench of decay. Sebastian drove the point of his sword forward, felt it pierce skin, and the thing retreated, only to be replaced by another, equally hideous visage and a pair of groping hands that clawed at his face.

Beside him, Galt was hacking and stabbing with his sword; then Sebastian heard the metal doors creaking open behind him and a voice cried, 'Inside, now!'

Sebastian pushed Keera and Salah towards the opening and saw that human arms were pulling them into the light. Now Cal and Max were retreating inside, followed by Cornelius. Only Sebastian and Galt were holding back the waves of shrieking, leaping creatures. Sebastian began to edge back; he shouted to Galt to come with him, but the warrior seemed oblivious to everything but the brutes attacking him.

He was swinging the sword like a madman and his face and shoulders were spattered with their dark blood. Sebastian started to move forward to help him, but he was pulled back inside the building. He could see that the things were all around Galt now; as he watched, horrified, one flung its arms around the warrior's shoulder and sank its teeth into his neck. Galt tried to raise his sword, but the things were swarming over him, pinning his arms to his sides. Sebastian saw that the door was closing – it was closing, and Galt was still outside.

'No!' he roared and tried to force his way out, but hands held him fast. He heard the door crash shut with a great clang and the huge bolts rasp across. Sebastian could see that there were scores of them on the door – presumably to keep those things out. He could still hear Galt's roars of pain and anger, mingling with the strange giggling sounds of the creatures; and then it was suddenly ominously quiet and Sebastian sank to the floor, dropped his bloody sword and buried his face in his hands.

There was a long silence. Finally he lifted his head and looked up at his rescuers. A shock went through him when he saw that they were children.

CHAPTER 18

SANCTUARY

There were six of them in all – four boys and two girls, their ages ranging from perhaps seven to fifteen summers. They were dressed in ragged, homespun clothes and were all armed. They stood looking down at Sebastian, their faces grim. Around them, those they had rescued were crouched, scared and exhausted but glad to be alive.

Sebastian pointed at the bolted door. 'We have to go out there again,' he said. 'Our friend – Galt – he's still out there. We can't leave him.'

The children turned to what must have been the oldest boy, a tall thin lad with a thick shock of curly black hair. He shook his head.

'There's no point,' he said. 'Your friend was bitten. He will turn.'

Everyone stared at the boy.

'*Turn*?' cried Cal. 'What do you mean?'

'I mean he will become one of the Night Runners – the things that were attacking you.'

'Don't be ridiculous!' snarled Cal. 'That's Galt out there, one of the finest warriors of the Jilith tribe. We can't just leave him. Now let us out before it's too late!'

'It's already too late,' the boy assured him.

'Nonsense!' Cal got to his feet and started to draw one of the bolts. Instantly every child raised a spear and levelled it at him. Their eyes showed only the cold, merciless stare of killers.

'I'm sorry,' said the boy, 'but if you even touch one of those bolts, we will kill you. This I promise.'

Cal stared at him angrily for a moment, and then, realizing that he was deadly serious, reluctantly lowered his hand.

'Now,' the boy went on, 'I must ask you all to examine yourselves carefully. Did any of you receive a bite?'

Everyone checked themselves as best they could. Sebastian found that though he was covered with blood, none of it was red. He ran his gaze over Max's flanks and haunches, knowing that the buffalope could not easily examine himself, but thankfully he found no trace of crimson amidst the shaggy ginger fur. As he did so, he was aware that the children were watching intently, their weapons held at the ready. However, it seemed that everybody had come through the ordeal unharmed. The boy seemed to relax a little and lowered his spear. The other children followed suit. For the first time, some of them allowed themselves a smile.

'Well, that's a relief,' said the dark-haired boy. 'It would have been terrible to have got you inside, only to be obliged to kill you.'

Cornelius gazed up at him. 'You'd have been prepared to do that?'

'If you were bitten, yes. Forgive me – it must seem harsh to you, but we have lived all our lives with the Night Runners and we know that the tiniest bite will turn a man into one of those things . . . and once inside here, it would mean the end for all of us.' He turned to look at Cal. 'Your friend out there was doomed from the first moment he was bitten. We have seen it a hundred times.'

Cal shook his head. 'This is easily said,' he growled, 'but you would feel differently if it was one of your friends.'

The boy shook his head. 'No, I would not,' he assured Cal. 'We all of us know that is the first rule of survival in this place. Aaron has taught us this. Never let your feelings get in the way of staying alive.'

'Aaron? Who's Aaron?' asked Keera.

'You will meet him in good time,' said the boy, 'and he will explain everything. But now you must be hungry. Come, we will find you food and drink.' He seemed to remember something. 'I am Phelan,' he said. 'I am the leader here. I answer only to Aaron.'

Max was astonished by this information. 'Aren't there any grown-ups?' he asked.

The children stared at him in astonishment, and some of the younger ones smothered giggles with their hands. Clearly they had not seen a talking buffalope before.

'How did you do this trick?' asked Phelan, grinning delightedly. 'Can one of you throw your voice?'

'The very idea!' said Max. 'I don't need any help to talk, thank you very much. I've been doing it since I was a calf. And I don't think it's very polite to be laughing when we have just lost a friend.'

'Of course,' said Phelan, twisting his lips into a grimace. 'You must forgive us. I'm sure our ways will seem very cold to you. But you will understand when you know more about us. So come, let us find you some refreshment.'

'Just a moment!' roared Cal angrily. 'How can you talk of food at a time like this? Are you forgetting about Galt?'

Phelan stepped forward and placed a hand on Cal's shoulder. 'It is pointless to think about him now,' he said. 'He is lost to you. But believe me, you *will* see him again before very much longer. And you will wish you hadn't. Now, come – you have had a poor welcome to our home. Food and drink will at least help to lift your spirits.' He indicated a flight of steep stone steps leading to a landing, then switching back on itself before continuing up. 'It's a long way up to our quarters,' he told them. 'But it's worth the climb.' He glanced at Max. 'Think you'll be able to get up there?' he asked.

'I'll do my best,' Max sighed.

'Very well.' Phelan instructed two of the older boys to guard the door and then led the way up. Max went after him, his hooves slipping and sliding on the smooth stone steps. After some hesitation, the others followed. Sebastian looked at Cal and saw that he was staring helplessly at the bolted door, as though still considering going out there. He placed a hand on Cal's shoulder.

'I'm sorry,' he said. 'Galt was—'

But Cal shrugged the hand away. 'Save your breath, elfling!' he snarled. 'Whatever points you earned back at the river just got wiped out. Galt was my closest friend. We grew up together. Now, because of this trip, he's gone. When this is all over, you and your midgling sidekick will have my sword to answer to. You might have put Keera under your spell, but I know you for what you are.'

'And what's that, exactly?' asked Sebastian.

'Trouble,' said Cal. And he turned away and marched up the stairs.

Sebastian shook his head; it was pointless now to hope that he and Cal could ever be friends. Galt's death meant there was a void between them that could never be bridged.

With a sigh, he followed the others up the stairs.

Phelan had not been exaggerating. They had to make their

way up fifteen flights of stairs before he led them along a landing to a large room; and Sebastian noticed that yet another flight continued upwards. Max was quite exhausted by this stage and complained loudly to anyone who would listen to him.

There were more ragged children in the room. Sebastian counted twelve in all, again ranging from just a few years to around Phelan's age. They all seemed intensely interested in these newcomers, and when they heard Max talking, they flocked around him, prodding and slapping, trying to elicit a response.

'Do you mind?' he protested. 'Get off! Ow! Stop that! Now, which one of you is in charge of the food?'

One end of the room was dominated by a huge stone fireplace in which a log fire blazed merrily. Phelan indicated a series of tattered couches and chairs around it and invited the guests to sit down. He instructed a couple of children to fill some clay bowls from a huge cauldron of stew that was bubbling over the fire; somebody else filled cups with water from large skins hanging in a corner. Phelan took a seat beside them and watched as they ate. Cal was staring moodily into the fire, spooning stew into his mouth and clearly uninterested in talking, so Phelan addressed his questions to the others.

'Have you travelled far?' he asked them.

'Some of us have come from Ramalat up on the east coast,'

said Sebastian, talking through a mouthful of what tasted like rusa stew. 'These three are Jilith from a village in the jungles of Mendip.'

Phelan nodded but didn't seem to recognize any of the names. 'You must forgive me,' he said. 'We have never known anywhere but here. I have no idea if these places you speak of are near or far.'

'Ramalat is a great distance,' said Cornelius. 'The Jilith village is just a few days upriver.' He thought for a moment. 'Actually, we're not the first from the village to come here. A man called Joseph visited many years ago when he was around your age. He only spent a few hours here but he told us he didn't meet anybody else. Perhaps there was nobody living here then.'

Phelan shrugged. 'It's a big city – there's no reason why he should have met anyone. Did he . . . stay here after dark?'

'I don't believe he did,' said Sebastian.

'Then he was lucky,' said Phelan.

'Does this place have a name?' asked Keera.

'We call this house Sanctuary,' replied Phelan. 'At least, that is what Aaron calls it.'

'Yes, you mentioned him before,' said Cornelius. 'What is he – a king, a general? And when do we get to meet him?'

'When he is ready,' said Phelan. 'One thing you learn about

225

Aaron is that he cannot be hurried.' He looked at Salah, who was gulping her food down hungrily. 'You don't have much to say for yourself,' he observed.

'Salah cannot speak,' explained Keera.

Sebastian had expected Phelan to look embarrassed but his smile never wavered.

'Of course she can speak,' he said. 'She just hasn't chosen to yet. Isn't that right, Salah?'

Salah looked up from her bowl of stew and smiled at the boy. Then she nodded and went on with her meal.

'Where are all the adults?' asked Sebastian.

Now the boy's smile *did* falter. 'You have already met them,' he said.

Sebastian was puzzled for a moment; then realization hit him. 'Oh my . . . you don't mean to say . . . those *things* out there are . . . ?'

'My parents are among them,' said Phelan. He gestured around the room. 'Most of their parents too. Not that we would be able to recognize them now. You can for a few days, when they have first turned, but then they become like all the others.' He shrugged. 'You grow used to it.'

'But how do they—?'

'Aaron will explain more when he sees you,' repeated Phelan. 'He has made a study of it. He knows many things. We call him Aaron the Wise.'

Sebastian frowned. 'Is *he* a child?' he asked.

This seemed to amuse Phelan. 'Aaron is not a child,' he said. 'You will understand when you meet him—'

'Ow, stop that! Don't you know it's rude to poke some-body?' Max's voice sounded muffled. Sebastian looked up to see that the buffalope had his head down in what looked like a bucket of fruit; however, some of the younger children were still creeping up and prodding him to see what kind of reaction they could get.

'Stop taunting the beast,' said Phelan; and, amazingly, the children did exactly as they were told, returning to their places around the room and getting on with whatever they had been doing before Max arrived. They all seemed to have jobs. Over in one corner of the room, a couple of girls were binding vines together to make rope. In another, a group of young boys were fashioning arrows.

'You clearly command obedience here,' observed Cornelius.

Phelan nodded. 'They understand how it works,' he said. 'Perhaps in some places they could afford to make the odd mistake. I'm sure it is how most children learn. But here, life is different. Disobeying an order might be the last thing you ever do.'

He smiled benignly but Sebastian felt a chill go through him. Something about Phelan didn't feel right. Sebastian's elf-sense was tingling – he had never encountered a boy like this before; one who smiled and was polite, yet underneath his genial mask was as cold and ruthless as any assassin.

Sebastian remembered that the boy had been quite prepared to kill any of the strangers who had been bitten. He wondered what terrible experiences had made him like that.

Phelan regarded their empty bowls. 'I would like to offer you more,' he said, 'but as you can see' – he gestured towards the other children – 'we have many mouths to feed.'

Sebastian waved a hand dismissively. 'Oh no, that's fine, I'm full as a tick.'

'How do you manage to forage for food,' asked Keera, 'with those things roaming about out there?'

'Oh, that's easy,' said Phelan. 'They only come out at night. By day they sleep in the dark shadows of the buildings. They are not a danger then. Unless you're stupid enough to go inside.'

Sebastian remembered how he had entered one of the buildings to investigate the noise. Happily he had encountered nothing more frightening than a flock of birds.

'If they sleep, then they are vulnerable,' said Cornelius. 'You need only find their resting places, go out by day and slay them while they slumber. It might take you a little while, but soon enough you would be rid of them.'

Phelan shook his head. 'You cannot kill them,' he said.

'Why ever not?' argued Cornelius. 'I understand that some of them were once your parents, but they are hardly the same thing now.'

'No, you misunderstand me,' explained Phelan. 'You cannot kill them because they are already dead.'

CHAPTER 19

A VISITATION

'What did he mean, *they're already dead*?' Max couldn't seem to get Phelan's last words out of his head. 'Dead people don't generally hop about like great big spiders, do they?'

Sebastian and Cornelius groaned. A short while earlier, Phelan had led the three friends to another room, where a collection of hides were piled in one corner. He had taken Keera and Salah to a smaller chamber further along the landing, while Cal had elected to stay where he was, in the communal room, staring moodily into the fire. Sebastian and Cornelius had dutifully stretched themselves out with the intention of snatching some much-needed sleep, but Max was having none of it. He was clumping nervously up and down the chamber, his hooves clunking on the stone floor.

'I mean to say,' he continued, ignoring the resentful glares

229

from his two companions, 'most dead things I know lie still and don't make a sound. So these Night Runner things can't *really* be dead, can they? Can they? Well, *can they*?'

Cornelius gave a groan of irritation. 'It would explain why our swords had no effect on them,' he said. 'And why their blood is that horrible greeny-black colour. Now shut up and go to sleep!'

'I will not!' Max continued pacing. 'It's always like this, isn't it? Wherever we go we encounter horrible, creepy, nasty things that want to kill us. Why can't you take me some-where nice for a change? A sunny meadow with plenty to eat and pretty butterflies flapping around my head.'

'We'll keep that in mind for our next adventure,' Sebastian assured him. 'Now please, can you settle down? We haven't slept properly in ages and I for one could do with some decent shuteye.'

'Oh, it's nice for those who *can* sleep, isn't it?' protested Max. 'I shall probably never sleep again. Every time I shut my eyes I see one of those hideous things swooping down at me. It's a miracle I wasn't bitten. I could have been like Galt, reduced to going around like some great big zombie for ever.'

'So no change there then,' murmured Cornelius and Max gave him a wounded look.

'Go on, mock!' he said. 'I don't like it here. As soon as the sun comes up, we should walk out of this ruddy city and follow the river all the way back to the Jilith camp. It might be a bit rough there, but at least the people in it know that when they're dead, they're dead. I don't care how long it takes, we should go.'

'We're not going anywhere until we've met this Aaron character,' Sebastian told him.

'Oh yes, I can just imagine what he'll turn out to be! A giant man-eating frog with a kelfer's head ... or perhaps some ruddy great spider with ten eyes and twenty mouths.'

'Don't be ridiculous!' said Sebastian. 'I have no reason to suspect that he's anything other than an ordinary human being.'

'No reason to suspect ...? Forgive me, but that gives me no reassurance at all. Whatever happened to your famous elf-sense, eh? I can't begin to count the number of times it's let us down.'

'Will you please belt up!' roared Cornelius.

'You'd like that, wouldn't you? All three of us fast asleep while unspeakable things come creeping up on us.'

'Those things are out there,' said Sebastian, pointing to a solitary window; the glass had long since shattered, allowing the night wind to come gusting through. Sebastian could see that it was protected by a series of thick metal bars – a fact that Max was quick to pick up on.

'What are the bars for?' he cried. 'Bars in a bedchamber? This is some kind of prison!'

'The bars are obviously to keep the Night Runners out,'

said Cornelius through gritted teeth. 'All the windows in the building are like that; and it's not a very effective prison if the door is left ajar.'

Max sniffed and paced over to the window. 'Just the same,' he said, 'you won't catch me going to slee—' He broke off as a familiar voice rose on the night wind.

'Cal! Cal, help me!'

Max's eyes grew big and round. 'That's Galt's voice!' he gasped. 'Ooh, I don't like this! It's getting all creepy again!'

In an instant Sebastian and Cornelius were up on their feet and peering down through the gaps in the bars. Sure enough, Galt stood far below, his big figure dwarfed by distance. He was gazing up at the window. It seemed incredible that his voice should carry such a distance; but even from up here, they could see how horribly white his features were.

'Cal, it's me, Galt. I'm all right, but you must come down and open the door for me before those things come back!'

Suddenly there was the sound of footsteps on the landing and Cal went racing past the doorway, closely followed by a frantic Phelan.

'Wait!' he yelled. 'Cal, hang on a moment!'

Cornelius and Sebastian exchanged glances and then went in pursuit.

'Wait for me!' yelled Max, but his hooves slipped on the stone floor and he went over onto his side with a grunt of surprise. Sebastian and Cornelius didn't hesitate. As they started down the first staircase, Phelan looked back at them over his shoulder.

'It's a trick,' he said. 'They always try this. I told your friend but he won't listen to me.'

'Cal!' shouted Sebastian. 'Wait, don't go down there!'

But Cal ignored them. He was racing down the steps three at a time, already nearly a whole flight ahead of them.

'Is there a lock on the main door?' shouted Cornelius.

Phelan shook his head. 'Only bolts,' he said.

'Right,' said Cornelius. He seemed to concentrate for a moment, then threw himself up into the air and went somersaulting over Phelan's head. He landed lightly on the next level, flung himself round the corner and whirled down the staircase in a blur of motion. Cal didn't have a chance. The little warrior's boots hit him square in the back, flinging him off balance, and he went down the last few steps on his chest like a human toboggan. He crashed into some railings at the end and lay still.

When Sebastian and Phelan reached them, Cornelius was turning the warrior over onto his back. Cal looked dazed and a trail of blood trickled from a gash on his forehead. He sat up and glared at Cornelius.

'Let me go,' he snarled. 'I heard Galt out there – he needs help.'

Phelan shook his head. 'I know that's how it seems to you – but I have seen this so many times before. Countless Night

Runners lie in wait for you should you open that door. If only one of them gets in here, we would all be doomed.'

Cal shook his head. 'But his voice sounds the same!'

Phelan sighed. 'I already told you. It takes time for them to turn fully. In the passing of one moon, he will be like all the others. He will look and sound as they do. In the meantime, the Night Runners are cunning – they make use of the fact that your friend's appearance has not changed much. He is bait, nothing more.'

Phelan sat down on the steps and his expression became troubled. 'It was like this with my parents when they were first taken,' he said. 'For many nights they stood under the window calling out my name. I was just a little boy – what did I know? I wanted to go to them and open the doors, and had to be restrained by those around me.' He reached out a hand and placed it on Cal's shoulder. 'Take it from me, the man you knew is gone. There is no way anybody comes back once they have been bitten. He is a Night Runner now, doomed to wander the streets of this city for eternity. Come.' He stood up and helped Cal to his feet, then began to guide him back up the steps. 'You need sleep, my friend. In the end that's the best medicine of all.'

Cal didn't protest. He trudged back up, head bowed, all the fight gone out of him. Sebastian gazed up after him, sorry for the warrior despite himself. Cal had taken every opportunity to be mean to him, but it was evident that he carried a terrible burden of guilt for what had happened to his friend.

Sebastian looked at Cornelius. 'Perhaps Max is right,' he said. 'Perhaps we should just get away from this place the first chance we get.'

Cornelius frowned. 'That would be foolish,' he said. 'The hard work is done now. Against all the odds we have found the lost city. Now all we need is proof of its existence and Thaddeus Peel will pay us a small fortune for it. Enough to finance another trip to the treasure island of Captain Callinestra!'

Sebastian stared at him in surprise. He had quite forgotten why they taken this job in the first place – to finance another trip to the island where they had found an incredible treasure hoard, only to lose what they had taken shortly afterwards.

'Oh, yes, the treasure. I knew there had to be a reason why we were putting ourselves through all this.' Sebastian gazed at his friend for a moment. 'But ask yourself, Cornelius: is it worth it? Even if we do eventually end up rich beyond our wildest dreams, will the price we have to pay for it outweigh the rewards? Three good men have already died on this trip. Karl and Samuel, back before we found the village, and now Galt. Tomorrow it could be one of us.'

'But that's the risk any adventurer takes,' Cornelius assured him. 'If adventuring were easy, everyone would be doing it, wouldn't they?'

Sebastian looked down at him, baffled by this logic.

'Come on,' said Cornelius. 'Let's get some sleep – it's too late to be doing so much soul-searching.'

They returned to their chamber and found a comical sight awaiting them. Max was trying to get back to his feet, but his hooves kept slipping on the stone floor, sending him sprawling again. A few of the younger children were doing their best to help him up, without much success. He glared at Sebastian and Cornelius.

'Well, don't just stand there,' he said. 'Come and give me a hand.'

Sebastian smiled. 'On one condition,' he said.

'What's that?'

'That you promise to stop talking and let us sleep.'

Max grunted, clearly not happy with the deal, but reluctant to spend the night on a cold stone floor. 'Oh, very well,' he said. 'I'm wasting my breath talking to you two idiots anyway. In the end you'll do exactly what you want. You generally do.'

CHAPTER 20

AARON

Sebastian was woken from a deep sleep. He had been dreaming that he was creeping through the deserted city at night, making as little noise as possible because he knew that, out there in the shadows, the Night Runners were stalking him. He had never been so grateful to be shaken awake.

He blinked at the person who was crouched over him. It was Phelan, and he was looking down at him with an urgent expression on his face.

'Aaron wishes to see you,' he said.

Sebastian looked around and realized he had been lying with his head pillowed against Max's shaggy flank. He shook his head to try and dispel the last shreds of sleep.

'What, *now*?' he asked. 'What time is it?'

'The sun is just rising,' Phelan told him. 'You are to come with me, you and the little warrior...' He glanced at

Cornelius, who was already sitting up and taking notice. 'He wishes to speak to both of you. And the comical talking creature. I have told Aaron all about him and he wishes to see him for himself.'

'All right.' Sebastian elbowed Max unceremoniously in the rump.

'Oh well, perhaps just another star fruit,' said Max. 'I'm watching my figure.'

Sebastian stared at him. 'What are you blathering about?'

Max directed his bleary gaze at him. 'Sorry,' he said. 'I was dreaming I was at a buffalope restaurant.'

'I've been to one like that in Golmira,' Cornelius told him, blinking the sleep from his eyes. 'Very tasty it was too. I had roast buffalope in hot pepper sauce, with a side order of suckling rusa. Dee-licious!'

'That's nothing to boast about,' said Max. 'And you misunderstand me. This place was run by humans, but the buffalope weren't on the menu, they were the *customers*. It was called Buffalopia. There were really smart candlelit troughs, and every so often a waiter would come by and throw in another bucket of fruit; and there were these giant tankards filled with ale and—'

'I'm sure this is fascinating,' interrupted Sebastian, 'but we have to go and meet Aaron now.'

'What?' Max looked apprehensive. 'Well, good luck to you, that's all I can say. Let's hope he doesn't bite your heads off.'

'What are you talking about?' asked Sebastian, getting to his feet. 'You're coming with us, you ninny – he's asked to see you.'

'Me? He doesn't need to see me. Why should he want to see me?'

'Because I have told him all about you,' said Phelan. 'I have said what a funny old thing you are.'

'Oh, well, thanks for that, I'm sure,' said Max, finding his feet with great difficulty on the slippery stone floor. 'I suppose you told him that I had a good bit of meat on my bones, did you? Yes, he's probably woken up hungry. That'll be it.'

Phelan looked at Sebastian. 'What's he on about?' he asked.

'Good question. Max seems to have got it into his head that Aaron is some kind of flesh-eating monster.'

Phelan laughed. 'He's been called many things in his time, but never that!' He turned to look at Max. 'There's no need to worry,' he said. 'Aaron isn't going to hurt you. He's kind and generous. Come along, you'll see.'

He led the way out of the room and the others followed, Max with visible reluctance.

'Why do I have to go?' he complained.

'Because he's heard about you and probably thinks he'll be entertained,' said Cornelius. 'Most people are, *the first time*.'

Max looked at him dolefully. 'What's that supposed to mean?' he muttered.

'Only that the novelty soon wears off.'

At the end of the landing Phelan turned to climb the next flight of steps to a level they had not yet visited.

'Oh yes, go on, insult me,' Max told Cornelius. 'You may as well, everyone else does! But if we get up these stairs and this Aaron character turns out to be some kind of unspeakable monster, don't expect me to help you out.'

'For goodness' sake, Max,' whispered Sebastian. 'Why are you so convinced he's going to be something awful?'

'Because that's what always happens,' said Max. 'Haven't you worked that out yet? We meet somebody and they seem all right, but in reality they're crafty and evil or they turn into wild animals or they've been plotting to murder you, or eat you or something even worse. Why do we never meet any nice people?'

'We *do* meet nice people,' protested Sebastian. 'Jenna Swift . . . Princess Kerin . . . Garth Bracegirdle, the landlord of the Brigand's Arms . . .'

'Peg o' the Hills,' said Cornelius. 'The Kid and his father.'

'Lemuel,' offered Sebastian, 'Cassius and the rest of the crew of the *Sea Witch*.' He thought for a moment. 'Osbert,' he added.

'Oh yes, well, now we're really scraping the barrel, aren't we? As I recall Osbert was a rather thick mule who could barely string a sentence together. All I'm saying is, if I had to start listing all the nasty scumbags we've encountered, I'd be here till doomsday.'

They came to a set of ornate metal doors, which Phelan pushed open with a flourish. He led the three friends into the room beyond and Sebastian stared around in amazement. Unlike the bare rooms they had seen so far, this one boasted fine furniture, gold drapes and handsome ornaments. The walls were hung with huge oil paintings – mostly portraits of stately-looking men and women; and the room was lit by a gigantic glass chandelier, upon which scores of candles burned brightly. Sebastian was reminded of the treasure trove of Captain Callinestra because so many fine objects had been crammed higgledy-piggledy into the room.

Along one entire wall stood a gigantic bookcase crammed with handsome leather-bound volumes like those Sebastian had once seen in the palace of King Septimus. But there were so many other things to catch the eye – furniture and statues and goblets and weapons and jewels and things that Sebastian could not even put a name to.

At the far end of the room was an elaborately carved and bejewelled throne, and upon it, dwarfed by its size, sat the oldest man Sebastian had ever seen. He had thought Joseph, back at the Jilith camp, was ancient, but this man was shrivelled and wizened by time, so that his pale blue eyes stared out from a face that was a mask of lines and wrinkles. He wore a simple white tunic; beneath it, his body was so emaciated, it looked as if the softest breeze would be enough to blow him away. Sebastian noticed that his bare legs were horribly twisted and marked with ancient scars and realized that he would not be capable of walking without the aid of crutches.

Phelan led Sebastian, Cornelius and Max up to the foot of the throne. He bowed his head politely and the others did likewise.

The old man smiled and bowed back. 'So,' he said, in a voice that was as dry and papery thin as his own flesh, 'at last you have come. And not before time.'

Max sighed. 'Oh no,' he said. 'Not another blooming prophecy!'

Aaron seemed amused by this. He tilted back his head and gave a wheezy laugh that threatened to turn into a hacking cough. 'Excellent!' he said. 'A talking buffalope. I knew such a thing was possible, but to have lived all these years and never seen it till now . . . What a strange world it is and no mistake.' He looked back at Max. 'No, Mr Buffalope, not a prophecy – just the belief that one day somebody would finally come here and survive the ravages of the Night Runners.' He turned to Phelan. 'Bring some chairs for my guests' – he looked doubtfully at Max – 'and some . . . cushions for the beast.'

Phelan immediately scuttled off to do the old man's bidding. There was no doubt that Aaron enjoyed all the

powers of a king and yet, despite his bejewelled throne, he wore nothing that would have marked him out as one – no crown, no splendid robes or badge of office. Phelan came back with a chair for Sebastian, a small stool for Cornelius and, after some frantic searching, a couple of plush silk cushions upon which Max duly settled himself. Phelan stood watchfully by, awaiting further instructions.

'What a fabulous room,' said Sebastian, looking around in awe.

Aaron nodded. 'This building was the king's palace,' he said. 'And this was his throne room. Once every room contained as much finery as this, but that is something we shall speak of later. We are all comfortable and we can speak freely. Tell me first where you come from and why you are here.'

There was a long silence. Sebastian and Cornelius looked at each other. Sebastian told himself that the best thing was simply to tell the truth.

'We have come from a port called Ramalat,' he explained. 'It's on the east coast of the known world, beyond the jungles of Mendip.'

'Yes, I know of it,' said Aaron. 'Your homeland?'

'Er . . . no, I'm from Jerabim, which is further west. And Cornelius here is from Golmira, way up in the frozen north. We—'

'Ahem!' said Max. 'I, on the other hand, am from the great

plains of Neruvia where, as a young calf, I lived as part of a mighty herd. But through a series of unfortunate events I came into the care of Sebastian's father, who looked after me and brought me to adulthood—'

'That's probably enough background,' Sebastian told him.

'I was only trying to give him the full story,' said Max.

'Yes, but I know you – you'll blather on for ages.' Sebastian turned back to Aaron. 'We were all in Ramalat after a sea-faring adventure; and it was there that we met a rich merchant called Thaddeus Peel. He had heard stories of a lost city in the jungle, so he paid us to mount an expedition to go and look for it. He told us that if we found it, we were to bring him back proof of its existence . . . and, well, here we are.'

Aaron nodded. 'Yes, here you are,' he said. 'And when you finally get back to Ramalat, you should tell this Thaddeus Peel that on no account should he or his people ever try to come here. Tell them that a terrible fate awaits them should they try.'

Cornelius nodded. 'You speak, of course, of the Night Runners.'

'I do, sir.'

'Can you tell us what they are?'

'They are the people who once lived and worked in this city,' said Aaron sadly. 'They are all that is left of a once mighty empire.'

'And how did they come to be in this frightful condition?' Cornelius asked.

Aaron waved a hand at the great bookcase to his right. 'Before you, you see an incredible wealth of knowledge,' he said. 'There are the answers to all your questions about this city. Phelan, go and pluck out any two books at random and give them to our guests.'

Phelan rushed away and was back in a moment, pressing a book into Sebastian's hands and another into Cornelius's. Sebastian examined his eagerly. It was beautifully made, the cover of rich brown leather, but where he imagined a title ought to be there was nothing but a series of odd-looking marks. Puzzled, he opened the book at a random page and saw lines of the same indecipherable dots, dashes and squiggles.

'What language is this?' he asked.

'A good question!' said Aaron. 'It is the language of the people who founded this city, thousands of years ago; it is called Chagwallish, the language of the Chagwallans.'

'Oh, the Chagwallans!' said Max, and everybody turned to look at him. He thought for a moment, then shook his head. 'No, never heard of them.'

Aaron smiled. 'Since I first came here as a young man, a member of an expedition from the Southlands, I have devoted much of my time to translating that language,' he said. 'It has been a long and irksome task, but I am stubborn and I have persevered and' – he gestured at his twisted legs – 'I certainly had plenty of time on my hands. Unable to come and go as other men do, I have devoted my life to study. Now, as I approach the end of my days, I am able to fully understand what came to pass here. It is not a nice story.'

'They never are,' said Max, rolling his eyes.

'Would you be interested in hearing it?' asked Aaron.

'We would,' said Cornelius.

'Absolutely,' added Sebastian.

'It's not too long, is it?' asked Max. 'Only I haven't had any breakfast yet.'

Sebastian gave him a sly kick in the rump and Max looked offended; but he settled down to listen.

Aaron paused for a moment, lifted a small goblet from a table beside him and took a sip of its contents. He set it down carefully and then, leaning back in his huge throne, he began to tell the story.

CHAPTER 21

OF KINGS AND EMPIRES

'It begins in a city called Chagwalla,' said Aaron, 'which in the ancient tongue means the Golden City. It was located across the Straits of Serim in the unknown world, where on our maps it says only, *Here Be Dragons*. The Chagwallans had a mighty empire, with their own language, their own gods and a powerful army that controlled their land with a rod of iron. In that city lived a man called Nasram and he was feared as the most powerful man alive.'

'Sounds a bit like King Septimus,' said Max. 'I'll bet he was every bit as evil too.'

'Oh, he was not a man to trifle with. But he was not a king – at least, not at first. He was a general who served a king, and that king was called King Daalam; for him, General Nasram waged many wars and conquered many cities. King Daalam was ambitious and had long sought to extend his empire; and so his thoughts turned to the unknown land across the sea. He commanded General Nasram to assemble a massive expeditionary force and sent it across the Straits of Serim to explore the world on the other side. King Daalam planned to claim it for himself and add it to his already vast empire. When he embarked on his mission, General Nasram commanded a fleet of fifty ships, every one of them packed with soldiers.'

Cornelius let out a low whistle. 'That's quite an army,' he said.

'Indeed. But Nasram wanted to be prepared for anything or anyone who might oppose him. After many days and nights of travel, the armada landed on the south-west coast of the known world and Nasram saw before him a seemingly impenetrable jungle, stretching east and west as far as the eye could see. Undeterred, he marched his men forward and they hacked their way through the dense undergrowth and just kept going.

'Every night the expedition would cut down enough vegetation to allow it to pitch its tents. Hunting parties were sent out to bring back enough meat to feed every last man – the jungles in those times teemed with wild animals. And so they marched for many moons, until finally Nasram's advance scouts brought back exciting news from up ahead: they had seen a great golden city, ripe for plunder.'

'Who lived there?' asked Sebastian.

'Another mighty empire called the Metyars,' explained

Aaron. 'A much more primitive society than the Chagwallans, but fabulously rich because of the gold mines on the outskirts of their city; gold that the Metyars used to make statues, jewellery and fine ornaments to offer up to their gods. They had no real concept of the worth of the gold, but used it to adorn themselves.'

'Rather like the Jilith,' observed Sebastian.

'The king of this empire was called Selawayo,' the old man continued, 'a proud man who in his own realm was every bit as powerful as Daalam. But he was totally unprepared for the arrival of these strangers from the unknown world. They fell upon his armies like wolves and vanquished them quickly and mercilessly. Selawayo was taken prisoner and his people turned into slaves, forced to mine their precious gold, not for their gods but for Nasram.'

'Don't you mean for King Daalam?' asked Cornelius. 'After all, he had sent the expedition.'

'Indeed. But General Nasram quickly became corrupted by his new found power. Why should he send all his wealth back across the straits to King Daalam, he thought, when he could be a king himself, here in the new world? So that is exactly what happened. He proclaimed himself King Nasram and decided to demolish the Metyars' old city and build upon it a fabulous new one dedicated to his own glory. He no longer thought of himself as a mere mortal but as some kind of god.'

'He sounds a proper bighead,' said Max. 'I hope somebody took him down a peg or two!'

Aaron shook his head. 'Sadly, no,' he said. 'There was to be no retribution in his lifetime. King Nasram forced all the captive Metyars to work on his new city and it began to spring up on the rubble of the old one. He named it Nasrama, 'the place of the Golden One'.

'A modest sort, wasn't he?' said Max.

'He also made a promise to Selawayo, who was now a king in name only and lived as a captive in Nasram's court: when work on the city was complete, he would free the Metyars from slavery and let them go back to their old ways. But Selawayo could not have guessed at the scale of the project. Year after year the work went on. Thousands of slaves perished in their chains and were thrown into a mass grave on the outskirts of the city; their children took their places and whole families lived and died in servitude and ended up in that same mass grave. The Chagwallans treated the Metyars like animals and kept them chained up in pens like common cattle . . .' Aaron glanced at Max. 'No offence,' he said.

'Oh, none taken,' said Max. 'As you said, common. Not like us buffalope.'

'Indeed. Eventually Nasram grew old and died in his bed, wrapped in satin sheets. His son became king and carried on his father's work, and that man's son after him, and still the work went on, until finally, when a man called Sesam was king, the city was finally finished. The Metyars asked that Nasram's promise be honoured; but Sesam merely sent them back to the gold mines, still in chains, and told them that they would now be digging gold for *his* glory. The Metyars were still slaves, with nothing but a handful of rice a day for their troubles.

'One day an old Metyar woman begged for an audience with King Sesam and, surprisingly, he granted it. He must have been in a good mood that day! This woman was called Thalis and was considered an oracle – somebody who could speak with the gods and predict future events. Thalis stood defiantly before Sesam in this very room and warned him that he must honour the agreement that Nasram had made all those years before. If he did not, she told him, there would be a terrible price to pay.

'Sesam laughed at her audacity. "What price?" he asked her.

' "This city will no longer be a place for the living," she told him. "It will be a place of death, where the dead will walk the streets every night and no living man will be safe."

'Sesam laughed again and told his soldiers to take the old woman away and execute her for daring to speak to him in such an impudent manner; but when the guards went to take hold of Thalis, there was a brilliant flash of light and a great cloud of smoke; and when the smoke had cleared, Thalis was nowhere to be seen.'

'That reminds me of that hag, Leonora,' growled Cornelius. 'She pulled a stunt like that on me once.'

'Thalis was never seen again,' continued Aaron. 'Some said that the gods had carried her up to their paradise to live her life anew. Others said that she was a changeling and had transformed herself into a tiny bird and flown away. Whatever the case, Sesam should have paid heed to the warning he was given, but he chose to ignore it. And then the bad things began to happen.'

'It couldn't get much worse,' said Max. 'Could it?'

'Sadly, yes. One day a rumour came to Sesam. Guards at the huge cemetery where the slaves were buried said they had seen dead people walking at night: they were pale and thin and moved with amazing speed. At first Sesam dismissed this as ridiculous – but then he heard that some of the guards had abandoned their posts and were now walking around in the cemetery with the others.

'Then the sickness spread to the big pens where all the Metyars were kept chained together. Some of them were dying for no apparent reason, but when night came, they rose up again and bit whoever they were chained to; when their guards went in to try and separate them, they were bitten too, and those men fell ill – nobody who was bitten lasted more than a few hours.

'King Sesam was beginning to realize that something was terribly wrong. He sent a large force to take care of the matter, but these soldiers did not return and were seen wandering around the outskirts of the city, pale and thin; when anybody approached them, they attacked like wild animals, clawing and biting.

'The people of Nasrama understood that this was some kind of terrible contagion – a contagion that spread like wild-fire through the city. As more and more people were attacked and transformed, so the unaffected took to barricading themselves in their fine homes. But they couldn't stay there for ever: in the end they were driven out by the need to find food. And any who stayed out after dark never came home.'

Max rolled his eyes. 'Oh, this is a cheerful little story,' he moaned. 'Haven't you got anything a bit more jolly? An outbreak of plague, perhaps? A nice cosy massacre?'

Aaron shrugged his thin shoulders. 'I only tell you what I have learned,' he said, 'and the story is very nearly told. Soon only the king, his family and his closest friends were left alive in the deserted palace. When the contagion first began to spread, Sesam had ordered that every door and window should be fortified. But soon, even the huge stores of food in the palace began to run out. One morning Sesam's body-guards deserted him. They made a desperate attempt to flee the city; but that night they were back beneath the windows, hideously transformed and crying out to be let back in, their long white fingers clawing at the metal doors . . .'

'Oh, lovely,' said Max. 'Do you think we could leave it there? You're giving me the colly-wobbles!'

'Let him finish,' snapped Cornelius. 'And stop being so rude!'

Aaron waved a hand dismissively, but went on, 'Finally Sesam, his wife and his children drank poison, right here in this room, rather then venture out to meet their fate on the streets of his once-proud city. The dead now owned Nasrama. Soon the only things left alive here were the animals that occasionally wandered in from the jungle. Oddly, the Night Runners seemed to have no interest in them. They only pursued human prey.'

'What an amazing story,' said Cornelius. 'May I ask how you came to know all this?'

Aaron nodded. 'When I first came here as a young man, I found a journal. It was written by an old scribe called Lazarus, a servant of King Sesam, who lived through it all and was the last of the Chagwallans to die. At the end of the journal he penned a final note before taking poison himself. That too happened here, in this very room.'

'W-what did it say?' asked Max fearfully.

'It said simply this: *The city of Nasrama is cursed for ever. O wretched mankind, I warn thee. Stay away if you value your life, for this city now belongs to the dead.*'

'He had a way with words,' said Max. 'I bet he was a riot at parties.'

Aaron frowned. 'Before he died, Lazarus did two last things – things that certainly saved my life and the lives of many of those who came here with me. He went down to the entrance and drew back all the bolts. Then, in an upstairs window, he hung the Lantern of Krelt.'

'What's that?' asked Max.

'It is a magical thing indeed – a lantern that burns eternally. It uses no fuel, but contains a crystal that absorbs the light of day and discharges it when darkness falls. After all these years, it still burns every night in the same window . . . and, of course, it is the thing that drew you to us.'

'Amazing. I should very much like to see this lantern for myself,' said Cornelius.

'And you shall,' Aaron assured him. 'Of course, it took me many years to learn how to translate the language of the Chagwallans, but finally I was able to set the story down in our own tongue. When you are ready to leave, I shall give you the version I have written. That will provide the proof you need; and hopefully a warning to all strangers to stay away from here.'

Cornelius nodded. 'I thank you,' he said. 'I'm sure that Thaddeus Peel will accept that as proof of the city's existence.' He thought for a moment. 'So . . . you said you came here as a young man?'

Aaron smiled. 'Oh yes. That's another story. Would you care to hear it?'

'Absolutely,' said Sebastian.

'Definitely,' added Cornelius.

Max opened his mouth and his two friends glared at him. 'Please, do go on,' he said.

And Aaron continued with his story.

CHAPTER 22

AARON'S STORY

'On the southern shores of the known world there is a port called Veltan—'

'I've heard of it!' said Sebastian excitedly. He looked at Cornelius. 'I believe that's where Jenna was headed with that cargo of cloth. She could be there right now.'

Aaron nodded. 'Yes, Veltan trades with Ramalat and has done so for centuries. Veltan was my home when I was a child. My family was poor but I managed to make a decent life for myself and I suppose you could say I was a success in my chosen career. But like many young men, I yearned for adventure and the riches that might come with it. When I was in my twenty-third summer, I heard of an expedition setting off in search of a lost city in the jungle . . .'

'That sounds familiar,' observed Cornelius with a wry smile.

'Indeed. Your Thaddeus Peel is not the only one interested in old stories, my friend. At any rate, a large team of people was needed, and desperate to get away from what I saw as a humdrum existence in Veltan, I managed to convince the expedition leader, Bartholomew Tate, to take me on as a mule handler.' Aaron laughed his wheezy laugh. 'Not a very prestigious job, but one that would allow me to seek the adventure I craved. So the expedition set out – not a mighty force like Nasram's; just a hardy group of men and women determined to make something of their lives. We followed the course of the river Sleed, the mouth of which empties into the harbour of Veltan.'

Aaron closed his eyes for a moment as though picturing the scene. 'It was hard going. Like Nasram before us, we had to hack our way through the thickest vegetation. Some of us succumbed to jungle fever and others died from serpent bites and attacks by wild animals; but we kept going and eventually, after many trials and tribulations, one morning we cut through a screen of vegetation and found Nasrama waiting for us. It seemed completely deserted, but we quickly discovered that it was piled high with priceless treasures.' Aaron paused as if remembering his first sight of the city. He waved an arm around him. 'What you see here is but a fraction of what was on offer to us. We quickly realized that it would not be the work of days to remove it all but would take considerably longer.'

A pained expression came across his emaciated features. 'Then darkness fell, and the Night Runners came for us. It was terrifying: they swarmed out of every shadow and we could do nothing but run for our lives. Some among us, including Bartholomew Tate, were taken and we did not see them again – at least not in their usual form. I myself suffered a terrible accident. In my haste to escape from my pursuers, I fell down a steep drop onto some jagged stones.' He indicated his withered legs. 'Snapped these poor things like two twigs in a score of places but, thank the gods, my friends picked me up and carried me onwards.

'Then we saw our salvation – the light of the Lantern of Krelt – and found the door unbolted. The Night Runners had never ventured inside because there was nothing left alive in there; of course, every room in this palace has windows to allow in the light of day – a bad place for a Night Runner to seek refuge, but perfect for us. Sesam's bars and bolts had not saved him in the end, but of course, this place became our sanctuary – hence the name.'

'Excuse me asking,' said Max, 'but why didn't you just get out of the city and head back the way you came?'

Aaron grinned. 'I was in no position to head anywhere, Mr Buffalope. My legs were broken, and even if my friends had been prepared to carry me all the way back to Veltan, it was unlikely that I would have survived such a long and arduous journey. Besides, nobody was ready to go back just yet. You must understand that we had suffered many hardships on the journey here. Some of our party had perished in that terrible jungle. To return now, empty-handed, would have meant resuming the lives we had known back in Veltan. Of course, without proper medicine, the legs never set properly. Even now, I can only drag myself along with the aid of crutches. It is the price I pay in exchange for great riches.'

'Riches?' Sebastian raised his eyebrows.

'Oh yes.' Aaron looked around. 'In those days the palace was not as it is now, stripped of all items of value. Every room was a treasure trove. We vowed that we were going to have that treasure for ourselves, however long it took!'

Aaron shook his head and smiled ruefully. 'But what good were riches to us when we could not spend them? There was so much treasure around us, we could only have carried a tiny part of it away. And yet we would not leave it here for others to discover. What a conundrum!'

'I can see it might be a problem,' agreed Cornelius. 'We had a similar one ourselves, not so long ago. We found some treasure and could only carry away a small part of it.'

'Which we promptly lost,' added Max.

'Even now we find ourselves dreaming up ways to return and claim the rest of it,' said Sebastian. 'This very expedition was undertaken to finance another trip.'

Aaron nodded sympathetically. 'We would not consider taking only a small part away,' he said. 'We felt we had earned the right to enjoy all of it. We decided to send a party back to Veltan, to bring back an army to help us. But we never saw those people again. We wasted months waiting for them to return. Either the Night Runners got them or they succumbed to wild animals or sickness – who can say?' He sighed. 'We discussed the idea of trying again, but in the end we dismissed it. I made it my self-appointed task to devise a way to get us, and our treasure, out of the city and back to Veltan.'

'That's easier said than done,' observed Sebastian.

'I knew it was not going to be accomplished easily – indeed, it has taken me many years. Meanwhile I, and the men and women of my party, made a life for ourselves here in Sanctuary. A hard enough life, for sure, but we could hunt for food during the day and stay safe in here at night; we survived well enough. Some of my companions married and in time, of course, there were children, and when those children grew, they married and in turn had more children and—'

'How long have your lot been living here, then?' asked Max, incredulously.

'Long enough for a young, optimistic fellow to turn into the shrivelled creature you see before you,' said Aaron, with more than a trace of sadness in his voice. 'I don't keep exact figures but—'

'A blooming lifetime,' finished Max.

'May I ask a question?' said Sebastian.

'Of course.'

'I've been wondering ever since we got here. Where are the other adults?'

Aaron sighed. 'Gone,' he said.

'Gone?' muttered Max. 'Gone where?'

'I think he means dead,' murmured Sebastian.

'Oh, right. What, all of 'em?'

'Yes, I'm afraid so,' said Aaron. 'Until recently, we still had a few left. But an outbreak of fever a few moons back killed two of them. The children seem to have hardier constitutions – they don't get sick like the adults did, and . . . well, grown-ups seem to be more prone to the yarps.'

'The what?' cried Sebastian.

'Oh, it's a term we use to describe what happens to people when they spend too long cooped up in one place. They tend to go a little . . .' He made a drilling motion at the side of his head with his index finger.

'Crazy?' suggested Cornelius.

'Yes. It manifests itself in many different ways. They run off into the jungle and we never see them again. Or they fight each other to the death. Or they throw themselves into the river and the water dragons get them. The last three adults in our party went out hunting one morning, around two moons ago. They all seemed rather . . . edgy. They never returned – at least, not in their original forms. We don't know how exactly, but the Night Runners got them. So that left just me and the children. We managed somehow – Phelan and the older children are proficient hunters, but many are too young to do very much at all. I was despairing of them ever escaping from this place and then . . .'

'And then what?' asked Max suspiciously.

'And then my prayers were answered. You arrived to help me complete my task.'

There was a puzzled silence at this.

'I'm sorry,' said Sebastian. 'I don't quite follow . . .'

'I am now too old and frail to make the journey back to Veltan. I shall stay on here and live out my remaining days with my things around me. And if it all becomes too much, I can simply do what Sesam and Lazarus did before me . . . As for the children – well, I thought Phelan here would have to command the expedition to Veltan, but – no disrespect to him – he is not old enough to have such a responsibility thrust upon him.' The old man gazed at Cornelius. 'But you, now – you may be short on stature, but you have about you the bearing of a military man. I think you could handle the job.' He looked at Sebastian. 'And you, though still young, are certainly older than Phelan.'

'I'm seventeen,' said Sebastian. He thought about it for a moment. 'Probably eighteen by now – I must have had a birthday somewhere back down the trail.'

'Eighteen. A good age! Just a few years younger than I was when I first arrived here.'

'And let's not forget,' said Max, 'that they both have me to look after them. I mean, I don't like to boast but—'

'I can see you are a fine asset,' Aaron agreed.

'I beg your pardon?' said Max.

Cornelius looked thoughtful. 'So you're asking us to escort the children – and the treasure – back to Veltan?' he said.

'Correct,' said Aaron.

'And . . . how are we to do that exactly?'

Aaron indicated a nearby table: on it lay something covered with a white cloth. 'Phelan, do the honours,' he said, and the boy hurried over to pull aside the cloth, revealing a strange-looking craft made of wood.

'The ark of Aaron,' he explained.

Max stared at it. 'I'm not being funny,' he muttered, 'but you won't get very much into that.'

The old man glared at him. 'That's just a model of it, you ninny! The real one is moored on the river.'

'Oh, right,' said Max. 'I knew that.'

'I designed it myself,' Aaron went on proudly. 'See how deep the bows are? The hold is loaded with treasure – everything that was once stored in this building. It has taken us many, many moons to get everything safely aboard.'

'But . . . who built it?' asked Cornelius. 'Surely not the children?'

'Oh no, we still had plenty of adults when we started work on this. As you can no doubt imagine, it has been an

incredibly slow process, finding the wood, cutting it, allowing it to season properly and then actually putting the thing together. It has taken many years. And over those years, our workers have fallen prey to the Night Runners.'

'Well, they must have been careless,' said Max bluntly. 'Those things only come out at night, so surely all your lot had to do was stay inside until the sun came up?'

Aaron shook his head sadly. 'It's not quite as straightforward as that, I'm afraid. True, the Night Runners cannot venture into the sunlight – the touch of it destroys them. But they *can* lurk in dark, windowless rooms waiting for careless people to come foraging for food or fuel. And there are many places like that in this city.'

Max snorted. 'Remind me not to go into any of them,' he told Sebastian.

Cornelius was strolling around the model ark, inspecting it closely. 'It certainly looks imposing enough,' he said. 'Where did you get hold of the plans?'

'I had to design it,' said Aaron. 'Another reason why it's taken so long. And I'll admit I didn't get it right first time. But as I'm very fond of saying, you can't make an omelette without breaking eggs.'

Max brightened a little. 'An omelette,' he said. 'That would go down very nicely!'

Cornelius glowered at him. 'He's talking about a hypothetical omelette, you nitwit!'

Max frowned. 'Don't think I've ever had one of those,' he said. 'A bit of cheese would do me – I'm not fussy.'

Cornelius did his best to ignore Max. 'We came down that river on a raft,' he said. 'The river Sleed, I think you called it? We passed through some horrendous rapids. We even came over that huge cascade upstream and were lucky enough to survive the fall. You really believe this heavy craft can handle such rough treatment?'

Aaron smiled. 'It won't have to,' he said. 'There *are* no rapids between here and Veltan.'

'Well, I appreciate you followed its course upriver when you first set out, but that was a lifetime ago – you can't be expected to remember every detail.'

Aaron shook his head. 'Oh no, you misunderstand. I found some old charts that mapped the course of the river. According to them, the great waterfall is the last obstacle. From here it's a nice calm stretch all the way to Veltan. It's simply a case of going with the current.'

'That's what *I* was told,' said Max.

'*We* didn't have charts,' said Cornelius defensively.

Aaron smiled. 'It ought to be simple enough,' he said. 'A lot easier than the journey down river you have already endured. And somebody must take up the challenge! My life is nearly over but those children will arrive in Veltan with great riches at their disposal. They will be set up for life.' He looked shrewdly at his companions. 'And so, of course, will you.'

'Us?' Sebastian looked at him blankly.

'Well, I wouldn't expect you to change your plans without seeking some kind of reward. Shall we say twenty per cent of the value of the treasure to share out as you wish?'

Sebastian and Cornelius exchanged glances.

'That seems a most generous offer,' said Cornelius, 'if, as you say, what is in this room is only a tiny part of the treasure . . .'

'Oh, it is! Trust me when I say that if you undertake this task, you will be rich men indeed. I don't know what this Thaddeus Peel has offered you but—'

'It's not a fortune,' said Cornelius. 'I can tell you that much.'

'But you know nothing about us,' said Sebastian. 'How do you know you can trust us?'

'I don't,' admitted Aaron. 'But I consider myself a good judge of character; and I simply have no other choice. I am coming towards the end of my life. These children will be all alone in the world – they are orphans. And you, good sirs, represent their one chance of escaping from this hell on earth and finding a new and prosperous life in Veltan. I hope you will agree to help them.'

'Well—' began Cornelius, but Aaron lifted a hand to silence him.

'No, I don't want you to decide here and now. This enterprise has been so many years in the preparation, what difference can a few more days make? Have a think about it. Later, Phelan will take you to look at the ark so you can judge for yourselves how robust it is. And he will show you the treasures that are stored down in the hold. When you have considered everything carefully, then come back to me and tell me your decision.'

He sat back in his ornate throne and his narrow shoulders slumped with exhaustion. 'I swear, these days even talking seems to wear me out. I pray you will excuse me and allow me to rest a little. We will speak again soon.'

'Of course.' Cornelius bowed his head and he and the others followed Phelan back out through the huge doors.

Just before he left the room, Sebastian glanced back once again at the frail, skinny old man on his fabulous throne, surrounded by riches that he would never be able to spend. He tried to imagine what kind of life he must have endured in this place while he drew up his plans for escape. Sebastian thought that it was one of the saddest stories he had ever heard; and he knew in that same moment that he would have to help the old man to achieve his dream.

CHAPTER 23

AARON'S ARK

They headed for the communal room, but Cornelius hung back and told Phelan to go ahead without them.

'We have a few things we need to discuss,' he said. 'In private.'

'That's all right. I'll see about sorting you out some breakfast,' said Phelan.

'Oh goody, what are we having?' asked Max excitedly.

'Well, for us it's generally rusa stew, but I think I know where I can lay my hands on some fruit,' said Phelan. 'After we've eaten we'll go and have a look at the ark.'

'Good, we'll look forward to it,' said Cornelius as the boy made his way towards the big room. The Golmiran swung round to look at the others. 'Well, what do we think?' he asked them.

'I think my stomach's gurgling,' said Max.

'Your stomach is *always* gurgling,' said Cornelius. 'I'm speaking of Aaron's request.'

Sebastian frowned. 'I don't really see how we can refuse,' he said. 'Those poor children – we can hardly leave them to their fate.'

'True. And it ought to be easy enough. If Aaron's right about the absence of rapids, then it's plain sailing all the way to Veltan.'

'See, you're doing it again,' complained Max. 'Whenever you say something like that, it turns out to be anything *but* plain sailing. Look at that ruddy raft.' He mimicked Cornelius's hearty voice. '*All we have to do is point it into the current!* No mention of rapids, waterfalls or ruddy great dragons!'

'You're such a pessimist,' observed Cornelius.

'No, I'm a realist,' said Max. 'There's a big difference.'

Cornelius gave a dismissive wave of his hand. 'If Aaron hasn't exaggerated about the treasure – and judging by what's up in that throne room, I've no reason to believe he is – then we could come out of this rich beyond all measure. There'd be no need to think about returning to Callinestra's island. And of course, once we're in Veltan, what's to stop us from chartering a ship round the coast to Ramalat? Then we can deliver Aaron's book to Thaddeus Peel and we'll have another payday from him.'

'Oh yes, it all sounds wonderful, doesn't it?' said Max. 'I

seem to remember you saying similar things about that pirate treasure. And what did we get out of that? Nothing. Nowt. A big fat zero. Things are never as easy as you make out, Golmiran.'

'I hate to admit it, but he's right,' admitted Sebastian. 'It's not straightforward. For one thing, what about Keera, Cal and Salah?'

'What about them?' asked Cornelius.

'Well, they only signed on to help us find the lost city. We've done that now. What are they going to say if we tell them we're moving on down river to Veltan?'

Cornelius shrugged his shoulders. 'They don't have to come with us,' he said. 'They're free to head back to their village any time they like.'

Sebastian stared at him. 'On their own? For goodness' sake, Cornelius, what chance would they have out there?'

Cornelius laughed. 'Those three were raised in the jungle – they'd handle it better than we would.' He thought for a moment. 'Anyway, if they decide to come with us, we could offer them a share of the treasure. That would be an incentive.'

'You clearly didn't learn much about the Jilith during our stay, did you?' Sebastian shook his head. 'Offering them gold and jewels would be meaningless. You may as well offer them the wind or the sun.'

'Well, we'll just have to tell them we're going and it's up to them to decide what to do. I mean, they're adults, aren't they?'

'Salah isn't,' Sebastian told him.

'No, but . . . she'll probably go along with whatever Keera decides. And Cal – well, I'd say he'd do the same. That man is devoted to her. It's a shame she's so intent on being with you.'

'That's not my fault,' protested Sebastian.

Cornelius sighed. 'At any rate, we'll have to go in and face the music.' He gave Max a warning glance. 'Whatever happens, you keep your big mouth shut. This is sensitive stuff and I don't want you putting a ruddy great hoof in it.'

'Charming,' said Max. 'I'll try not to mess things up for you.'

They moved on along the landing and in through the open doorway. Sebastian scanned the room and saw Keera and Cal sitting on cushions in one corner. Their expressions were blank, as though they were already bored with each other's company. Salah was playing a game of tag with a crowd of other children. She was laughing delightedly and as Sebastian watched, Phelan ran up behind her and tapped her on the shoulder. She turned and looked at him, her eyes flashing with excitement.

'Well, at least Salah seems to have made some friends,' said Sebastian thoughtfully.

As they approached, Keera looked up and her expression

changed to one of delight. She jumped to her feet and hurried towards Sebastian.

'There you are,' she said. 'I was beginning to worry about you. I'll go and get you some food.'

'Oh, that's OK, I can—'

But she had already rushed off towards the fireplace, where a cauldron of stew was bubbling over the flames. A moment later, she was back with two bowls and a couple of pieces of flat bread, which she handed to Sebastian and Cornelius. She indicated a bucket of fruit standing a short distance away. 'Phelan left that for Max,' she said.

'Oh,' said Max, 'things are looking up!' Plunging his snout straight into the bucket, he began to eat noisily. Sebastian and Cornelius settled themselves down on some cushions and started on their breakfast.

'What about you?' Sebastian asked Keera.

'We have eaten,' she said. 'Or at least, I have. Cal didn't seem to have much of an appetite.'

Cal glared at her. 'Can you wonder?' he snarled. He looked at Sebastian. 'I'm sick of all this waiting around. What news from this mysterious Aaron? Do you have the proof you need?'

'Umm . . . not yet,' said Sebastian, chewing a chunk of gristly meat. 'No, not . . . not quite.'

'I've told you before not to question the Chosen One,' said Keera.

Cal laughed at her. 'There you go again,' he said. 'I'll question who I please!'

'You forget yourself. Remember, I am Maccan's daughter. He would be most displeased to hear you speak to me in such a way.'

'He'd be even more displeased if he saw how you've been carrying on,' snapped Cal. 'But if you want to speak with your father, I'll gladly escort you home. Just say the word.'

There was an uncomfortable silence before Cornelius weighed in with more information.

'Aaron wants a favour from us first. He is dying, but he has asked us to take the children down river to a city called Veltan. He fears for their safety when he is no longer around to look after them.'

'Veltan?' Cal sneered. 'Never heard of it. Nobody said anything about it when we undertook to help you.'

'No, I appreciate that,' said Sebastian. 'But . . . well, we can't leave the children to their fate, can we? So once everything is prepared, we will be sailing down river. Aaron has a boat and—'

But Cal was shaking his head. 'It's out of the question,' he said. 'You may do as you like but me, Keera and Salah, we'll be heading back to our village.'

Keera glared at him. 'That's not for you to decide,' she told him. 'My place is with Sebastian.'

'No,' roared Cal, loud enough to turn heads all around the

room. 'Your place is with the Jilith! You think I'm going to go back to your father and tell him that you have decided to carry on down river with . . . *him*?'

'If that's what I decide, that's what you must tell him,' snapped Keera. 'Don't you dare presume to speak for me!'

Cal's eyes filled with tears of frustration. 'Keera, don't you see, these people are no good for us. Look what's happened since we fell in with them. Galt has gone and you've completely lost sight of reality. You're coming back with me if I have to drag you by your hair!'

'Can we try and keep things a little cooler here?' said Sebastian. 'We only want the best for everyone. Nobody is going to be made to do anything they don't want to do.'

'Keep out of this, elfling,' said Cal, 'or by Okrin, I'll teach you a lesson you'll never forget.'

Sebastian could feel his own temper beginning to fray. 'Cal, nobody made you come with us. As I recall, you volunteered to come, mostly so you could keep an eye on Keera.'

'Yes, and a fat lot of use that's been to me. She's been bewitched by your fanciful words ever since she first laid eyes on you. She thinks there's something special about you, but I can see you for what you are.'

'You see nothing,' Keera shouted at him. 'You're so full of envy you cannot recognize true greatness when it stands before you.'

Cal stood up suddenly and made a dismissive gesture at

Keera. 'You know what? Do what you like. I wash my hands of you! You can go on this fool's errand if you wish, but me and Salah, we are heading back right now.' He glanced over towards the group of children and got to his feet. 'Salah,' he said. 'Come with me. We're leaving.'

Salah stared at him, her eyes wide. Then she shook her head.

He glared at her. 'Come along, Salah, none of that. I am responsible for your welfare. You're to come with me now.'

Salah opened her mouth and grimaced, as if trying to take a breath, then began to gesticulate. Suddenly she stopped.

'No,' she said; and everybody turned to look at her in complete amazement. Salah lifted a hand to her mouth as though she couldn't quite believe it herself. Then she laughed incredulously, and it wasn't her usual silent laugh but a loud chuckle. She looked at Cal and spoke again, with only a little hesitation. 'No, C-Cal. I'm . . . s-s-staying here . . . with Ph-Phelan.'

There were gasps and exclamations all around the room. Phelan ran over to Salah and hugged her, and Sebastian understood the look he had seen in her eyes earlier. He turned to Keera and the two of them shared a laugh of disbelief. Cal muttered an oath, turned on his heel and strode out of the room. Sebastian started to go after him, but Cornelius pulled him back.

'Let him go,' he said.

'You think he'll leave?' asked Sebastian.

'By himself? I doubt it. I imagine once he's had a chance to simmer down a bit, he'll realize that he may as well come with us. But you know, it's up to him. Tell you the truth, I almost wish he *would* leave. It would improve the atmosphere around here no end.'

Salah and Phelan came over, beaming delightedly. Sebastian saw that they were holding hands like sweethearts.

'What happened?' he asked Salah.

'Phelan happened,' she said. 'He told me . . . I w-w-would speak . . . when I was r-ready, and finally . . . I was!'

'It's wonderful news,' said Keera. She reached up and clasped the girl's free hand in hers. 'I only wish we had some way of telling Joseph what has happened. He would be so thrilled to learn of it.' She looked at Salah intently. 'So, you wish to go with us down river?'

Salah nodded and glanced at Phelan. 'I go . . . w-where Phelan goes.'

Phelan grinned. 'That's settled then,' he said. 'Now, you'd best finish up your food. We have some way to travel if you are to visit the ark today. And we must be back in Sanctuary before nightfall.'

CHAPTER 24

DOWN TO THE RIVER

They set off a short while later – Sebastian, Cornelius, Max, Phelan and another boy of perhaps twelve summers, a red-headed, freckled lad whose name was Olaf.

Keera and Salah would have gone with them but found themselves enlisted by a second group, leaving later that morning, who were setting out in search of some fresh meat. Sebastian wasn't surprised when Cal appeared from nowhere to announce that he too would accompany the hunting party. He hardly acknowledged Sebastian and Cornelius as they passed by.

'Still taking every chance he can to spend time with Keera,' observed Sebastian.

Cornelius gave him a wry smile. 'Anybody would think you were jealous,' he said.

'Don't be daft. It's just pathetic, that's all. Everyone knows she's not interested in him.'

They trooped down the many steps to the ground floor, where a couple of young boys sat guarding the huge metal entrance door. They nodded to Phelan, peered out through the observation slot, then started to draw back the massive metal bolts, standing on tiptoe to reach the highest.

The door swung open on oiled hinges. Phelan and Olaf leaned out and glanced quickly up and down the street before stepping through. Sebastian noticed that they held their swords out before them, ready for trouble, so he and Cornelius unsheathed their own swords as they went out. Max ambled after them and winced as the door slammed shut behind him. They stood there for a moment, gazing around.

'What are we looking for?' Sebastian asked Phelan. 'There's no danger of any Night Runners surely?'

Phelan shook his head. 'They're not the only things to fear around here,' he told him.

'Oh great,' said Max. 'There's something you haven't told us about.'

Phelan laughed. 'You're too suspicious,' he said. 'But you have to be careful. Sometimes animals come wandering out of the jungle. A friend of mine turned a corner one day and walked right into a gruntag. Last thing he ever did.'

Sebastian studied the boy thoughtfully, thinking that

Phelan's outlook was way beyond his tender years. It was as if he was talking about the loss of a hat, not another human being. But he had endured such a harsh life here in this ruined city, perhaps it was no great surprise.

'You must be looking forward to leaving this place,' Sebastian said.

Phelan nodded eagerly. 'It's all I've dreamed of ever since I was old enough to think,' he said. 'But of course, Aaron can't be hurried on anything. Now I really feel that it might be about to happen.' He and Olaf glanced up and down the street again before setting off; the others followed.

'Why exactly are we doing this?' asked Sebastian. 'Going to see the ark, I mean? Why was Aaron so keen on us looking at it before we made up our minds?'

'He wants us to inspect it,' said Cornelius, 'to see if it's strong enough to carry us all down river.'

'As if we'd know,' said Max scathingly.

'Oh, I like to think I know a thing or two about boats,' said Cornelius.

'Is there anything you don't know about?' grunted Max unkindly.

'Just one. How to get a buffalope to keep a still tongue!'

Sebastian looked around. 'Phelan, I don't know how you find your way around this city,' he said. 'Every road looks exactly the same to me.'

Phelan laughed easily and glanced back over his shoulder.

'I have been finding my way along these streets since I was old enough to walk. There is not one alleyway that I have not mapped.'

'You have *maps*?' Cornelius asked him.

Phelan nodded and tapped his forehead. 'In here,' he said. 'The best kind.'

'Oh, right,' said Max. 'Much better than those daft things that people draw on paper.'

They walked on through a maze of crumbling grey stone buildings. Everywhere empty windows gazed down upon them and Sebastian shivered.

'I feel like I'm being watched,' he said.

'You are,' said Olaf, in a surprisingly deep voice. 'The dead are watching us from every shadowy corner, just waiting for night to fall.'

Max looked at him. 'Who invited laughing boy?' he asked.

'Olaf has every reason to be gloomy,' said Phelan protectively. 'He saw both his parents taken by the Night Runners just a few summers back.'

'How terrible,' said Sebastian; and he nudged Max in the flank.

'Er, yes . . . tragic,' muttered Max dutifully.

In the unnatural stillness, Sebastian found that he was alert to any sudden movement. Once a tiny javralat came racing out from an open doorway, making his heart thump in his chest; a short while later, a flock of the big black birds flapped out of an alley, their shrill screeches echoing on the still air.

'What are those things?' he asked.

'Scraws,' said Phelan. 'Carrion birds. They dine on the leftovers that nobody else wants.'

'I know the feeling,' commented Max.

Phelan and Olaf never hesitated: they moved left and right through the maze, ever watchful, ever decisive; and after perhaps an hour of walking, they reached a place where the jungle had invaded the streets to such a degree that roots and vines covered the grey stone like grasping talons. A short distance further on, the last buildings had crumbled into heaps of shapeless stone. Then lush green undergrowth enfolded them and they found themselves walking along a narrow jungle trail.

Sebastian looked back and was astonished to see that after only a few steps, the city was completely lost to view. It occurred to him that a passing traveller would have no idea it even existed. How many people must have come past, unaware of its proximity – and of their lucky escape? He thought about Joseph's visit all those years ago – how fortunate he had been not to linger until nightfall.

Eventually Sebastian's keen ears picked up the sounds of water up ahead. The trail widened out before them and they found themselves standing on the banks of the river. Upriver they could hear the distant sounds of the waterfall, but it was lost to sight round a bend. Sebastian surmised they were a good distance downstream from where they had first come ashore.

'Shadlog's teeth!' he heard Cornelius say, and turning his head, he saw the ark up ahead of them. He could understand Cornelius's concern. The huge craft was resting on a steep slope, its prow pointing hopefully towards the water; but it was held in position by a complex arrangement of poles and struts and braces, all of which had been made from rough timber. That was worrying enough, but even more startling was the fact that the ark looked nothing like the model in Aaron's room. That had been lovingly crafted from smooth, planed wood; the real thing was rather less appealing – a haphazard jumble of logs, branches and rough-hewn planks, all strapped together with jungle vines.

The group approached it, and the closer they got, the more anxious Sebastian became.

'I . . . I'll be honest,' he said, trying to sound diplomatic. 'It's not what I was expecting.'

Max was more blunt. 'It looks like a death trap,' he said.

Phelan scowled. 'I know it's a bit rough and ready. We tried hard to follow Aaron's plans, but . . . well, we only had simple tools and hardly anybody to use them.'

'Has Aaron seen this?' Cornelius asked.

Olaf shook his head. 'Are you kidding? He'd do his nut! But he never leaves his room now and we didn't have the heart to tell him it looks nothing like it's supposed to.'

They had moved into the shadow of the ark's hull. Sebastian could see that the gaps between the planks were plugged with an oily black substance. He pushed an index finger into it and it came away coated with a sticky layer. 'What's this stuff?' he asked.

'It's resin from the beebob tree,' said Phelan. 'Aaron's idea. He reckoned it would keep everything watertight.'

'Hmm.' Cornelius frowned. 'Good thinking, but I don't imagine he meant it to be used quite so liberally.'

'We had to do it that way,' said Olaf defensively. 'It's all right for Aaron, making a scale model with proper tools and everything. It's a bit different when you're hacking away at a tree trunk with a stone axe.'

'I can see that it would be,' admitted Cornelius. 'You've done a brilliant job under the circumstances.'

There was an uncomfortable silence and then Max asked the question they'd all been too polite to ask:

'Do you think this heap will actually float?'

'Well . . .' said Phelan.

'Because it looks to me like it'll just go straight to the bottom of the river.'

'No, it won't,' said Olaf. 'At least, we don't *think* it will.'

'I kind of expected it to be in the water already,' said Sebastian. 'I mean, how do we actually get it into the river?'

'Ah, that's the clever bit,' said Phelan. He led them down the bank to the prow and pointed to the jumble of props beneath the hull. 'We just cut through this one branch here' – he indicated a central prop – 'then the whole lot collapses under it and the ark slides down the bank into the water.'

'That Aaron's idea too?' asked Cornelius.

'Yeah. He says it can't fail.'

'That's right,' agreed Olaf. 'Mind you, it did last time, didn't it?'

Phelan threw the boy an angry glare but it was too late.

'Last time?' cried Sebastian. 'What do you mean, *last time*?'

Phelan looked uncomfortable. 'Well, it's just that this isn't the first ark we've built. There were . . . earlier versions. What Aaron calls . . . prototypes?'

Sebastian and Cornelius exchanged worried looks.

'How many of them?' asked Cornelius.

'This is the third,' said Olaf. 'You know what they say. Third time lucky!'

'Yes,' said Max. 'I believe I've heard several idiots saying that. Would it be too much to enquire what happened to versions one and two?'

Phelan frowned. 'Well, version one . . . we decided to float that one straight away, didn't we, Olaf? And it did float really well . . . for a few days.'

'Luckily we hadn't loaded the treasure into it when it sank,' said Olaf.

'Yes, very fortunate,' said Sebastian. 'And . . . version two?'

'Ah, well, that's when Aaron came up with the idea of this

launch down the riverbank,' Phelan told him. 'Only we must have lifted the prow up too high, see? We got all the treasure loaded into it – took us weeks, it did. We said goodbye to Aaron and everything. Then everyone climbed aboard and I chopped the supporting log away and . . .'

'And what?' growled Cornelius.

'It came down too hard,' said Olaf. 'The whole thing split across the middle. It didn't even slide down towards the river.'

'So then we had to unload all the treasure and take it back to Sanctuary piece by piece,' said Phelan glumly. 'Aaron was very surprised to see us.'

'Still,' said Olaf, 'this time he's sure he's got it all worked out properly. The angles and everything. He says it's now or never, because he hasn't got the strength to give it another go.'

There was another long silence while everyone digested this piece of information.

'Tell me,' said Cornelius at last. 'What did Aaron do before he set off on that expedition to find the lost city? I mean . . . I'm guessing here, but I suppose he was some kind of a teacher – a scholar, something like that.'

Phelan looked at him in surprise. 'Oh no, nothing like that. He was one of those people who go around telling jokes for a living. What do they call them? Oh yes, a jester!'

Sebastian stared at him. 'You are joking?' he said.

'Oh no, I leave the jokes to him – he's a killer when he gets going! Next time you see him you must ask him to tell you the one about the merchant and the pigs. It's a riot!'

Cornelius started to chuckle; a chuckle that quickly developed into a full-blooded roar of laughter. 'A fool!' he cried. 'Sebastian, it looks as though you missed your vocation. You could have turned your hand to designing boats.' He looked at Phelan's puzzled expression. 'Excuse our amusement,' he said, 'but Sebastian here used to be in the same line of work as Aaron.'

'I don't know what you're laughing at,' sighed Max. 'Maybe I'm being picky but I don't much like the idea of trusting my life to a boat designed by a jester.'

'What's wrong with that?' asked Sebastian. 'Just because a man tells jokes for a living it doesn't mean he can't think big thoughts.'

'You've told me some of your thoughts,' said Max. 'None of them are going to give the great philosophers any sleepless nights.'

Cornelius walked back along the ark's hull. 'Let's go and take a look inside this thing,' he suggested. Max started to follow him, but the little warrior turned back and held up a hand. 'Maybe you'd better wait here,' he said. 'If that support snaps, this thing could wind up in the river before it's time to leave.'

'What are you trying to say?' muttered Max indignantly, but he obeyed the order and stayed where he was, watching the others with a gloomy expression. 'If you feel any creaking below you, get out of there fast,' he advised them.

Cornelius found a gangplank and set it against the side of the boat. He and Sebastian walked up onto the deck, closely followed by Phelan and Olaf. Sebastian couldn't help noticing that when the four of them stood close together, the planks sagged dramatically beneath their combined weight.

'Still quite a bit of sap in this wood,' observed Phelan, stamping a boot down hard. 'When everyone's aboard we'll have to make sure that we space ourselves out a bit.'

'You could always put some supporting braces below decks,' suggested Cornelius. 'To take the strain.'

Phelan shook his head. 'I don't think there's room for that,' he said. 'Come and take a look.' He led them through a doorway set into the central wheelhouse. Within, they found a surprisingly spacious enclosure containing bunks and benches, with just enough room for everyone to stretch themselves out to sleep. In the centre, a set of rickety steps led down through an open hatch.

Phelan pointed down them. 'Go and have a look,' he said. Cornelius started to descend and Sebastian followed. It was dark down below, but an ancient oil lamp hung from a hook on the wall. Cornelius found his tinderbox and eventually managed to get the lamp lit. He held it at arm's length to illuminate the hold. As he looked around, he gasped and Sebastian did likewise.

The entire length and breadth of the area was stacked with booty. Now Sebastian understood why Phelan had said that there would be no space for a supporting brace. He was reminded of Captain Callinestra's treasure, a small part of which they had appropriated and ultimately lost in the sinking of the *Marauder*. The children of Sanctuary had clearly decided to leave none of the hoard behind. In the soft glow of the lamplight Sebastian saw the shimmer of gold and precious jewels: crowns and necklaces, open sacks of coins, jewel-encrusted scabbards and beautifully tooled swords. There were statues and paintings and medals and things that Sebastian couldn't easily identify, but it was evident that Aaron had not been exaggerating when he boasted of the wealth stored in the ark. It must have been worth a thousand king's ransoms.

'It looks . . . heavy,' said Sebastian.

Cornelius nodded. 'I'm beginning to appreciate what a responsibility this is,' he murmured. 'Getting those children to Veltan will only be part of the operation. If word got out that they had this kind of fortune at their disposal, there'd be villains queuing up to relieve them of it.' He considered for a moment. 'We'd have to find them a safe place to store it. We might even have to consider making an arrangement with a – a bank.'

Sebastian frowned. 'Are you sure?' he muttered. 'My father used to hate those places – said they weren't to be trusted.'

'With respect, Sebastian, your father might have been prosperous in his heyday but he didn't have this kind of wealth at his disposal. They can hardly keep all this under their mattresses, can they? At any rate, that's something to think about later. First of all, we have to be as sure as we can be that this vessel will actually make it to Veltan.'

'So . . . we're accepting the assignment?'

Cornelius turned back to him and grinned. 'Of course we're accepting it! Sebastian, if we pull this off, we'll be set up for life.'

'And Thaddeus Peel?'

'Oh, sucks to him – we'll sort him out later, if we're in the mood. Come on.'

They turned and made their way back up to the deck, where they found Phelan and Olaf waiting anxiously for them.

'Well?' said Phelan. 'What do you think?'

Cornelius adopted a cool demeanour. 'I have just one question for you,' he said. 'When were you thinking of leaving?'

CHAPTER 25

ONCE A FOOL

'Three days' time?' cried Max. 'Do you think that's a good idea?'

He was reclining on cushions in the corner of the communal room, having just devoured a bucket of fruit that some of the children had procured for him.

Cornelius turned to look at the buffalope. 'Good idea or not, that's when we're leaving,' he said flatly. 'But don't worry, I'm going to spend the time wisely. I'm taking a work party up there every day to make a few improvements of my own.'

'Oh, so now you're an engineer,' observed Max caustically. 'Honestly, there seems to be no end to your talents.'

Cornelius shrugged. 'I'd hardly call myself an engineer,' he said. 'But I can see that it would be a good idea to strengthen the hull and the deck. Any fool could do that.'

Max turned his gaze in Sebastian's direction. 'Well, a fool designed the boat, so anything's possible,' he said.

'What's he on about?' asked Keera, who as ever was at Sebastian's side.

'Hmm?' Cornelius looked at her. 'Oh, nothing,' he said. 'Ignore him, I think he got too much sun today.'

Night had fallen only a little while earlier, and in the big hall the younger children were running around playing one of their boisterous games, the older ones huddled in little groups, talking animatedly or eating bowls of stew taken from the big pot. Salah sat with one group, talking as though she had been doing it all her life. There was a sense of anticipation in the air: word had got around that they would soon be leaving for Veltan. Sebastian wondered how they would cope with their new found wealth and a completely different life in a bustling port – assuming, of course, that they made it there in one piece. A quick head count told him that there were fifteen children in all, including Phelan and Salah, with ages ranging between three summers and fifteen.

Phelan appeared through the door and made a beeline for Sebastian. 'Aaron wishes to speak with you again,' he said; but when Cornelius also started to rise from his seat, the boy shook his head. 'Just Sebastian this time,' he insisted.

'What's it about?' asked Sebastian, but Phelan simply shrugged his thin shoulders and beckoned impatiently. The elfling nodded and followed Phelan out of the room and up the staircase.

The boy led Sebastian to the big doors and pushed them open, but made no move to follow him inside. Sebastian found the old man sitting on his huge golden throne. A more modest chair was set out beside him.

'Ah, Sebastian, thank you for coming,' he said. 'Please, sit beside me for a little while. I would very much like to talk with you.'

Sebastian did as he was asked. 'How are you this evening?' he asked politely.

'I am well,' said Aaron. 'And all the better now Phelan has told me you've decided to accompany the children to Veltan.'

'Yes,' said Sebastian. 'We will undertake your mission. But . . .'

'Yes?' asked Aaron anxiously.

'Well, I wish you'd consider coming with us. I'm sure if we made some kind of stretcher, we could easily carry you down to the ark. And there are bunks inside – we could make you comfortable enough.'

'I've no doubt you could,' agreed Aaron. 'But what would be the point? Even if I survived the journey, I'd have only a very short time in an unfamiliar world. It's different for the children. They are adaptable; they are just starting out. But this room is all I have known for much of my life. I would rather die here, surrounded by the things I love. Besides there's one last thing I wish to do before death claims me.'

'What's that?' asked Sebastian.

'Oh, nothing of importance,' murmured Aaron dismissively. He gazed thoughtfully at Sebastian. 'Phelan told me something interesting about you,' he said. 'It appears we have something in common.'

'Really?' Sebastian was initially puzzled, but then Aaron's meaning became clear to him. 'Oh, you mean that we were both once jesters?'

Aaron chuckled. 'Once a fool, always a fool,' he said.

'Oh, no . . .' Sebastian raised a hand in denial. 'I gave it a try, that's all. My father was in the business – he was quite successful in my neck of the woods. You might have heard of him. Alexander, Prince of Fools?'

Aaron shook his grey head. 'I'm afraid not,' he said.

'Well, no matter. At any rate, he passed away suddenly. My mother and I were starving, so I set out to try and fill his boots. Quite literally. It was the only thing I could think to do. But it was a disaster. Every audience I played to seemed to hate me and nobody ever laughed at my jokes.'

'Oh dear.' Aaron looked genuinely sympathetic. 'And who were these difficult audiences?'

Sebastian thought for a moment and was surprised to arrive at the conclusion he did. 'Actually, it was only one audience; but an important one. A whole bunch of noblemen and women at the court of King Septimus in Keladon.'

Aaron looked as though he couldn't believe his ears. 'So you allowed the reaction of one audience to persuade you that you had no skills as a jester?'

Sebastian nodded. 'Pretty much,' he admitted. 'But you've no idea how bad I was. I was lucky to get out of there alive!'

Aaron considered the matter. 'Let me ask you this, Sebastian. Did you never try performing for the best audience of all?'

'Who would that be?' asked Sebastian, mystified.

'Why, *children*, of course! Children are the finest audience any jester could ask for. They have no preconceptions, they don't worry what the person sitting next to them might think if they laugh. Children are a joy to perform for, and yet they are the true test of any jester's skills.'

'I never performed for children,' Sebastian said.

'Well, then, perhaps you should! You have a captive audience of children downstairs. Let's face it, none of them are going to walk out on you – not if they value their lives. And the nights are so long in this city. When I was younger and still able to drag myself around on crutches, I used to do my old routines for the children here. How they laughed! Those children have grown up and gone now, but there's a whole bunch down there who've never enjoyed a performance by a jester.' An idea seemed to occur to Aaron and his face brightened. He snapped his fingers. 'Yes, of course!' he said. 'Why didn't I think of that? Sebastian, at the back of the room over there you'll find a wardrobe. Go and open it for me, will you?'

Sebastian did as the old man suggested. The wardrobe was an ancient mahogany one with beautiful brass inlays. He opened the door, revealing a selection of simple white robes.

'Look behind the other garments and see what you find,' suggested Aaron.

Sebastian pulled aside the other clothes and found a beautiful jester's outfit in black-and-yellow striped silk. A matching three-pronged hat hung from a hook on the back of the door.

'This is beautiful,' cried Sebastian. 'Yours?'

'Indeed. My old costume. I took it with me everywhere I went – even on an expedition into the jungle: you just never knew when you might need it. Bring it to me, will you?'

Sebastian carried it over, holding it as though it were some holy relic. Aaron smiled and stroked the smooth material with a blue-veined hand. 'Ah, yes, it looks as though it was made yesterday, does it not?'

'It certainly does. This is fine fabric – it must have cost you a fortune.'

'I was lucky enough to have a friend who was a dressmaker. She created this costume for me . . .' Aaron's voice seemed to fail him for a moment and his eyes misted with tears. 'Even after all this time, it hurts to remember that I left her behind,' he said. 'I chose adventure and lost somebody very dear to me. I always imagined that I would return with a fortune in gold and jewels and make her my wife. But of course, things rarely go as you plan them to.'

Sebastian couldn't help thinking of a similar situation of his own: it had been his mother he had left behind. He knew that regular payments of gold crowns were being made to her, but it had been so long since he had seen her. He told himself he must try and find his way back to Jerabim before much longer.

Aaron lifted a hand to wipe away the tears. Then he looked at Sebastian. 'Why don't you try the outfit on?' he said.

'What, *me*? Oh no, I couldn't—'

'Of course you could! It looks about your size.'

'Yes, but . . . I've finished with all that nonsense.'

'Why do you say it's nonsense?' asked Aaron sternly. 'Let me tell you, young man, being funny is a serious business. Please, indulge me. There's a room through there where you can change – and a full-length mirror.'

'Very well.' Sebastian found the small room, stripped off his tattered clothes and pulled on the jester's outfit, which fitted him perfectly – much better than his father's old costume ever had. He settled the hat snugly on his head, then regarded his reflection doubtfully in the mirror. Sure enough, the outfit could have been made for him. He returned to the main room and approached the throne.

Aaron beamed when he saw the transformation. 'It's

perfect,' he said. 'I see now, Sebastian, that it is not chance that has brought you here, but fate. I want you to have that costume.'

'Oh no, I couldn't possibly take it,' protested Sebastian.

'You can and will! If it stays here in this place of death, then it dies with me. If it goes with you, who knows what new adventures may await it? Now' – Aaron clapped his hands together – 'I ask of you one more thing. I want you to go downstairs and perform your act for the children. Let them decide whether you're a jester or not.'

Sebastian stared at him. 'But . . . they might . . .'

'What? Laugh at you? Hopefully, they will. Now go on.'

'But you don't understand. I can't. I'm just not funny. And besides, the jokes . . . I don't—'

'Don't try to tell me you cannot remember your routine,' said Aaron. 'Once committed to memory, it's something you never forget. I should know, even after all these years: it's there at the back of my mind, ready to be recalled at a moment's notice. Go on, your audience is waiting.'

Sebastian sighed. He turned and went downstairs feeling decidedly stupid in the unfamiliar clothing. He hesitated outside the door of the big room, but finally took a deep breath and stepped inside.

The effect was dramatic. The large group of younger children who had been running around yelling suddenly stopped in their tracks to gaze at him; then, lured by the distinctive costume, they stampeded towards him, laughing delightedly and pulling him into the room. The older children soon came over to see what was going on.

At one end of the room was a raised section that might once have been used as a stage. Sebastian was pushed and prodded onto it and the children settled themselves cross-legged around him, gazing up in anticipation. It was strange. They could never have seen a jester, and yet the brightly coloured costume somehow told them that he was about to perform for them.

For a moment he was lost: he didn't know what to do or say. And then some lines from his father's old routine came to him and he launched straight in.

'Two snakes are crawling through the jungle,' he said. 'One of them says, "Hey, are we poisonous?" The second snake says, "I'm not sure, why do you ask?" And the first snake says, "I think I just bit my tongue." '

A few cautious chuckles greeted this joke and some of the children nudged each other. He pressed on.

'Two lupers are eating a jester. One looks at the other one and says, "Hey, does this taste *funny* to you?" '

Bigger laughs this time.

'A guy goes to the doctor and says, "Hey, Doc, I keep thinking I'm a pair of curtains." The doctor says, "Pull yourself together!" Another guy comes in and says, "Doc, I keep waking up and finding myself lying under my bed." The doctor says, "You must be a little potty!" A third guy comes in and says, "Hey, Doc, I keep thinking I'm a bridge." The doctor says, "What's come over you?" The guy says, "Two equines, a buffalope and a hay wagon!" '

The routine was flowing from him like clockwork and he even found himself mimicking his father's little gestures. He delivered every line with increasing confidence; soon the children's laughter threatened to lift the roof off the building. After a little while Sebastian found himself deviating from the established script and starting to improvise.

'So this Night Runner mother is playing with her baby and she says, "Oh, Junior, you've got your father's eyes. Make sure you give them back when you've finished with them!" '

They loved that one – being invited to laugh at the thing they feared most in the world. It got a great response.

'Hey, what do you call a Night Runner in a bell tower? A dead ringer!'

Likewise.

'Did you hear about the polite Night Runner? Every time he met someone, he said, "I'm pleased to eat you!" '

Now the children were literally roaring with laughter and Sebastian was on a roll. When he found a scrap of paper in one pocket, he decided to try the 'Letter from my mother' routine. This was one of his father's finest moments – it had been copied by jesters the length and breadth of the known world.

'I had a letter from my mother back in Jerabim,' he told the children, adopting a serious tone; and then pretended to read from the slip of paper:

'Dear Sebastian, I hope you are well. I'm writing this very slowly – I know you're not a quick reader. You'll see some big changes when you come home because we've moved house. It was your father's idea. Somebody told him that most accidents occur within two miles of home, so he decided we should move.'

The laughter now was coming in waves. Sebastian had to keep pausing to let it die down before he continued.

'The weather here hasn't been too bad. It only rained twice last week – the first time for three days, the second time for four days. It's been so windy, one of our hens laid the same egg four times.'

Roars of laughter filled the room.

'Your brother has an important new job. He has seven hundred men under him. He's cutting the grass at the town cemetery. I am enclosing three socks because you said in your last letter that you'd grown another foot.'

They were screaming with laughter now and Sebastian had to make a real effort not to join in with them.

'Well, son, I must finish up now. Your father's dinner is on the stove and there is a terrible smell coming from your loving mother. P.S. I meant to put ten croats in with this letter but I have already sealed the envelope!'

The audience was in stitches and, encouraged, Sebastian kept going, the jokes spilling out of him in a never-ending stream – old jokes, new jokes, ones he'd just made up. He looked across to the corner where his friends were sitting and saw that Keera, Phelan, Salah and Cornelius were laughing along with everybody else. Even Max looked like he was enjoying himself and Cal's usual sneer had been replaced by a grudging smile.

Inspired, he started improvising jokes about them; jibes about Cornelius's height ('He's so short, he needs turn-ups on his underpants!') and Max's ability to break wind ('He's famous for doing farmyard impressions. Not the noises, just the smells!'). By the time he'd reached the end of the routine, the children were hysterical and the place in uproar. He took a bow at the end and left the stage to the sound of children applauding and yelling for more. As he went to sit with his friends, he seemed to be walking on air; he imagined Aaron up in his throne room, smiling to himself as he heard the sounds of applause drifting up the staircase.

'You were great!' observed Cornelius incredulously as

Sebastian threw himself down on a cushion. 'I can't imagine why you gave it all up.'

'You were so funny!' cried Keera.

But Max looked as though he was about to burst into tears.

'What's wrong with you?' Sebastian asked him.

'Your father would have been so proud, young master. If only he had lived to see that performance. So much better than everyone expected!'

'Thanks,' said Sebastian. 'I think.'

Everybody glanced warily at Cal, expecting some kind of put-down, but he just shrugged his powerful shoulders.

'You were good,' he said; and left it at that.

'I suppose that has to be Aaron's old costume,' observed Cornelius.

Sebastian nodded. 'He gave it to me as a parting gift,' he said. 'You know, I wish he'd agree to come with us. I hate the thought of leaving him all alone here. He said that there was one other thing he needed to do but I can't imagine what that might be.'

All eyes turned to Phelan, but if he knew what that something was, he wasn't telling.

CHAPTER 26

THE DEPARTURE

The next three days passed in a fever of preparation.

Each morning, Cornelius and Sebastian set out with a work party to make their final adjustments to the ark. These consisted mostly of adding extra struts and braces at what Cornelius had determined were 'danger points'. Sebastian had no idea what difference they would make but he bowed to Cornelius's superior knowledge, saying that what he knew about boats could be written on one fingernail. After all, his homeland Jerabim was in the middle of a desert!

Max went along with them to provide muscle, which proved useful when a large gruntag came lumbering out of the undergrowth – to be faced with a buffalope charge. Keera and Salah came along with them one day; Sebastian gave them a guided tour of the treasure in the hold, but it meant very little to the Jilith – they described the precious jewels and gold coins as 'pretty'.

In the evening, safely back at Sanctuary, Sebastian went to spend some time with Aaron. The old man was a fountain of knowledge on just about any subject and Sebastian found his conversation fascinating. It was becoming increasingly hard for him to think about leaving Aaron behind.

Almost before he knew it, it was the eve of their departure and he went up to the throne room one last time. As he pushed open the doors, Phelan came towards him, looking furtive.

'What's going on?' Sebastian asked him.

'Nothing,' he said. 'Just some last-minute business. I'll see you downstairs.' He went out, closing the door behind him.

Sebastian approached the throne and noticed immediately that a few things had changed. Many of Aaron's precious possessions seemed to have been removed – and lengths of jungle vine trailed along the floor, disappearing behind wooden boxes that had been placed strategically around the room. The vines appeared to have been soaked in a sticky black substance, much like the resin used to waterproof the ark.

'What are those for?' asked Sebastian, but Aaron simply made a dismissive gesture.

'Nothing for you to worry about,' he said. 'Just a few arrangements for after you've all departed. Something in the way of a surprise.'

'A surprise for who?' asked Sebastian.

'Ah, now that would be telling! Come and have a seat. As tonight is a special occasion, I have opened a bottle of wine I've been saving.' He indicated a dusty old bottle standing on a table with two golden goblets. 'I used to have quite a collection of fine wines,' he said, 'but over the years it has gradually dwindled away. A few bottles here, a few there – you know how it is. But I always swore that I would not drink this last bottle until my task was complete.'

Sebastian sat down in his usual seat and, filling the goblets with the dark-red liquid, handed one to Aaron. 'What's so special about this wine?' he asked.

'Oh, this one bears King Sesam's crest. This would have been from his very own reserve.'

'Won't it have gone off by now?' asked Sebastian.

Aaron chuckled. 'A fine wine improves with age,' he said. 'Everybody knows that.' They both lifted their goblets and sipped at the contents; then spat it out with a sound of disgust. 'So much for that theory!' spluttered Aaron; and then he laughed delightedly. 'Imagine – all those days and nights I longed to open the ruddy bottle and when I finally do, it tastes like buffalope pee!'

Sebastian laughed too. He liked the old man immensely and enjoyed being in his company. Why wouldn't he agree to accompany them to Veltan?

'Look,' he said. 'About tomorrow . . . Surely there's

some way we can persuade you to change your mind?'

'We've been through this before,' said Aaron, shaking his grey head. 'I'm staying here. I have things to do.'

'What things?' cried Sebastian. 'I mean, please don't take this the wrong way, but you're helpless on your own. Who will bring you food and drink?'

'I shall have no need of it,' Aaron assured him.

'But you'll die.'

'All men must die, Sebastian. And I'm already living on borrowed time. I've had my life. Now I'm more concerned with the youngsters, about making sure they have an opportunity to escape from this awful place. Come . . .' He lifted a waterskin from beside his seat and rinsed out the goblets, then filled them to the brim. 'A toast,' he said. 'And since the fine wine is long past its best, we shall have to make do with water.' He raised his goblet. 'Here's to the children. To their new life in Veltan – and to those who will help make it happen.'

Sebastian drank, and the water tasted surprisingly cool and sweet.

The following morning Sebastian woke at first light to find that he was alone in the small chamber. He grabbed the animal-skin backpack that Keera had made for him, into which he had already folded his jester's outfit. Then he went down to find Cornelius packing his own things for departure; Max was watching him and offering plenty of unwanted advice. Most of the children were awake, throwing their various bits and pieces into their own packs, while Phelan, Salah and Keera wandered around giving instructions.

Max saw Sebastian approaching and gave him a disparaging look. 'Oh, so you're finally up?' he observed. 'Amazing how some people can sleep at the most inappropriate times.'

'I was tired,' Sebastian told him. 'What's for breakfast?'

Cornelius jerked a thumb towards the fireplace, where the usual pot of rusa stew was bubbling aromatically over the flames. 'Same as always,' he said. 'Between you and me, I'm getting a bit sick of that stuff.'

'We've only been eating it a few days,' Sebastian told him. 'These poor kids must have been eating it all their lives. Still, I know what you mean. The first thing I'm going to do when we get to Veltan is order something exotic. You know – something with some spices in it. It's a big port: they're sure to have some fancy restaurants there.'

'I think you may be getting ahead of yourself,' said Cornelius calmly. 'Perhaps you should have said if we get there. As in, *if* the ark doesn't sink and *if* the water dragons don't gobble us up and *if* Aaron's right about there being no more rapids between here and Veltan.'

Max studied the little warrior for a few moments. 'You're a right little ray of sunshine, aren't you?' he said.

Cornelius smiled. 'Coming from you, that's probably quite a compliment.'

A quick breakfast was eaten, mostly in silence. Everybody was aware that this was the big day, their chance to escape from Sanctuary. Nobody was sad to leave the place. It had been their prison for far too long. Instead, there was an atmosphere of rising excitement.

As usual, Keera came over with a bowl of stew for Sebastian – as if he were incapable of serving himself. 'Here,' she said, pressing it into his hands. 'Did you sleep well?'

'Fine, thank you.' Sebastian looked at her thoughtfully. 'Keera, are you positive you want to come with us? I'm sure that Cal and you could make it back to your village if you decided that was the best thing. I'd understand.'

Keera looked insulted. 'I told you before, my place is with you.' She glanced across the room at Cal, who was sitting near the fireplace, wolfing down his own breakfast. 'Cal says that he will come too.'

'Really?' Cornelius seemed none too happy at this news. 'Surely he'd rather head back to his own people. He's fulfilled any obligation he made to us.'

'He says he promised my father he would look after me,' said Keera. 'So he will not abandon me, no matter what happens. I have told him to go back, but he just won't listen.' She looked at Sebastian. 'He is jealous of the two of us.'

'Er . . . um . . . well, there's absolutely no reason why he should be!' protested Sebastian, aware that Cornelius and Max were enjoying his discomfort.

'Of course there is! He knows that you have asked me to be your *mate*.'

'Er ... yes, I've been meaning to have a word with you about that. You see, Keera, where I come from, a mate is just—'

But he was interrupted by a sudden crash. Glancing up in surprise, he saw that Phelan, his meal finished, instead of stacking his clay bowl to be washed as usual, had simply flung it against the nearest wall, smashing it to pieces. For a moment everybody stared at him in silence. Then Salah, who was sitting beside him, grinned and flung her own half-eaten meal against the wall, making a great splash of stew and broken pottery. Suddenly the idea caught on and all the children were throwing their bowls at the wall, the sound of the shattering clay echoing around the empty room.

'What's got into them?' asked Max irritably. 'They're behaving like ... like animals!'

'It's a symbolic gesture,' Sebastian told him. 'It's their way of saying that they're never coming back to this terrible life.'

Max grunted. 'I understand that,' he said. 'But what are they going to eat out of when they're on the ark? Their pockets?'

'He's got a point,' said Cornelius.

Phelan got to his feet and looked around the room. 'It's

almost time,' he announced. 'But first we go to bid farewell to Aaron.'

'Yes,' muttered Max. 'And perhaps you'd like to tell him about the horrible mess you've made with all that broken crockery.'

'It won't matter to him,' said Phelan mysteriously.

All the children shouldered their packs and followed him up the stairs. Sebastian and the others did the same; Sebastian felt particularly awkward when Keera took his hand as if they were sweethearts. Only Cal chose not to accompany them, saying that he had not been invited up before and didn't see why he should bother to go now. Nobody felt like pointing out that he was being rude so they left him to it.

Aaron was sitting on his throne, bidding farewell to the long, respectful queue of children. Sebastian noticed that the old man knew them all by name and had a special last thought to impart to each. He was like a doting grandfather taking leave of his grandchildren.

As they drew nearer to the throne, Sebastian noticed Cornelius gazing thoughtfully at the resin-soaked vines running across the stone floor.

'What *are* those things?' he whispered.

'I'd say they are fuses,' Cornelius muttered. 'And presumably the boxes he has placed around the room are stuffed with explosives, like the thunder-sticks we used in Brigandia.'

Sebastian was horrified. 'But . . . why would he have explosives in here?' he hissed.

Cornelius shrugged. 'Perhaps he's planning to go out with a bang.'

Sebastian would have asked more questions but they were now approaching the throne.

Cornelius stepped up first and bowed to Aaron.

'Ah, Captain Drummel,' said the old man. 'I am putting all my faith and the lives of these children in your capable hands. It is a great responsibility. Please don't let me down.'

'I won't,' Cornelius assured him.

'Good man. I have a parting gift for you.' Aaron reached down by his feet and lifted a small glass lantern. It looked old and battered and there seemed to be no chamber for oil. Aaron placed it carefully in Cornelius's hands. 'The Lantern of Krelt,' he said. 'Now wherever you travel at night, a light shall go with you.'

Cornelius was clearly surprised. 'But surely you must leave this for others who may come to this city?' he reasoned.

Aaron shook his head. 'There will be no place for it when I am gone,' he said. 'Take it with my best wishes, and may good fortune travel with you.'

Cornelius bowed his head and stepped aside. Sebastian, still holding hands with Keera, took his place.

'My good friend the jester,' said Aaron. 'I trust you are a happier man now that you know you can be funny. I have a gift for you also.' He produced an old leather-bound journal, which he pressed into Sebastian's hands. 'As I promised, here is my account of the fateful history of this cursed city. Take it and give it to your Mr Peel with my best wishes. And tell him to heed its warning well.' He studied Keera for a moment. 'And who is this delightful creature?'

'Er . . . oh, this is Keera,' said Sebastian, tucking the note-book carefully into his pack. 'From the village of the Jilith. She's my, er . . .'

'His *mate*,' said Keera, putting as much emphasis on the word as possible.

Aaron nodded approvingly. 'She is a vision,' he said. 'Little wonder you hold onto her so tightly, Sebastian. I sense there may be wedding bells when you get to Veltan . . .'

Keera giggled girlishly and Sebastian felt his face reddening.

'Wedding bells?' he cried. 'Er . . . oh well, there are no plans to . . . to . . .'

But Aaron had now turned his attention to Max. 'And my dear Mr Buffalope,' he said gravely. 'I hope you were not too disappointed to discover that I wasn't a flesh-eating monster!'

Max looked surprised by the remark. 'I can't think what you mean,' he said. 'I was the one who kept telling everyone that you would turn out to be a nice old chap. It was these two who were worried.'

Sebastian and Cornelius gave him looks of sheer disbelief.

'Well,' said Aaron, 'time waits for no man. It only remains for me to bid you all a fond farewell.'

Sebastian leaned closer to whisper, 'Those ropes on the floor . . . Cornelius tells me they're fuses.'

Aaron smiled. 'Does he now? Well, he's an observant fellow, isn't he?'

'But why would you—?'

'Goodbye, Sebastian. And good luck.'

'But, wait, you can't—'

'*Goodbye*, Sebastian.' Aaron's expression was firm. It was clear he would entertain no more talk on the matter.

Sebastian and the others turned to leave. They followed the trail of children down the long flights of stairs, Cal tagging onto the end of the line at the next level.

Max was making very hard work of it, his hooves slipping and sliding every few steps. 'I shan't be sorry to say goodbye to these blooming stairs!' he announced at one point. 'I take my life in my hooves every time I venture down them.'

Finally they reached the ground floor, found the entrance door open and stepped out into the brilliant sunshine. Sebastian was one of the last ones out and he found Phelan waiting for him. He turned to slam the door shut behind him, but Phelan lifted a hand to stop him.

'We're to leave it open,' he said. 'Aaron's orders.'

'What?' Sebastian stared at him. 'But if we do that . . .

tonight, when the sun goes down . . . the Night Runners . . .'
Realization dawned on him. 'Oh,' he said.

'It's his last project,' said Phelan, his voice expressionless.
'We can't kill the Night Runners with swords or spears, but if
they're blown into tiny pieces – even *they* won't be able to
walk around any more. Aaron means to take as many of them
with him as he can. The black powder is his own invention.
It's powerful stuff.'

Sebastian made as if to turn back but Cornelius reached out
a hand and grabbed the hem of his tunic.

'Leave it, Sebastian,' he said. 'It's Aaron's choice. Let him
end it as he sees fit.'

Sebastian sighed. 'It seems such a waste,' he said bleakly.
'That man has a mind like no other. Think of what he could
achieve if he were only to live a little longer.'

'Destroying large numbers of Night Runners may be his
greatest achievement,' said Cornelius. 'At any rate, it's what
he has decided to do and it's not for us to question it.'

Phelan walked up to the head of the column, where he
joined Salah and Olaf. They began to lead the way through
the abandoned city. Phelan and the older children stayed out
in front, while the youngsters walked together in the middle
and the adults brought up the rear. Everyone who could
handle a sword held it out, ready for any trouble.

But for much of the way, trouble seemed to be in short
supply. Phelan cut expertly back and forth through the

streets and alleyways, and apart from the odd flapping flock of scraws, there was no sign of life. After an hour they were well on their way to the river.

Keera kept looking up the column to see if Salah was all right but she was too busy chatting to Phelan to take much notice. 'How quickly that child has changed,' she commented. 'It is as if she has become a woman in the blink of an eye.'

Sebastian smiled. 'She seems very close to Phelan,' he admitted. 'I wonder how Joseph will react when she doesn't come back to him.'

'I don't think he was expecting her to return,' she said. 'He is an old man nearing the end of his days. Sending her on this adventure was his way of telling her to start her own life.'

'And what about your father?' asked Sebastian.

'What about him?'

'Well . . . you *are* going back to him sooner or later . . . aren't you?'

She smiled enigmatically. 'That's really up to you,' she said.

'Oh, but Keera, you know that I already—' He broke off suddenly because a strange thing had just happened. Keera's lovely face had fallen into shadow – yet the sky was cloudless; it was as if the light was somehow beginning to fail. She asked him if everything was all right, but he looked around in dismay. The column had come to a halt and everybody was staring at each other, trying to fathom what was happening.

Then Cornelius gazed up at the sky, holding one hand to shield his eyes. 'Shadlog's breath!' he cried.

Sebastian turned to look and was astonished to see a huge black disc moving across the face of the sun. He had to avert his gaze immediately because the sight threatened to sear itself permanently into his vision. 'What's happening?' he gasped.

Cornelius scowled. 'I've seen something like this once before,' he said, 'as a boy in Golmira. I think it's called an eclipse – when the moon passes across the face of the sun. If this is what I saw then . . .' He looked around decisively. 'Phelan, get moving!' he snapped. 'Fast as you can!'

Phelan didn't waste time asking questions. He quickened his pace and everyone followed. The darkness was gathering by the moment. Sebastian saw that Cornelius was looking anxiously at the buildings around them, and then he sensed, rather than saw, something moving in the shadows. A terrifying sound reached him – a high-pitched giggle that he recognized only too well. It was as though the blood in his veins had suddenly turned to ice.

'RUN!' bellowed Cornelius as the last of the light slipped away and they were plunged into darkness.

CHAPTER 27

RUN FOR YOUR LIVES!

They came scrambling out of every doorway, those gaunt, pale creatures with their flapping cloaks and long bony fingers, and the sound of their frightful cries filled the air. Sebastian saw them coming and, still holding Keera's hand tightly, put his head down and started to run. But he soon realized he couldn't go too quickly: the small children in front of him couldn't run fast and he was in danger of trampling them in his haste.

Without a word, he released Keera's hand and grabbed the nearest child, a little fair-haired girl, tucking her under his arm and running along with her. Keera took the hint and grabbed a tiny boy, and even Cal threw a girl across one brawny shoulder. Max galloped alongside a couple of small children and urged them to scramble up onto his back. Cornelius, hampered by his size, could only shout at the children around him.

'Run!' he roared. 'Run like you've never run before! We have to make it to the—' He broke off with a grunt of surprise as something leaped out of a window and came flapping towards him like a huge bat. He met the attack with a quick swing of his sword and the creature shrieked and tumbled away minus its head.

Sebastian kept up the pace. He was aware of movement on either side of him and held up his sword, ready to fight off any attack. 'How far to the river?' he yelled.

'Not too far!' Phelan shouted back. 'Just keep— Argh!' He stopped to fend off a Night Runner making for Salah. Flailing his sword at it, he sent it tumbling aside.

As they turned down a narrow alleyway, Sebastian glanced back into the darkness and was dimly aware of a series of dark shapes following in their wake, some racing along the ground, others clinging to the walls. He glanced down at the little girl he was carrying. She looked surprisingly calm, as if this was something she encountered every day.

'We'll be fine,' he assured her and she just nodded.

But immediately a Night Runner was lunging down at them; at the last moment Max accelerated and tossed the assailant aside with an almost casual flick of his horns. On his back the two children shouted jubilantly.

'Thanks,' Sebastian cried.

'Don't mention it,' said Max, sounding surprisingly calm.

Sebastian sensed rather than saw something leaping up

behind him and braced himself for an impact; but the creature swooped effortlessly over his head and came down upon a small boy, throwing him forward onto his face. The creature shrieked triumphantly and prepared for the death blow, but in that instant Sebastian saw Cornelius reach into his belt. The little warrior's hand came up and something flashed through the air – something spinning end over end as it sped towards its target. The dagger struck the Night Runner between the shoulderblades with a dull thud, forcing it to release its grip. It leaped aside, leaving the boy sprawled on the ground. Cornelius was there at once, helping him to his feet, and they ran on together.

Sebastian's heart was thudding in his chest and the child under his arm was beginning to feel heavy. He glanced at Keera and saw she was still running beside him, her sword at the ready; then he realized they had reached the place where the stones of the city met the green of the jungle and he began to hope that they might make it to safety.

Perhaps they won't follow us beyond the city, he thought; but it was a vain hope. Still the creatures came on, cackling and gibbering. They followed their quarry out of the city and along the narrow trail that led to the river. Now they were bursting out of the dank vegetation on either side, their white faces staring, their mouths hanging open in anticipation. Sebastian saw Max swing his head hard to one side, flinging two more Night Runners back into the undergrowth. His heart was hammering, his breath laboured, and the child he was carrying felt like a ton weight.

We're not going to make it, he realized desperately. *They'll overrun us, here on the trail.* But then, up ahead, he saw the place where the trail opened out onto the riverbank and there, further to the right, was the great hulking shape of Aaron's ark; they all swerved towards it.

Suddenly there was a flash of light, so bright they thought at first that daylight had returned; the Night Runners stopped in their tracks, shielding their eyes. But then the light turned yellow, and far behind them they heard the great roar of an explosion. The following shock wave seemed to shake the ground beneath them. Turning, Sebastian saw a huge column of fire and smoke billowing up above the tree tops, accompanied by bright orange flames rising high into the sky.

'Aaron!' he cried; and he knew that the old man was gone. A succession of images flashed through his mind: Aaron sitting on his golden throne, lighting a tallow candle as the Night Runners came creeping up the staircases, the dull sound of their feet on the stone steps. He would have waited till the last possible moment, Sebastian thought, until the flapping, groping shapes were all around him and pressing in for the kill . . . and then he would have lit the fuse.

For a few moments everything seemed frozen. The great tower of flame lit up everything with a strange red glow. The Night Runners were all looking back as if they knew exactly what it meant; and then Cornelius rallied the children with a yell.

'To the ark!' he bellowed, and they obeyed without hesitation.

Sebastian was relieved to see that the gangplank was already in position. Phelan ushered Salah onto it. Reluctantly she obeyed him. His friend Olaf stood beside him, sword raised, and now the younger children were all scuttling up, threatening to knock the flimsy wooden board loose. Sebastian helped the little girl he'd been carrying along, then Keera's child and then Cal's.

Now the adults turned at bay: the Night Runners, sensing that they were close to losing their quarry, came on with renewed ferocity. They were fully visible in the red glow and a terrifying sight they made, white faces contorted, fingers clawing at the air. Sebastian pushed Keera towards the gangplank.

'No, not without you!' she yelled.

'You must do as I tell you!' he shouted. 'Please!'

She turned to climb into the ark, but had taken just a few steps when a Night Runner flew straight at her. Cal saw it coming and flung himself in the way. He and the Night Runner collided and went tumbling down the riverbank towards the prow of the ark. Keera hesitated, looking down.

'Keep moving,' Sebastian yelled, and then had to lash his sword at another Night Runner. The curved blade traced a deadly arc and the Night Runner's arms went tumbling to the ground, but it kept on coming till a second swing cleaved it in two at the waist. It struck the earth with a thud and Sebastian was horrified to see that its mouth was still opening and closing.

'Phelan, get aboard!' yelled Cornelius. 'You too, Olaf.'

'But who'll launch the ark?' cried Phelan.

'Will you just do as I say?' roared the little warrior; and the two boys turned and raced up the gangplank. 'Max, you're next!'

Max looked doubtful. 'I'm not sure that thing will take my weight,' he said. He butted a Night Runner clear over the heads of its comrades. 'Maybe I should hang on until last.'

'You go NOW,' cried Cornelius. 'That's an order.'

'Yes, Chief.' Max began to walk up the gangplank, which sagged dramatically beneath his bulk. Under different circumstances it might have looked comical, but Sebastian found himself wondering what would happen if the wood snapped in two.

But soon Max was stepping onto the deck of the ark and turning to look anxiously down at his comrades. Now there were just three men left on the riverbank.

'Sebastian, your turn!' said Cornelius.

'What about Cal?' asked Sebastian. He looked around frantically and saw the big warrior beside the water, struggling with three Night Runners. They had him pinned to the ground and one was kneeling triumphantly on his chest, leaning forward to deliver the death bite.

'NO!' Sebastian didn't hesitate. He ran down the bank and lashed at them with his sword, spilling them left and right. One went somersaulting over Cal's head and crashed into the shallow water. It turned, baring its teeth, preparing to spring straight back at Sebastian; but suddenly a long olive-green snout shot up out of the water. A huge pair of jaws snapped around the Night Runner's waist and dragged it below the surface. Sebastian stared at the ripples on the water, then leaned over to help Cal to his feet; but the big warrior seemed dazed. He stared at Sebastian stupidly.

'Come on!' Sebastian urged him. 'We can still make it to the ark.'

But Cal shook his head and stood there looking at Sebastian, a curious expression on his face.

'What's wrong?' asked Sebastian; and then something slammed into him, knocking him sideways. All at once a Night Runner was sitting astride him. Its arms shot out and its long taloned fingers clamped around Sebastian's wrists, pinning them to the ground. Sebastian struggled to throw the creature off, but then froze as he realized that its features were horribly familiar. It was Galt's face that stared down at him, but the warrior was hideously transformed. His once ruddy cheeks were sunken and white and his beard was matted and filthy. The eyes, though, were unchanged. Galt

opened his mouth – wide, impossibly wide – a mouth that bristled with misshapen yellow teeth and from which a long tongue lolled.

'Galt!' yelled Sebastian. 'No! It's me – your friend!'

He glanced desperately around for Cal but the warrior seemed to have disappeared. He had left Sebastian to his fate!

Galt's head began to descend and Sebastian steeled himself for the impact of those terrible teeth . . . but then there was a flash of light, more pure, more intense than Aaron's explosion – and a shaft of sunlight hit Galt in the face. He threw back his head and bellowed as though he had been run through with a sword. Releasing his grip, he lifted his hands to cover his eyes.

Sebastian stared around in amazement. The light was returning!

Galt scrambled away and ran screaming for cover. Sebastian sat up. A wash of brilliant sunlight was now moving along the riverbank and the Night Runners were retreating before it, covering their eyes and throwing themselves into the densest vegetation. Smoke was rising from their bare skin, and as he watched, one of them blackened like a tree branch and burst into flames.

Sebastian risked a quick glimpse up at the sun and saw that the strange black disc was moving on again; sunlight was now streaming like fire from a crescent-shape beside it.

Grinning delightedly, he turned to look for Cornelius. His friend was still standing at the foot of the gangplank, sword dripping with green gore. His expression was grim and he was gazing at something further down the riverbank. Sebastian turned his head to look.

Cal stood near the water's edge, one hand resting against the hull of the ark as if he was too weak to stand. He turned to face Sebastian, who was shocked to see how pale he looked. The warrior motioned to him.

'Get aboard,' he shouted, and his voice sounded hoarse. 'I'll cut through the supports.'

'But, Cal, we can still—' Sebastian's words died on his lips as he saw the bite mark on Cal's muscular shoulder; there was a trail of fresh blood. Crimson blood. Sebastian felt as if someone had punched him in the chest. 'No . . . wait,' he gasped. 'Maybe we can—'

Cal shook his head impatiently. 'Get aboard,' he said again. 'Quickly. I can't stand this light much longer.'

Sebastian looked helplessly at Cornelius. 'There must be something we can do,' he said.

'There is,' the little warrior murmured. 'We must do as he says. Come on.' And he turned and walked up the gangplank.

Sebastian got to his feet. He looked at Cal and searched desperately for the right words. 'I'm so sorry,' he said. It sounded weak and pathetic, but it was all he could think of.

'Me too,' growled Cal. 'Now I won't have the chance to

settle things with you as I promised.' Sebastian could see that Cal's eyes were streaming with tears. It clearly required all his effort to keep them open. 'Now,' he croaked, 'for the last time, get into the ark before it's too late.'

There was nothing more Sebastian could say. He turned, climbed the gangplank and stepped aboard. He found all the others waiting for him. Keera came forward, a look of concern on her pretty face.

'What's wrong?' she whispered.

Sebastian sighed. 'It's Cal,' he said. 'He's been bitten.'

She stepped up to the rail and stared down at Cal. He gazed back up at her in silence for a moment; tears spilled down his dirty face. The sound of the rippling water seemed loud in the silence that followed. Then Cal turned to look at Sebastian.

'Look after her!' he said; and he stepped towards the prow, his sword clasped in one huge hand. He studied the haphazard assembly of struts that held the ark in position and looked up, his face contorted in agony.

'May Okrin go with you!' he cried; and raising the sword, he swung it down hard against the wood, slicing clean through the main support. He stepped back quickly. The struts fell away and went rolling down the bank towards the river. For a long time nothing happened.

'So much for that idea,' said Max bleakly.

Everyone looked at each other. Then something occurred to

Sebastian: they were all still grouped together in the stern.

'Move to the prow!' he shouted, and everyone ran to obey him – everyone except Max. Sebastian glanced back at him. 'Come on!' he yelled. 'We need you!'

'Oh, it's nice to be wanted for a change,' said Max haughtily. 'Let's face it, this is another thinly veiled comment about my weight, isn't it?'

Cornelius glared at him. 'Just move, you great bag of wind!' he bellowed.

'Charming.' Max took a step forward. Then another. The ark began to creak alarmingly.

'Keep going,' said Sebastian. 'I think . . . I think it's working!'

Max snorted, but kept on going until he reached the prow. He stood there, looking around. 'Any more bright ideas?' he asked.

And suddenly there was a grinding sound and the prow dropped towards the riverbank. The ark thudded down with a force that threatened to smash it in two. For a moment it just sat there, prow pointing hopelessly towards the water, seemingly stuck fast . . . but then it began to slide – slowly at first but with increasing speed – towards the river. The bows ploughed into the water, throwing up a great wave, and Sebastian gripped the rail, fearing that it would just keep going down into the lair of the water dragons . . . But no, thankfully the prow rose and levelled out. The ark slid silently across the surface of the water, heading for mid-stream.

A great cheer went up from the children and arms were raised defiantly in the air.

'Yes!' gasped Cornelius. 'Aaron, you were a ruddy genius!' He hurried back towards the wheelhouse, beckoning to the children to follow him.

Sebastian went back to the stern and saw the riverbank slipping quickly past. Cal stood staring hopelessly after them. As Sebastian watched, he lifted one hand to wave. Then he started wading into the shallows.

Sebastian gasped. The water dragons! He was about to shout a warning but then he realized that Cal knew exactly what he was doing. He did not want to face an eternity of roaming the streets of that awful city. He wanted the water dragons to take him. Sebastian turned away, unable to look; when he finally glanced back, there was no sign of Cal. Sebastian shook his head, trying to dispel the horror of what had just happened.

He turned to see Keera coming back to stand beside him. She looked enquiringly at their launching place.

'What happened to Cal?' she asked him.

Sebastian could not look at her. 'He went back into the jungle,' he told her.

She nodded. 'Perhaps he'll be all right,' she reasoned. 'Perhaps the bite wasn't too serious. Most likely he'll make his way back to the village and Danthus will be able to take care of him.'

'Most likely,' he said; but he knew that she didn't believe what she was saying any more than he did. It was just something to make her feel better and he wasn't going to deny her that comfort.

They didn't say anything for quite some time after that. The ark was now heading downstream and began to pick up speed as the current took it.

Cornelius and Max came back to join them.

'Phelan's taken over at the wheel,' said Cornelius. 'And we're staying afloat. That's as much as we can hope for at this point.'

'Frankly, I'm amazed,' said Max. 'I thought this thing would go down like a barrel of stones.'

Cornelius smiled. 'Perhaps Aaron was not such a fool after all,' he said.

Max gave him a withering look. 'We've still got a good distance to go to Veltan,' he reminded them. 'Don't be jinxing us by saying rash things.'

'We'll just have to stay optimistic,' Sebastian said; but he was thinking of Aaron – the man who had spent much of his life devising this escape plan but had not lived to see the moment when his great project finally came to fruition. Sebastian hoped that wherever he was now he knew that all his work had finally paid off.

CHAPTER 28

THE VOYAGE

Darkness fell around them and still the ark drifted on, its prow pointing stubbornly down river. The younger children got themselves settled on the animal skins and woven blankets that had been placed in the wheelhouse. Cornelius fetched his backpack and carefully took out the Lantern of Krelt.

'Thank goodness it wasn't damaged,' he said.

All eyes turned towards it, and suddenly, magically, it lit up, flooding the wheelhouse with a clear bright light.

'Amazing,' whispered Sebastian.

'Incredible,' added Cornelius.

'What's the big deal?' asked Max. 'It's only an old lamp.'

Sebastian glared at him. 'A lamp that never needs refuelling,' he said. 'A lamp that has burned every night for thousands of years.'

'All right, keep your hair on! I just think you humans are easily impressed, that's all. A magical barrel of pommers that keeps replenishing itself – now that would be something worth having.'

'It's funny how your idea of something wonderful always involves food,' observed Sebastian.

He felt a tug at his sleeve and, looking down, saw the little blonde girl he had carried to safety. She was gazing up at him, her face serious.

'Hello, Chosen One,' she said. 'I'm Ellan.'

'Hello, Ellan,' he said. 'You can call me Sebastian if you like.'

She nodded. 'Thank you for saving my life,' she said.

Sebastian's heart seemed to melt within him. He crouched down to the same level as her. 'You are more than welcome,' he told her. She put her arms around him and gave him a fierce hug, then went off to find herself a place to sleep. Sebastian stood up again. 'Isn't that cute?' he said.

Max was unimpressed. 'I carried two of them and neither have been round to thank *me*,' he muttered.

'I'm sure they're both very grateful,' said Cornelius. 'I'd better take the lantern and have a look in the hold – make sure we aren't springing any leaks.'

'Isn't there a hurricane lamp down there?' asked Sebastian.

'There is, but I'm nervous crawling around in the hold with something that could start a fire at any moment.'

'Good point,' said Sebastian. 'Be careful with the Lantern of Krelt, though. Whatever you do, don't drop it. It's probably the only one like it in the known world.'

Cornelius went down the steps, taking the light with him.

'Don't worry about us!' Max called after him. 'We're quite happy to stand around in the dark.'

Cornelius's voice drifted up from below. 'Well, I could skip this inspection,' he said. 'But if we sink in the middle of the night, don't blame me.'

'No, you carry on,' said Max hastily. 'Have a really good look.'

Sebastian felt another tug at his sleeve and turned, thinking that the little girl had come back. But it was Keera; her face was very grave.

'Can we talk?' she asked him. She nodded towards the doorway. 'Outside,' she added.

'Of course.' Puzzled, he followed her back to the stern. It was a calm, still evening and exotic jungle fragrances drifted on the air. A full moon rode serenely in the sky, reflected in the gently rippling water. Sebastian looked at Keera and was alarmed to see that her eyes were wet with tears. 'What's the matter?' he asked her.

'It's Cal,' she said. 'I can't stop thinking about him.'

He nodded. 'It was awful, what happened,' he admitted. 'But there was nothing else we could have done. We couldn't bring him with us. The bite, he—'

'I know that,' she said. 'But I feel guilty. He cared so much for me, Sebastian. He wouldn't have been bitten at all if he hadn't got in the way of the creature that was attacking me. And yet I treated him horribly because I was blinded by my feelings for you.'

Sebastian frowned. He realized that this was all true enough, but he just said, 'People can't help the way they feel.'

She nodded. 'I've been thinking about this very carefully,' she told him. 'And . . . well, I'm sorry to tell you that I cannot be your mate any more.'

He stared at her and then realized that she was using the word in the Jilith sense. For a moment he nearly punched the air in relief, but stopped himself just in time. 'Umm . . . oh,' he said. 'I see. Why . . . ?'

'Because I cannot betray Cal's memory,' she told him. 'He gave his life for me. He made the ultimate sacrifice. Now he rests in the arms of Okrin and I must honour him as a true warrior.' She gazed up at Sebastian; her face was enchanting in the moonlight. 'I understand how disappointed you must be . . .'

'Oh yes, I should say so! But, I'll . . . I'll try and live with it, obviously.'

'If you want me to go away, I will jump off this boat right now,' Keera offered. 'I will swim to shore and make my way back to my village . . .' She made for the rail but Sebastian grabbed her arm.

'NO!' he said. 'Er . . . no, I don't want that. This thing about mates . . . well . . . where I come from, it has a different meaning.'

'It does?' She turned back to look at him.

'Yes. In my world a mate is somebody you just *like*. You know – you talk with them, hang around with them, maybe eat or drink together. You . . . you tell each other jokes. Maybe . . . maybe we could have that kind of friendship?'

She considered for a moment and then shrugged her shoulders. 'This would be enough for you?' she asked.

'Oh, yes, I think so. And I'm sure it would be more agreeable to Jenna.'

'Ah, the captain woman! Your wife.'

'She's not my wife,' said Sebastian hastily. 'But we're . . . close.'

Keera smiled sadly. 'So now I won't have to fight her for you?'

'No,' said Sebastian. 'I think it's all for the best.'

She nodded. 'I'm glad we settled this,' she said. 'And I think Cal will rest happier too.' She reached up and gave Sebastian a kiss on the cheek. 'This is permitted between your kind of mates?' she asked him.

'Oh yes,' he said, smiling. 'That's no problem.'

The wheelhouse suddenly filled with light and the lamp came bobbing out of the doorway. Cornelius made his way towards them, his face unusually anxious.

'Everything all right?' Sebastian asked him.

'Not exactly,' said Cornelius. 'I've just finished inspecting the hold. I'm afraid we're taking on water.'

CHAPTER 29

THE PORT OF VELTAN

Four days later, the ark, listing dramatically to starboard but still just about staying afloat, rounded the final bend in the river. Sebastian, standing in the prow, was delighted and relieved to see the bustling port of Veltan waiting up ahead of them. Beyond it, the river mouth opened out into the vastness of the open sea.

'Cornelius!' he yelled, and the little warrior came scrambling out of the wheelhouse to join him, followed by a small crowd of cheering children. Everybody started to hug each other in delight.

'Now there's a sight for sore eyes,' cried Cornelius. 'I was beginning to think we might not make it.'

It had been a nightmarish four days and three nights, during which everyone had had to work in shifts, baling out with whatever came to hand – buckets, goblets, ladles, all had been put to use and everybody pushed to the very edge of exhaustion. But now it looked as though their worries were finally over and they could celebrate their amazing escape from the city of Chagwalla.

Ships of various sizes rode at anchor alongside a huge wooden jetty. They ranged from humble fishing boats to great three-masted schooners, their mighty sails furled. On and around them, legions of men and women moved to and fro, packing or unpacking their cargoes. As the ark drew nearer, Sebastian saw that many small dwellings were clustered along the harbour front. Beyond them, a mighty city rose up on a steep hillside – scores of whitewashed buildings, huddled together as if for safety. Here and there were more opulent palaces with great golden domes, marble spires and turquoise minarets. There was clearly much wealth in Veltan and, Sebastian mused, there would be a good deal more once the contents of the ark's hold was unloaded.

'There's an empty berth right there,' said Cornelius, pointing to a place between two majestic ships. He turned and gestured into the wheelhouse, where Olaf was currently piloting the ark to its final destination. 'Max is going to be so disappointed,' the little warrior observed. 'For the last two days, he's been announcing to anyone who'd listen that we were doomed!'

Sebastian grinned. 'Where is he, anyway?' he asked.

'He's having a lie-down. Said he was feeling seasick again.'

Sebastian shook his head. 'I didn't realize you could get seasick on a river,' he said.

'Probably just an excuse to take another nap,' said Cornelius. 'Actually, I'm glad of the silence.' He thought for a moment. 'We'll have to play this right. We can't let everyone go tearing off into the city or our treasure will be looted before you can say Shadlog's trousers. I think it's best if you all stay here and keep an eye on it. I'll nip into Veltan and find the right people to escort it up to a bank.'

Sebastian looked doubtful. 'You sure that's the best thing to do?'

'Absolutely. Well, it's like I said before: that much treasure needs to be stored in a vault. You can't just throw it in a heap and hope for the best. And some of these children are too young to know what to do with it. There will be other things to sort out – somewhere for them to stay and so forth. They won't want to be split up after spending all their lives together so we'll need to find a big property, somewhere with plenty of rooms . . .' Cornelius looked up at him. 'Of course, if you'd rather head into town and sort it all out, I don't mind staying with the ship.'

'Oh no, you go ahead – you're better at that kind of thing. Besides, I want to ask around, see if anybody has seen anything of Jenna. Oh, I hope she's still here! Hey, supposing she is? Won't she get a surprise!'

'Yes, particularly when she claps eyes on Keera.'

Sebastian shrugged. 'Oh, it's not going to be quite so bad now. At least she's just a mate – and I mean that in *our* sense of the word. It would have been a great deal more awkward if Keera still thought she was my second wife.'

Cornelius laughed. 'What a complicated life you lead, Sebastian!' he observed. 'I thank my lucky stars the ladies never seem to find me as appealing as they do you!' He hurried back to the wheelhouse to advise Olaf on mooring the ark. Sebastian stayed where he was, staring at the approaching jetty. This place reminded him of Ramalat – it had the same urgency about it, as though everybody had a job to do and needed to get it done as quickly as possible. He scanned the ships around him but couldn't see one that looked like the *Sea Witch*.

He heard the clump of hooves behind him and turned to see Max looking dolefully at the approaching port.

'We made it then,' he said, seeming to take absolutely no pleasure in the fact. 'And there was me thinking we'd have to swim the last few leagues.'

Sebastian shook his head. 'How did you ever come to be such a misery-guts?' he asked.

'I had a hard life,' said Max, 'when I was young.'

'Really. Well, it seems to me the hard times are finally over. Once we sort out all that treasure in the hold, we'll be rich. Think of it, Max! There'll be no reason to ever go adventuring again.'

Max sighed. 'Now why do I find that so hard to believe?' he asked.

The ark nosed slowly towards the jetty and then swung round to lie alongside. Sebastian picked up a mooring rope and flung it to a man who had appeared on the quayside and addressed them.

'Avast there,' he said. 'The harbourmaster will be with you presently.' He wrapped the rope expertly round a mooring post.

'Er . . . oh, arrrh!' said Sebastian, trying to sound suitably nautical. 'Er . . . avast yourself . . . shipmate!'

The man gave him a puzzled look and walked off.

Cornelius and Keera appeared on deck; the children followed, chatting excitedly as they gazed in wide-eyed wonder at the city that lay before them. They flocked up to the bows and watched in awe as Cornelius jumped nimbly onto the jetty. He looked up at them. 'Now,' he said, his expression stern. 'Nobody leaves the ark until I get back, understand? I want you all to keep an eye on what's below decks. And don't forget to keep baling out that water. We haven't come all this way only to sink in the shallows! I'll return presently with some wagons and an armed escort.'

'Don't be too long,' Phelan called down. 'We want to see the wonders of Veltan, don't we, Salah?'

'Yes. I can't wait to see the k-k-king's palace!' she said.

'All in good time,' Cornelius assured them. 'First we have to make the necessary arrangements.'

Sebastian leaned over the rail. 'I was thinking,' he said. 'What do we do about Thaddeus Peel?'

Cornelius smiled. 'Let him stew. Right now, we have bigger fish to fry. When we next find ourselves in Ramalat, we'll look him up, if only to give him Aaron's journal. If that doesn't put him off sending another expedition, nothing will. And of course, we'll tell him that there's not a bit of treasure left in the place.' He tapped the hull of the ark with his knuckles. 'We won't mention that it was us who brought it out of there! Anyway, I'll be back shortly.' He turned and strode away along the jetty.

Keera studied the huge city with evident trepidation. 'It looks so big,' she said. 'And there are so many people!' She turned her gaze towards the vast sea beyond. 'And that must be the thing you spoke of. The ocean.'

'Yes,' said Sebastian. 'But don't worry, we've no reason to venture out there. I plan to make only one more sea journey, to Ramalat – hopefully in Jenna's ship.' He glanced up and saw that a couple of smaller children were already trying to clamber over the side. 'Stop that,' he told them. 'You heard Cornelius – we must wait until he returns.'

Phelan and Salah stepped forward and pulled the children safely back onto the deck. Now that they had arrived safely, everybody seemed to be revelling in a new sense of freedom.

There was an air of wild excitement and Sebastian could only wonder what they would be like once they stepped ashore.

'You cannot blame them for wanting to stretch their legs,' said Keera. 'They have spent so many nights behind locked doors.' She looked at Sebastian. 'You are troubled?'

Sebastian frowned. 'I can't seem to shake the feeling that it's all been too easy,' he said.

'Easy?' She was puzzled. 'I wouldn't say getting here has been *easy*. If I'd had to bale out one more pan of water, I would have screamed!'

'That's not what I mean. I'm just talking about the last leg of the trip. Aaron said there would be no rapids and, sure enough, there were no rapids. Max said the ark would sink, but it didn't sink. In my experience, if things *can* go wrong, they generally *do*. I hate to sound like Max, but how come we've arrived in one piece with no major problems?'

Keera smiled. 'Why can't you just accept that everything is fine?'

'Because I—'

'Ahoy there!' said a deep voice, and Sebastian glanced down to see a man striding towards him – a heavy-set man wearing a tricorn hat, red frock coat decorated with gold braid, and highly polished shoes decorated with silver buckles. He had a jolly red face and a bulbous nose. 'I'm Rollo Tandy,' he announced proudly. 'Grand Harbourmaster of Veltan.'

'Oh, and I'm Sebastian Darke, Prince of Fools,' said

Sebastian, without thinking. 'Er . . . I mean, Prince of Pirates . . . er, Explorers . . . I'm Sebastian Darke,' he finished lamely. 'Pleased to meet you.'

Rollo Tandy ran a doubtful eye over the badly listing ark. 'I must say we get all kinds of craft in this harbour, but that's a new one on me. Build it yerself, did yer?'

'Umm . . . no, this was built by these children, under the direction of a brilliant man called Aaron . . .' Sebastian realized that he had never learned Aaron's second name. 'It was designed as a rescue boat. They have lived in the jungle all their lives and now we have brought them to civilization.'

'Very noble of you, I'm sure!' said Rollo. 'Well, you've brought them to the right place. And let me tell you, there's no finer port in the known world than the great city of Veltan. May I enquire what is your cargo?'

'Well, it's just their . . . their possessions, really,' said Sebastian. It was vague but it wasn't really a lie. 'Their . . . various bits and pieces. They are orphans. My friends and I found them in a lost city in the jungle of Mendip.'

'Really?' Rollo looked very interested at this news. 'Ever since I was a boy I've heard stories about a fabulous lost city in the jungle. Is this the place you speak of?'

'It may be. But I would advise you to forget I ever mentioned it. It is a terrible place, sir, filled with creatures from your worst nightmares; a fate worse than death awaits anyone who is foolish enough to go there.'

'And he calls *me* a misery,' muttered Max.

'Do you require help off-loading your cargo?' asked Rollo.

'Er . . . no, my friend has gone into Veltan to make the arrangements.'

'Very well. If you would just like to step ashore and sign the necessary papers; and of course there's the little matter of the mooring fee.'

'The . . . what?'

'The mooring fee. Two gold crowns. That must be paid, young sir, otherwise the craft and its cargo become property of the King of Veltan.'

'Oh, er . . .' For a moment Sebastian panicked. He had no money at all with him. But then he felt Phelan push something into his hand, and when he looked down, he had two golden coins in it. 'That's no problem,' he said brightly. He climbed over the rail and jumped down onto the jetty. 'Phelan, you're in charge till I return,' he announced over his shoulder.

He followed Rollo along the jetty to a small wooden office. They went inside and the harbourmaster sat down at a finely carved desk, its surface covered in charts and scrolls.

'Now, take a seat, young sir, while I search out the relevant documents,' he said.

Sebastian dropped into a seat opposite him and took a look around the interior of the hut, which was crammed with all kinds of nautical equipment. There were ancient maps tacked to the wall, lanterns hanging from hooks, stuffed parrots perched on a branch – and even a dusty pile of wooden legs. And then Sebastian saw something else. Something he recognized. Propped up in one corner of the hut was the figurehead from a ship – a battered life-size image of a woman with long hair streaming out behind her. The woman's nose had been sliced off and one cheek flattened.

For a moment Sebastian couldn't remember where he'd seen it before, but then it came to him. 'The *Sea Witch*!' he cried delightedly.

Rollo glanced up from his papers and turned to look at the figurehead. 'You . . . recognize that, young sir?'

'Of course I do. That's Jenna's ship. Jenna Swift, a captain out of Ramalat. Does this mean that she's still—?'

He broke off, perplexed by the expression on Rollo's previously jolly face. 'Is something wrong?' he asked.

Rollo stared at him forlornly. 'She was . . . dear to you?' he asked quietly.

'Yes, she . . .' Sebastian was experiencing a terrible sinking sensation in the pit of his stomach. 'Why do you look at me like that?' he asked. 'Has . . . has something happened to Jenna?'

The harbourmaster sighed. 'I met her only the one time,' he said. 'She seemed a most remarkable young woman. And the boy who sailed with her – the one everyone called The Kid – he was a bright spark, that one! She came in with a cargo of cloth, maybe one moon ago. Said she was eager to get back to Ramalat and meet up with her young fellow . . .' He gazed sadly at Sebastian again. 'There were storm warnings. I advised her to wait a few days, let them blow over, but she was fearless! Told me that she would face any storm to clip a few days off her journey. Said her love would keep her safe.' Rollo's big shoulders slumped. 'The wreckage started coming ashore five days ago. The figurehead was the last thing we found, just down the coast from here. We put out boats to have a look for any survivors but we found nothing. I'm sorry, lad.'

Sebastian sat there, gazing across the paper-strewn desk. He was aware of a pain in his hand and, glancing down, saw that he had been gripping the gold crowns so tightly, a trickle of blood was flowing from his palm. He opened his mouth to speak, but nothing came out.

'Believe me, if I thought there was any hope, those rescue boats would be out there still. But we searched for days and found nothing but wreckage. They couldn't have survived out there. The—'

'No!' The single word was a croak. 'She . . . she can't be dead. Not Jenna. She . . . she only went for a short while. Needed the money, you see. Some crazy treasure-seeking adventure we had, but . . . we lost it all. Every last bit of it ended up at the bottom of the ocean . . .' Sebastian was still staring at his hand, the rivulet of blood trickling down his arm now. But then the hand seemed to blur as tears filled his eyes. 'She . . . she might have got to shore,' he said. 'Don't you think?'

Rollo shook his head. 'I'm sorry, lad,' he said. 'They would have been out in the open sea. I did try to warn her. She was headstrong, that one.' He waved a hand dismissively at the paperwork. 'Forget this for now,' he said. 'We can do it later. You need to have a bit of time to yourself.'

Sebastian nodded. He swallowed hard and got to his feet. His legs seemed to have lost all their strength and he had to put out an arm to support himself against the doorframe as he left the hut.

Across the jetty, in the ark, there was still an air of celebration. The children were laughing and calling out to each other; but they fell silent when they saw Sebastian walking slowly and carefully back to them. He was trying in vain to hold back the tears. He clambered up the gangplank and saw Max's mournful face looking at him.

'Young master?' he said. 'Whatever's wrong?'

'Jenna . . .' he croaked; and couldn't find any more words. He pushed past the others and went to sit in the wheelhouse, his back to the door. Alone in the silence, he felt his grief sweep through him like a dark tide and could no longer hold back the tears.

EPILOGUE

The days passed agreeably enough. In the afternoons the big house rang to the sound of children's laughter. Cornelius had found them a perfect home a short ride from the city; it was surrounded by gently rolling meadows, dotted here and there with tall, graceful trees.

In the afternoons Sebastian liked to go out to the big paddock and chat with Max, who had grown sleek and fat on a steady diet of his favourite fruits and grains. Money was no object now and they wanted for nothing. Whatever they needed could be obtained from the merchants in Veltan, and whenever gold crowns were in short supply, it only required a trip to the bank, where those who oversaw the vast fortune that had been brought from Sanctuary were happy to dispense bags of gold coins as if they were no more valuable than the packets of sweets the children loved to buy from the city markets.

Sebastian and Keera had been cast as parents to an extended family of children who ran and played and sometimes argued in the big empty rooms of a mansion house that had once belonged to a prosperous oil merchant. Cornelius was the wise uncle who visited sometimes and kept a small room to himself, up on the top floor. He was still travelling here and there, pursuing his various schemes. Though now a rich man, he was never happy to sit still.

Sebastian could not say that he was happy either. He was able to put on a reasonable show, but he knew that he was just going through the motions, ticking off the days as they slipped slowly by. He was pleasant enough to Keera, though he knew that she could never be anything more than a friend. She seemed to have accepted that, just as she had accepted the fact that she would never see her village again. Somehow, that all seemed so far away and long ago. But she seemed to enjoy her role as housemother to the children, and they in turn adored her. She had made friends with some of the ladies who lived in neighbouring properties and they were teaching her to act in a manner that befitted a prosperous lady of Veltan. One day, Sebastian thought, she would notice one of the many young men who cast admiring glances at her whenever she travelled into the city to do her shopping; a romance would inevitably follow. Of course, he would do nothing to oppose it. He had loved two women in his life, both of them lost to him for very different reasons.

He could not make himself love Keera, no matter how pretty she was; and even if one day his feelings changed, the death of Cal would always be there to drive a wedge between them.

After he and Max had talked, Sebastian would walk across the meadows to a spot where he could look down over the cliffs to the ever-restless ocean. Sometimes he would sit there for hours, watching intently, thinking that he might see a small boat making its way back to shore, but he never saw anything like that; and besides, Rollo Tandy had promised to send a messenger if ever any word came about Jenna or The Kid.

But there was no word; and the passing days lengthened into moons and the seasons turned, now swelteringly hot, now cool and breezy, now dark with restless clouds that threw down rods of chill rain at the shivering earth.

One afternoon Sebastian left the big, echoing house and walked down to the meadow. He found Max waiting for him at the gate, his great mournful face staring as if in silent accusation.

'I'm ruddy well bored,' Max said.

Sebastian nodded. 'Me too,' he admitted.

'It's all right being rich for a while,' explained Max, 'but then you start to wish for a few hardships.'

Sebastian looked at him. 'Whatever do you mean?'

'I mean, I've got nothing to moan about,' said Max. 'I

suppose I could moan about having nothing to moan about, but that doesn't really work for me. I mean, what's life for if you can't have a good moan?'

Sebastian rubbed the buffalope's head affectionately. 'I thought this was what you wanted,' he said. 'The chance to take it easy.'

'I thought so too. But now I find myself thinking back to the adventures we've had, and yes, there were uncomfortable moments, and yes, we didn't always get what we wanted to eat, but by golly, we made our mark upon the world, didn't we?'

Sebastian smiled. 'We did,' he agreed.

'And that's the first time I've seen you smile since we arrived in Veltan,' added Max.

'Is it? Well . . . perhaps I'm beginning to accept what happened.'

'Hmm. That why you go out every day and stare at the sea? I know what you're looking for, young master, but you have to accept that Jenna's gone.'

'I know,' said Sebastian. 'You don't have to remind me.' He lifted his head and gazed across the rolling meadows. On the horizon he noticed something unusual against the clear blue sky. A distant cloud of dust.

Max saw what he was looking at. 'Something coming,' he observed. He paused for a moment. 'Something coming fast.'

Hope started to rise in Sebastian's chest. He knew it was ridiculous, but somehow he couldn't help himself.

He imagined a breathless messenger, leaping down from his horse to announce that a miracle had occurred. A longboat had drifted into the harbour, and in that longboat, two half-starved figures, barely conscious but needing only food and water to bring them back from the brink of death . . .

But after a while he could see that it was Cornelius on his dwarf pony, galloping towards them as if his very life depended on it. And surely Cornelius would not be bringing such news? And yet the speed at which he was riding! He was hunched low in the saddle, urging the pony forward as if this were a matter of life and death; now he was close enough for Sebastian to see the grim expression on his face.

He crossed the intervening space in moments and reined the pony in hard, making it rear up on its hind legs. He stared at Sebastian and Max and they could not remember ever seeing him look so tormented.

'What is it?' asked Sebastian. 'Cornelius, what's wrong?'

'I have come to say farewell. I leave for Ramalat on the morning tide.'

'You're leaving?' asked Max. 'But . . . why?'

'A message has found its way to me,' said Cornelius. 'From my parents in Golmira. They are in trouble and they need my help. I do not know how long ago it was sent, but of course I must go to them.'

'Golmira?' mused Max. 'The frozen north. That would be a long journey. A journey full of terrible hardships.'

He and Sebastian exchanged glances. Sebastian gave Max a questioning look and he nodded his horned head.

'You'll need to book two more places aboard the ship,' Sebastian told Cornelius.

The little warrior looked at them in surprise. 'Oh, but . . . I didn't come to ask you to go with me. I only came to say farewell.'

'And we couldn't let you go on your own,' said Sebastian. 'What kind of friends would we be if we did that?'

Cornelius stared at them in silence for a moment. 'I won't pretend that I couldn't *use* some help,' he admitted. 'But . . . what about Keera? And the children?'

'They have everything they need,' said Sebastian. 'And they will still be here when we come back.'

'*If* we come back,' Max corrected him.

'Yes,' agreed Sebastian. '*If* we come back.'

Cornelius nodded. 'Are you sure?'

'Of course we're sure,' said Max. 'Now, get going and book those places before we change our minds. And be sure and tell the captain that he needs to think about bringing suitable food for a buffalope.'

A brief smile crossed Cornelius's face. 'Thank you,' he said. 'A man could not ask for better friends.' He reined the pony round and galloped off across the meadow again. Sebastian and Max watched in silence until he had dwindled to a tiny speck in the distance.

'I expect we'll live to regret this,' said Max.

'I'm sure we will,' said Sebastian. 'Now, make sure you eat your fill of pommers tonight. They might be the last you'll have for quite some time. I'll see you just before dawn.'

'I can hardly wait,' said Max. He plunged his head into a bucket of fruit and started chomping away for all he was worth.

Sebastian turned away and, whistling tunelessly to himself, walked back to the big house to break the news.